CODE NAME
CAMELOT

CODE NAME
CAMELOT

AMAZON #1 BESTSELLING AUTHOR
DAVID ARCHER

Get David Archer's Starter Library FOR FREE

Sign up for the no-spam newsletter and get THE WAY OF THE WOLF,
plus the first two novels in David's bestselling *Sam Prichard* Series, and
lots more exclusive content, all for free.

Details can be found at the end of CODE NAME CAMELOT

"If you live among wolves you have to act like a Wolf"

– Nikita Khrushchev

PROLOGUE

JUAREZ, MEXICO

THE STREET WAS one of the seedier places in Juarez, a place where *gringo* tourists didn't usually show their faces. The tall American who was leaning against the bar was out of place, but as long as he didn't mind spending fifteen dollars for a bottle of beer, the bartender wasn't going to object to his presence. He was already on his third bottle, and Felicita had been sitting with him for quite some time. She liked the *gringos*, and seemed to have a special knack for getting them to pay attention to her.

As long as she also got them to pay the twenty dollars required for one of her blowjobs, that was fine.

This *gringo* had been coming around for several days, and Eduardo Hernandez, the bartender, had gotten to know him pretty well. The white man was tall, a couple of inches over six feet, with neatly trimmed blonde hair and blue eyes, and it was obvious from his general condition that he worked out regularly. His name was John Baker, he'd said, and he was in town on business. Considering that the town was Juarez, Mexico, it was no secret that the business involved drugs.

Again, that didn't matter much to Eduardo. A substantial number of his customers were in that same business, which suited him fine, since that meant they could afford the ridiculous prices he had to charge just to stay afloat. He had seen more than a few of them having private conversations with John the *gringo*, and though he hadn't seen money change hands, he knew without a doubt that it had.

John hooked a finger at Eduardo, and when the bartender looked, he pointed at the glass in front of Felicita. Eduardo grinned, then reached for the special bottle reserved for the drinks the customers bought for the whores, the watered-down drinks that cost Eduardo only pennies, while he charged the customers as high as ten dollars each. He was fully aware that John liked to keep the girl happy, and since the girl went back to his hotel with him almost every night, he suspected that they may have come to some private arrangement that was cheating the bartender out of his cut of the money she made.

She knew how things worked, though, and as long as she could keep John buying those drinks, she knew Eduardo wouldn't complain about her keeping the extra money she made in the night. She made it her business to keep John smiling, flirting with him and promising even more exciting pleasures to come. It was working, and her glass was staying full, which meant that her purse would not be as empty as it often was.

ONE

NOAH FOSTER HAD been an exemplary soldier for more than five years. After joining the Army shortly before turning eighteen, he had demonstrated a willingness and ability to learn his craft that very few had ever matched, at least in the opinion of his instructors. He'd also demonstrated an incredible ability to adapt to almost any situation, to remain calm even in the face of overwhelming problems, and to carry out his orders without hesitation or delay.

Second Lieutenant Abigail Mathers, of the Judge Advocate General's office, read through his file with interest. Sergeant Foster was sitting in the stockade at that moment, preparing to face a court-martial that would almost certainly find him guilty of multiple counts of murder and other crimes, and sentence him to die. Lieutenant Mathers had been assigned as his defense counsel and was fervently wishing that she had never even heard his name.

It was a hopeless case. Sergeant Foster, according to the witnesses against him, had willingly and with malice aforethought killed First Lieutenant Daniel Gibson, Corporal James Mathis, Pfc. Charles Mason, Pfc. Jack Lindemann, Pfc. David Clark and Pfc. William Gould, apparently to try to conceal other crimes.

The biggest problem was that there was no question of whether he had killed them, because he had already admitted to it in his own statement. The only matter to be settled in court-martial was whether he had done so in order to cover up the fact that, as some members of his unit had reported, he had killed five civilian females, or because—as he claimed—his platoon leader and several other members of his unit had engaged in the recreational rapes and murders of several young Iraqi girls, girls whose only offense was the fact that they were alone and unprotected when Gibson and the others came upon them.

Mathers read through the general details of Foster's statement, essentially the report that he had made after walking into his unit's rear area with several members of his platoon disarmed and under arrest.

His story was that he had been assigned as cover fire, positioned as a sniper as his unit advanced in suspected ISIL territory, but there had been no firefight. Instead, the platoon had found five unaccompanied civilian females, who seemed to be engaged in some sort of agricultural chores.

Foster had made his report, he said, with the assumption that the guilty would be punished. He claimed he had absolutely no idea that it would be turned around and used as evidence to charge him with committing murder to cover up the very crimes he said he was trying to report.

Mathers closed the file and got up from her desk, then left the JAG offices and headed across the compound toward the stockade. Foster was a prisoner there, and she wanted to look him in the eye and hear his story for herself.

The duty officer at the stockade said it would take a few minutes to get Foster up to the interview room, and invited her to have a cup of coffee. She passed, and went to wait in the interview room for her client. Foster was brought in about ten minutes later, and took the seat across the table from her.

"Sergeant Foster," she began, "I'm Lieutenant Mathers, with

the JAG office. I've been assigned as your defense counsel, and I've just started working on your case. Looks pretty nasty, so far. Can you tell me your side of the story?"

"I've already told it several times. Isn't it in the file?"

Mathers nodded. "I read it," she said. "Reading a formal statement and hearing it straight from the man's mouth are two different things. Personally, I'm inclined to think that I can discern the truth more easily by watching your facial expressions while you speak. So how about it? Gonna tell me what happened?"

Noah shrugged his shoulders. "I had been assigned as a sniper that day," he said, "to provide covering fire as my unit moved in on what was supposed to be an outpost of ISIL terrorists. Instead, the lieutenant and the platoon found a number of civilian females, and decided to let off some steam with them. Some of the girls, judging from their bodies after I got there, looked to be as young as twelve, maybe thirteen, and only one of them was still alive by then. Lieutenant Gibson had called me down from my position and offered me the opportunity to join in the fun with the last one, but instead, I attempted to put a stop to the situation." He smiled, sarcastically. "The lieutenant didn't want to hear my objections.

" 'Sergeant Foster,' he said, 'these are ISIL sympathizers, and as such they are to be treated exactly the same as enemy combatants. As it happens, we decided to attempt interrogation and met with resistance. Now, I'm offering you the opportunity to engage in some interrogation of your own.'

"I stared at him, and tried to figure out what was going on. I said, 'Lieutenant, we can't be doing this.'

"He acted like I hadn't said anything of importance. 'And why not, Sergeant?' he asked. 'Do you see anyone else around here, to make any objections? How I run my unit is up to me, and this looked to me like an opportunity to let my men get some much-needed R&R. There's one left, are you going to take advantage?'

"I looked down at the girl that was being held by both arms, and I could see the look in her eyes, pleading with me to do something to save her life. I turned back to the lieutenant.

" 'No, sir,' I said. 'I can't be a participant—' but he cut me off. He held up a hand to stop me, then called out, 'Anyone else?' When no one answered, he looked back at me, shrugged his shoulders, and then shot the girl through the head."

"Wait a minute!" Mathers said. "You're saying your platoon leader actually murdered this girl, right in front of your eyes. Is that what you're telling me?"

Noah looked at her, one eyebrow lifted. "I thought you said you read my interrogation report? That would've been in it."

Mathers nodded slowly. "Go on," she said.

"Well, I stepped back, because I was startled at what just happened. The guys who had been holding the girl, they jumped back, wiping off the blood that splattered them, and I stared at them all.

" 'Have you guys gone nuts?' I asked. 'Are you all crazy?'

"Lieutenant Gibson turned around and grabbed me by the front of my shirt, and pulled me down so that he was looking me dead in the eye. 'Sergeant Foster,' he said, 'you will stand down. What happened here today was something these men have needed for a while, and something that will stay between us all. Not one word will be said when we get back to the rear, do you understand me? Not one single word.'

"I looked down at the girl he had just murdered, and then at the bodies of the others who had been with her. I doubted any of them was over sixteen, and probably were out there doing whatever their fathers had told them to do. Now, they were all dead, raped and murdered by a bunch of guys I thought I knew, guys I had fought beside, people I trusted. And the one who should have kept them all under control was the one who told them they could get away with it, and even he participated in rape and murder. Hell, even while I stood there protesting what he was doing, Lieutenant Gibson murdered that last girl right in front of me."

"And that's when you took action?"

"Yes. I did what, to me, was the only logical thing to do. I drew my side arm and shot him the exact same way. Corporal Mathis objected—he said, 'Jesus, Sarge! What the hell,' or something like that, and I started yelling, 'Just stop it! I want all of you to just stop, right now. What you're doing is wrong, and could be construed as an act of war against Iraq itself. These are civilians, the people we're supposed to be here to protect.' I kept my service pistol in my hand, as I looked at Mathis and the others. 'I have to make a report on this, and I want to know who was actively involved before I got down here.'

"Mathis stood there for a moment, with Gould and Lindemann beside him. He said, 'Foster, come on, man, Jesus, Sarge, you can't report this! Okay, things got a little out of hand, but God, you just killed the lieutenant!'

"I said, 'Corporal, what I'm seeing here is the rape and murder of civilian girls, some of them barely even old enough to be classified as teenagers. I think that's a little more than just things getting out of hand. When we get back to the rear, I'm going to have no choice but to place you all under arrest and file a complete report.'

"That was as far as I got. Mathis raised his rifle and pointed it at me. He said, 'We can't let you do that, Sarge.' I saw that his eyes were wide, and he seemed frantic. I watched Gould and Lindemann out of the corners of my eyes, and saw that each of them was nervously clutching his rifle, watching me.

"I looked back at Mathis, and realized that he was on the verge of killing me in his panic over being punished for what he and the others had done. I thought I would try to defuse the situation, so I lowered my pistol and shrugged. I said, 'Maybe we can put this off on the LT, we can say he wigged out, killed all these girls himself. No need to put any other names on it.'

"Mathis stood there for a moment, and I could see the wheels turning in his head. He was trying to decide whether to trust me or not, whether to believe that I'd really let it go at that. If I reported that it was only the lieutenant who was actually involved in the murders, and the others made sure their stories agreed with mine, there would be no investigations, no charges. Of course, the trouble was I had just made the statement that I would be placing them all under arrest when we got back to the rear. He knew me well enough to know that I wouldn't have said that unless it was exactly what I meant to do.

"He grinned, and then he said, 'Sorry, Sarge, you're like a bulldog; you don't let go of something once you got it in your teeth.' He raised the barrel of his rifle so that it was aimed at my head, rather than my chest, and I figured I had about a split second to live.

"The pistol was in my right hand, and its added weight would slow that arm, no matter how insignificantly, so I swung my left in an arc that brought it around and into contact with the barrel of his weapon. I slapped it to the left, at the same time leaning my head to the right, just as he squeezed the trigger. The bullet that was meant to take my life flew past my ear, but the flecks of burning powder didn't miss it. I could feel them, like tiny grains of flame that peppered my ear and cheek."

Mathers suddenly stood, and leaned across the table with her palms flat on it. "Show me," she said.

Noah leaned forward and tilted his head to one side so that she could look at his left ear. There were tiny black marks inside the cup of the ear, and on the earlobe.

Mathers nodded, and took out her iPhone to snap several pictures. "Those look like powder burns to me, alright," she said. "Go ahead."

"Well, while he was trying to shoot me again, I brought up my pistol and fired twice, taking Mathis in the gut with the first round, and through the heart with the second. While all that was going on, Lindemann reacted by leveling his own M-16 at me, so I continued to swing my right hand around until it was in line with his body, and then squeezed the trigger once more. Lindemann fell back, but his rifle was set to three round bursts, and he squeezed the trigger in reflex as he went down. His bullets missed me, but they hit Private Mason, who was standing behind me, in the face."

"Mason was an accidental casualty, then?"

"Yeah. Then Gould freaked out; he spun and ran, while a couple of the other guys began firing in my direction. We'd been standing in the middle of a little group of small buildings, probably related to whatever they call farming in that area, and I threw myself behind one of them. Gould yelled out, 'Come on, Sarge, there's no point in this. We're all on the same side, remember?'

"I wasn't interested in trying to argue with him, or anybody else, for that matter. There was a hole in the wall that I was hiding behind, leading inside the small structure. From what I could see, it looked like it might be some sort of simple shelter, maybe a place to get out of a sandstorm. Whatever it was, it offered me a chance to improve my position without being seen, so I crawled through the hole and into the building. There were a number of holes in the walls, some of them just big enough to peek through, while others were as big as the one I had used to get inside. I moved from one to the other, being careful and keeping out of sight, and was able to get a fair idea of where the rest of the men were; then I rolled out and across the little lane between the buildings, and got behind a different one. A couple of shots were fired at me, but none got close.

"Funny thing was, my new position gave me a clear view of one of the men, but he didn't see me. That was Clark, and since I had no choice but to consider him a hostile at that point, I took him out with a single shot from my M4. Instantly, the rest of them opened fire on the little building I was using for a shield, so I had to run behind another. Gould yelled out, 'It didn't have to be this way, Sarge.' I could tell the general direction his voice came from, but couldn't pin it down because of echoes.

"Those echoes made it difficult to know which way to move, because I couldn't tell where the rest of the men were taking cover. Gould was their corporal, and at this point, he was more likely to have their obedience and support than I was. That meant that if I could take him out, there was at least a fair chance the rest would give it up. I moved to the other end of the shelter I was hiding behind, to try to get some idea of which direction he might be in from my position.

"I yelled, 'We've got four dead already, Gould, do you want to make it worse? Give it up, man, we can come up with a story about what happened here.' He laughed, and I could tell that it was coming from behind another of the little buildings. He was about thirty meters from my position, but not in my line of sight because of the structure he was using to hide behind. I had to move to another position, or it wasn't likely I was going to be able to take him down, so I rolled again, over behind a different building, because it would put me in a position to get behind Gould. I figured that if I could take him out, there was that small chance that the rest would surrender, and I had to take a shot at it.

"I fired a burst in the opposite direction from where I wanted to go, to focus their attention in that area, and then I sprinted around the end of the building I was hiding behind. Seemed like there were almost a dozen of those little structures, and I had no idea what their purpose might be, only that they were made of a thick, Adobe-like material. That made them ideal as shields, since our little 5.56 ball rounds wouldn't penetrate them. Anyway, I got where I wanted to be, and when I looked around the end of the shelter, I saw Gould with his back against another one, facing loosely in my direction. My motion, leaning around the end of the building to see where he might be, caught his eye, and he opened fire instantly. I ducked back behind the structure, waited until he let up on his trigger, and then jumped out from behind that wall. I made it a good six feet away from the corner he'd seen me look around, which put me in a place he didn't expect me to be, and then I fired once with my M4, a single shot that took him between the eyes.

"I yelled, 'Gould is dead, and none of you is as good as me at this stuff, and you all know it. We can keep this up if we have to, but it'd be a lot simpler if we just go back and let the officers figure out what to do.' I waited for almost a minute, and then Private Hansen called out that he wanted to give it up. The other six in our unit followed him just a couple of minutes later, so I told them all to unload their weapons and clear them before I stepped out from behind cover. I watched carefully as they did so, then had them recover the weapons and dog tags from the men we lost. Once those weapons were also cleared, I ordered them into formation and marched them back to our rear area.

"I made my report, detailing what I had discovered when I was called down from my cover-fire position. I left no details out, including the fact that I had killed five of my own men, while the sixth, Private Mason, was killed accidentally as a result of my killing Private Lindemann. I also included details of the five civilian girls who had been raped and killed, complete with photographs I had taken on my phone."

Mathers sat back and just looked at him for a moment. "You're aware that the rest of your unit all says that you were the one who was raping and killing those girls, and that it was Lieutenant Gibson who tried to stop you. According to their statements, you killed him and Corporal Gould, and then killed the rest as they were trying to escape from you."

Noah shrugged. "You asked me to tell you what happened, so I did."

"Sergeant Foster, you are about to face court-martial on multiple charges of murder under UCMJ Article 118, as well as multiple charges of sedition under UCMJ Article 94, Section 894. Ironically, there's no mention of charges regarding the five girls, because by the time another unit was sent out there to try to gather evidence and collect the bodies, all of them had vanished. All they found out there were the bodies of your men, the ones that you killed."

"I didn't kill Mason," Noah said. "His death was an accident. I have no idea which way he would've come down on this issue."

"Yes, well, the Article 32 hearing has already determined that there is sufficient evidence to bring charges against you. What that means for me is that I have to try to find a way to keep you from being hung at Leavenworth. Now, considering that you have just told me this story with about as much emotion as your average donkey might display, would you like to give me some kind of an idea of what I might be able to use to do that?"

Noah studied her face for a moment. "You need to get into my psychological profile," he said. "It's a long story, but I suffer from something called blunted affect disorder, which means I don't have any emotions. That's why you're not seeing any when I talk to you." His face broke into a big smile, suddenly. "But I can fake it for you, if you want. I got years and years of practice."

Mathers stared at him. "With a psych problem like that, how on earth did you get into the Army?"

"Like I said," Noah replied, "I got years of practice at pretending to be human. It wasn't hard to get past the doctors, and I'm smart enough that the qualification tests were pretty simple. Uncle Sam jumped at the chance to get me, and by the time I finished basic training, there were a whole bunch of officers who decided they had found the perfect soldier." He shrugged his shoulders and cocked his head to one side. "Maybe they're right. Three tours of duty over here, and credited with more than a hundred and twenty confirmed kills. Not hard to do, when you can't feel fear and don't have a conscience."

Mather shook her head. "Do you realize that if anyone overheard those words, they would convict you without a moment's hesitation?"

Noah laughed, but there was no mirth in it. "Lieutenant, do you honestly believe there is any possibility that isn't going to happen, anyway? I figure they probably already have my room reserved on death row at the Disciplinary Barracks at Fort Leavenworth. Wouldn't want to make a bet on that, would you?"

Matters got to her feet and picked up the notepad she'd been scribbling on. "Look, Sergeant Foster, as strange as it may seem to you, I really do want to do everything I can to give you a real defense. The problem is that I have nothing to work with. If I put you on the stand, the members of the court are going to listen to you speak and conclude that you are every bit the psychopath your buddies have made you out to be. Other than some pictures of what might be powder burns, I have absolutely nothing in the way of physical evidence to corroborate your story, and I sincerely doubt that any of your former compatriots would be willing to speak up on your behalf, even if you're telling the gospel truth."

"Of course they won't," Noah said. "The other guys would kill them if they did. No, no matter how you look at it, I'm headed for conviction, and probably the death penalty." He leaned forward, his hands clasped calmly on the table. "Lieutenant Mathers, go and put some effort into a case you have a chance to win. Find someone who still has a chance, and put everything you've got into them, because I don't have one."

Mathers leaned her head to one side, staring at him in what he took to be complete shock. "You're just giving up?"

"Oh, now, I didn't say that. I said I'm fully aware that I'm going to be convicted. What I'm hoping is that you'll do exactly what I mentioned earlier, and get hold of my psychological profile. About the only chance I've got to avoid the hangman's noose is for you to get me declared either insane or incompetent. Let's face it, as crazy as I am, that shouldn't be too difficult. With any luck, you'll be done with me in a couple of weeks. So, go on, find the case you can win and put all your effort into that one. Just do what you can to keep me alive, would you?"

The lieutenant gathered up everything she had to take with her, and nodded once. "Sergeant, I really do wish that I could do more. The trouble is that we've got absolutely zero forensic evidence, no physical evidence, and no one to speak up and confirm your story. Maybe, given your psychological history, we can get a directed verdict of not guilty by reason of mental insufficiency. If the members of the court could be convinced that you can't understand the difference between right and wrong, then maybe we can go for commitment to a mental facility, and get you some real help. If that happens, you might even get your life back, someday."

Noah shrugged. "Possible," he said. "More likely, we'll get a life sentence, but then I might be able to win transfer to a place like that on appeal. From what I've found in my reading, it's a whole lot easier to get a lenient verdict in an appeal forum than it is in a general court-martial."

Mathers narrowed her eyes and looked at him. "That's true," she said. "It might even be possible to get an appellate panel to overturn your conviction, which would take a whole lot less evidence than we have to come up with to walk out of this one unscathed. Do you think there's any possibility that one of your friends might speak up for you in an appeal?"

"I honestly don't know," he said. "Hansen might, if he were given immunity. He's a real religious kid, and I bet that the only thing keeping his mouth shut now is outright fear of what the others would do to him. Is there any chance an appeal would bring charges back against the rest of them?"

Mathers shrugged. "It's possible, but not likely," she said. "It would be entirely up to the appellate judge as to whether he would send the original charges back for review. To be honest, I doubt he would do so, simply because, A: judges don't like to overrule each other, and B: the original victims in this case were those girls, and a military court isn't likely to consider them important enough to take any action about. Besides, they never found the bodies. I mean, you're only charged with the murders of your own men; there's no mention of any crime against Iraqi civilian girls."

Noah shook his head and looked at the tabletop. "And this country talks about human rights all the time, how these Muslim countries mistreat their people so badly. Welcome to American hypocrisy—Ameri-pocrisy. There, I've coined a whole new word, and it means that America gets to tell everybody else how to live, as long as they don't expect us to live up to our own standards." He raised his head and looked Lieutenant Mathers in the eye once again. "According to this booklet they gave me, you'll probably be my lawyer for this whole thing, right?"

She grimaced and nodded. "Yeah, unless you get mad and fire me, or this gets stalled for years and I discharge out before we go to trial. Why?"

"Just hoping we can pull off this appeal gimmick," he said. "If we do, and I get out one day, then maybe I can write a book about this, or something. I didn't know those girls at all, but I have to think that they deserve to have the truth told about what happened to them."

Mathers stood there and looked at him for a long moment. "I'll do my best," she said, and then she walked out the door of the interview room. Noah sat there for another two minutes, before one of the guards on duty came to take him back to his cell.

TWO

MATHERS WAS FRUSTRATED. Over the past week, she had filed all the necessary paperwork that should have allowed her to have access to Foster's psych files, but no matter what she tried, it seemed like she was being blocked at every turn. After the last communication informing her that she would not receive the access she was requesting, she began to feel like there was something going on, something she couldn't see.

Being with the JAG office at Victory Base Complex at Baghdad meant that Mathers was one of dozens of military lawyers who assisted service members with everything from minor issues involving disputes with local landlords all the way up to major criminal charges, such as she was currently handling for Sergeant Foster. She got up and went to knock on the door of her commander's office.

"Enter," came the voice from inside. She opened the door and walked in. Two steps in front of the desk, she snapped to attention and saluted.

Captain Willis glanced up at her and returned the salute. "At ease, Lieutenant," he said. "What can I do for you?"

Mathers relaxed rather than actually moving into the at-ease position. "Sir," she began, "it's the Sergeant Foster case. I've got reason to believe there could be a valid defense in his psychological history, but every attempt I've made to get access to it has been denied."

Willis put down his pen and leaned back in his chair. "Lieutenant, have you considered the possibility that there are forces at work here that you simply cannot overcome?"

She leaned forward and put her hands on the front of his desk. "Not really," she said. "Do you know something I don't know?"

Willis gave her a grin that might have signified patience, if it had been bestowed upon an errant child. "I don't know anything that you couldn't find out, if you would simply do a little research. I'll simplify it for you, though. Do you have any idea who the victims were in this case? Particularly the highest-ranking victim?"

Mathers felt her eyebrows lowering and gathering together in the center, as she leaned her head to the right. "Lieutenant Gibson? I got a copy of his service record, just like I did for all of the victims. What's so special about him?"

The captain chuckled. "Didn't read that service record very closely, did you?" Willis asked. "First Lieutenant Daniel Gibson, son of Republican Congressman Charles Oliver Gibson of Virginia. Congressman Gibson has held his seat for more than fourteen years, and there are rumors that he may be preparing to run for president. Your boy popped a cap on his firstborn, and I can flat guarantee you that TJAG is probably getting more pressure to see Foster convicted and executed than in just about any other case in Army history."

Mathers stood there for a moment, still leaning on the desk. "According to Foster, it was Lieutenant Gibson who actually committed murder in this case, as well as committing rape and condoning both crimes among his men, and frankly, if he's the son of an American politician, then I'm more inclined to believe Sergeant Foster than ever. All that aside, what about the fact that we're supposed to provide the best possible defense? If I'm right, then Foster should not be standing court-martial at all. This is a man who apparently suffered a great mental and emotional trauma when he was a child, and now suffers from PTSD. The little bit I've managed to uncover suggests that he has no functioning emotional framework, which would indicate that he is incapable of understanding the difference between right and wrong on a moral level, and can only perceive it in the context of concrete rules. To him, those rules would indicate that the rapes and murders of innocent girls called for him to take action, which he did."

"And who was it that appointed him to dispense justice on the lieutenant and his men? Granted, *if* he's telling the truth, and that's a big if, then Lieutenant Gibson should have been brought to justice, but there are established procedures. Foster should have simply made a report upon his return to the rear, and allowed his superior officers to determine what charges, if any, the lieutenant should face. Nowhere in the Uniform Code of Military Justice does it ever state that a noncommissioned officer should judge, pass sentence and execute the same on an officer. All he had to do was keep his mouth shut until he got back, and make a report to his unit commander. Instead, he blew the brains out of a lieutenant with serious political connections. If you want to destroy your own career by trying to save this idiot's life, then by all means, be my guest, but if you are capable of listening to reason, then you should get it through your head that there is no way you're going to pull it off. The congressman wants blood, and blood he is going to get."

Mathers continued to stand there for another moment, then suddenly went back to attention. "Yes, Sir," she said, just before snapping a perfect salute and executing a parade-ground-perfect about-face. She walked out of the office without looking back to see if the captain returned the salute.

Back in her own office, she sat down in her chair and looked at the open file on her desk. Sergeant Foster looked back at her from the photo that was paper clipped to it, and she felt a sense of shame as she stared into his two-dimensional eyes.

"You had to go and kill a congressman's kid," she said. "How freaking stupid can you get?"

She looked at the latest communiqué telling her the sergeant's psychological profile was not going to be made available to her, and slammed it down on the desk. There was something sinister about this whole case, and she had already come to the conclusion that the captain had been right. If she put any serious effort into trying to save Foster, she'd be driving nails into the coffin of her own career in the Army, and since being a JAG Officer had been her dream ever since she was a teenager and saw Demi Moore in *A Few Good Men*, it would be destroying everything she had worked for. That movie had defined her interest in a law career, had made her want to be part of the military justice system.

Her father, a corporate attorney who was a senior partner in a major firm, hadn't been thrilled with her decision, but he hadn't fought her on it, either. His attitude was that she should get her idealism out of the way during her military years, so that she could properly pursue a career that would reward her financially. It was cases like this one, she admitted to herself, that made her wonder if he was right.

She wondered what JoAnne Galloway would do, referring to Demi Moore's character in the movie. Would she give up and let her client suffer for a crime he probably didn't commit? Would she fight on, knowing she was throwing away her own career? Pissing off a congressman like Gibson (and even worse, a potential president) would almost certainly be the end of any hope of making a name for herself, either in JAG or in private practice.

Galloway wouldn't care, she was sure, but then, Galloway was a fictional character who didn't have to look into a mirror each day and think, *If only I had been smart enough to walk away from Foster.*

She was scheduled to go and see her client in just a little over an hour, right after lunch. She honestly wasn't sure what she was going to say to him, and decided not to think about it while she ate. She took the file with her and left the office to head for the Officer's Mess.

Lunch didn't help, because as hard as she tried to avoid any thoughts about Sergeant Foster, those big blue eyes of his kept popping up in her mind. Granted, when he had told her his account of the situation, he had sounded almost like a robot, but there was something so purely innocent about him, despite everything he had seen and done in his military career, that she couldn't help believing he was telling her the truth. That being the case, she wasn't sure that she could live with herself if she didn't fight for him with everything she had.

When her lunch was finished, she walked over to the stockade and signed in. She was escorted to the interview room, and sat down at the table to wait for her client. He was brought in a couple of minutes later, and took the chair across from her.

"Lieutenant," he said. "Good to see you again, I wasn't sure you'd be back." He smiled at her to soften the comment.

"Sergeant Foster," she said, "I'm gonna level with you. Everything I'm doing to try to help you is being blocked at the highest levels, and I don't know that there's anything I can do that isn't going to make things worse. Are you aware that Lieutenant Gibson's father is a United States congressman and maybe running for president?"

Noah let an eyebrow go up a quarter inch. "Seriously? No, I didn't know. The Lieutenant and I didn't move in the same circles, so I never heard about that." He let out a low whistle. "Now that I know it, though, it makes sense why everything has happened so fast. I mean, I was arrested within two hours of making my initial report, which sort of discounts Colonel Blanchard's claim that he had sent investigators out to the scene of the crime beforehand."

Mathers felt her eyebrows crunching again. "What you mean by that?"

Noah shrugged. "Where everything happened, it's up in a mountainous region where there aren't any roads. Some places, we had to walk single file going out and coming back, and it took us more than four hours to walk back to the rear. Now, let's do the math. I gave my statement at about fifteen hundred hours, but I was arrested just before seventeen hundred. Since one of the men I brought in would have had to show the investigating unit how to get there, there's no way they could have made it out and back in that short a time."

"Helicopter. They probably flew out, that would only take minutes."

"No, Ma'am, with all due respect," he said. "The whole reason we were out there in that area was because we were searching for some antiaircraft batteries that ISIL had up and operating. A chopper flying over that area would have been shot down, no doubt about it. No, they definitely would have walked, and there's no possible way they could have gotten there, looked the scene over, supposedly discovered that the bodies of the girls were missing, and then come back to make a report that resulted in my arrest."

Mathers sat there and stared at him. "Is there any possible way that we can prove that?"

Noah shook his head. "Not a chance," he said. "In order to make it stick, you can bet Colonel Blanchard has got the whole unit ready to back up his version of how, and probably where, it happened. All the documentation will show the event taking place somewhere close enough to reach in that timeframe, I'd bet on it. They would have gone after the bodies of our men sometime later."

Mathers leaned forward, her hands open on either side of the file that was lying in front of her. "Sergeant, I'm trying everything I can think of, but the truth is that I've already been informed there's no possible way I can win. In fact, my CO told me this morning that if I continue to try, all I'm going to do is ruin my own career." She closed her eyes tightly for a moment, then opened them again and let them bore into his. "I've tried to decide what to do, and I—I just can't figure it out. A part of me says I need to do everything possible to keep you from getting the death penalty, or at least to make it feasible for us to try the appeal route we discussed the other day, but another part tells me to run from you as fast as I can. Like I said, though, I can't decide, so I'm going to leave this up to you. You tell me what to do, right now, and I'll do it. Do I keep trying, or do I just go through the motions and let them convict you?"

Noah sat forward and put his right hand over her left. "Your CO is right," he said. "If you keep trying to help me, this whole thing is going to blow up in your face and ruin your life, just the way it's ruining mine. There's no point in both of us going down. Give me whatever it is I need to file in order to fire you, so we can get you out of this mess."

Mathers sat in her chair, staring at the young man who was looking her straight in the eye as he gave her permission to send him to his death. She already knew enough about his condition to realize that he was simply making what he considered the logical choice, but that didn't assuage her conscience in the least. Without her help, he was going to be convicted, sentenced to death and executed, and probably within a very short time.

She had done a little research on death row at the US Disciplinary Barracks, and found out that there were several people awaiting execution there. Most of them had been waiting for years, but with the appeals process and changes in the White House, there were various reasons why they had not yet had their sentences carried out. Mathers didn't think Foster would get to hang out with them for very long. Her gut hunch said that his execution would happen within months of sentencing, with all of his appeals exhausted as quickly as possible.

"And what if I can't do that?" Mathers asked. "What if my conscience just won't let me walk away? Sergeant Foster, the biggest problem I'm facing right now is the fact that I believe you. Yeah, yeah, I know there's no evidence to back you up, but when

I sat here and listened to you the other day, all I heard was a man who was calmly recounting exactly what happened. You weren't telling me some elaborate story, you didn't try to come up with excuses for why no one corroborates your claim, you didn't try to protest that you are being mistreated—hell, Sergeant, all you did was answer my questions. A man who's truly guilty, a man who's trying to put one over on the system, he'll come up with all sorts of things to say to try to throw us off. He'll tell me how the men who are willing to testify against him are upset because he refused to participate in some ritual, or that their ringleader is gay and he refused an advance from him. You didn't give me any BS—you just told me what happened, without any embellishments. In my experience, and in my professional opinion, that is something that only a man telling the truth would do."

Noah smiled. "Lieutenant Mathers," he said, "what on earth do you think truth has to do with it? This case isn't about who's telling the truth, or there would've been a real investigation of my report. Since we know there wasn't one, then all this case really is about is pinning the blame for the congressman's son's death on somebody as quickly as possible. Now, I've admitted that I shot him, and they got all the other guys making statements saying that I did it just because I'm nuts, and calling me a liar about what really happened. People who just want to put something away as fast as possible don't want to take the time to examine the facts. It's easier just to point their fingers and say I did it, and here's what they're going to do to punish me, put the whole thing to bed in a hurry. That's all they want to do."

"That doesn't make them right," Mathers said. "You want my opinion, it makes them monsters. I went to law school because I believe in the law; I joined the Army because I wanted to make a difference in military law. Now I'm just supposed to walk away and watch you go into the lethal injection chambers? How am I supposed to live with myself, after that? You answer that for me."

Noah pulled his hand back. "Lieutenant, I'm not the one who

put you in this position. In fact, I'm the one who's actually in this position, not you. You have an out; I don't. You can walk away; all I can do is move forward, propelled along by a system that is being used by a political machine to cover up what really happened, to make me pay for Lieutenant Gibson's crimes. If you can show me any fairness in that, then maybe I can help you figure out how to live with yourself when this is all over." He rubbed his hands over his face, and she thought the gesture was odd. Most people used it to try to get themselves under control, but if there was one thing she knew already about Foster, it was that he never lost control in the first place. He put his hands down, and looked her in the eye once more. "Lieutenant, I don't want to feel like I've hurt someone who's innocent. Give me the form I need to file, so that I can release you."

"No," she said. "I don't want to do that."

"There really isn't much choice," Noah said. "You can't win, and continuing to try will only hurt your career. If I'm going to die, I'd rather die knowing that I at least tried to always do the right thing."

"Yeah, well that's pretty much how I feel, too. If they win, then sometime, maybe a few months, maybe a few years, they're going to kill you. When that day comes, it'll be over for you, but I'll have to keep living with it. Frankly, I don't know if I can. If I don't do whatever I can for you, then the day may come when I just can't cope with being me anymore." She looked down at the file in front of her and opened it up. "Sergeant Wolf," she said, "tell me about your childhood."

Noah's eyes went wide. "My childhood? Surely you've been able to get at least that much information, right?"

She nodded. "Yes, but I want to hear from you. Please, go on."

Noah let out a long sigh. "Okay, but you're getting the Reader's Digest condensed version. Seven years old, I saw my father kill my mother and then himself. Got sent to the foster care system, lived there for almost a year before my grandparents showed up to take me, lived with them for a short time until they figured out I was a Pinocchio, then they couldn't cope with me anymore and I ended up back in the foster system. Grew up there, spent most of my time in a couple different foster homes, until something happened that made everyone afraid of me. I joined the Army to get out of my hometown, and I finally felt like I'd found a place where I fit in. The same parts of me that were considered a problem in civilian life became assets in the military, and I got a stack of commendations about what a fantastic soldier I was."

Matters had been scribbling furiously, even though she had a recorder lying on the table taking in every word and shoving them into its memory chip. She looked up at him. "What do you mean, that your grandparents figured out you were a Pinocchio?"

Noah shrugged. "That's what a friend of mine used to call me, a Pinocchio. Pinocchio was a puppet who wanted to be a real boy, everybody knows that story. In my case, it sort of describes how I am, a real person but without any emotions, without any sense of what it means to be human. I don't know how to act like a real person, so I just mimic the people around me. That works fine, until I'm confronted with a situation that's so unusual that there isn't any right or normal way to handle it."

"Such as what happened with Lieutenant Gibson and the other men, right?"

"Yep. I've never had the opportunity to watch someone else decide how to handle that type of thing, so I just went with what I thought was the most logical thing to do. Since it was obvious to me that Gibson would rather kill me than let me report what he'd been doing, the logical thing seemed to be for me to kill him first. Same with the other men: since they wanted to kill me to keep me from turning them in, the logical choice would be for me to kill them first."

She scribbled for a few seconds more. "Here's a question," she said. "You said that you told the men who surrendered that you were much better at combat than they were, and that they couldn't win. Apparently, they believed you, but the question is, did you believe it yourself? Do you honestly think you're that good, that you could have taken all of them out?"

Both of Noah's eyebrows went up, and Mathers read his expression as a way of saying, *Well, duh!*

"Of course I did," he said aloud. "And every one of them knew it was true."

She suddenly raised her eyes from the pad she was writing on and looked directly into his. "Then why didn't you do it? Why didn't you go ahead and kill them all, so that no one could have contested your report?"

"I didn't need to, they surrendered."

"Yes, but if you had not offered them the chance to surrender, they would've kept right on trying to kill you. You would have been completely justified in eliminating them all. Why didn't you?"

Noah stared at her for a moment. "Most of those guys were pretty decent people, for the most part, but in all the years that I've been studying humans, one thing I've found is that they tend to be a lot like certain animals. Take wolves, for example: an individual wolf will almost never attack another animal or even a human, unless it feels threatened or is starving. However, an entire wolf pack, if the alpha is aggressive toward that animal or human, will rip it to shreds. It won't matter if they're hungry, because they probably won't eat it anyway. They'll just destroy it." He leaned forward. "Humans are a lot like that, if they have a leader who will disregard right and wrong. Humans tend to submit to authority, or at least most of them do. If an authority figure tells them to do something, or even worse, leads by example in doing something that's just plain wrong, something they wouldn't normally do on their own, they'll give in to the lure of the taboo and join right in. You understand what I'm trying to say?"

Mathers looked him in the eye. "Pack behavior," she said.

"That's what they call the tendency for people to join in on group actions that they would normally consider unacceptable. What you're saying is that you believe those men would never have done what they did if Lieutenant Gibson hadn't pushed the issue, hadn't actually allowed or even ordered them to do it. Right?"

"Right. So that means that, in some ways, they were still innocent. They didn't deserve to die just because they were scared of what I might do to them. Now, if they hadn't laid down their weapons, yes, I would've done what I had to do. But once they did, then it became my duty to bring them in alive and unharmed."

Mathers sat there and looked at him for another long moment, and then began scribbling again. "There you go again," she said. "The ironic thing is that the very problem you've got, this thing about not having emotions or knowing how to be human, is almost certainly what has made you one of the best men I've ever met. I know a lot of terrific people, but if they had been in your position out there, and known as surely as you did that they could have killed all of the others, you can bet your life that they would have come back alone and sworn up and down that the rest of their unit was wiped out by enemy missile fire. There'd be no search for bodies, so the story would hold up."

Noah sat silently for a moment, but then reached over and laid a hand on hers, stopping her pen from moving across the paper. "Lieutenant," he said softly, "I don't know about whether I'm a good man or not. I don't have any reasonable way to judge myself. But this much I have learned, and again, mostly by watching other people. Just because you can do something that may benefit yourself doesn't necessarily make it right to do so. That would be like if you found yourself alone in a building where hundreds of gold bars were stored, and knew with an absolute certainty that you could take a couple of them and no one would ever know." He leaned his head down a bit more, so that he could look her in the eye more directly. "It would still be stealing, now, wouldn't it?"

THREE

"IT JUST ISN'T fair," Mathers said. She was sitting on the couch in her apartment, leaning back against Major Arthur Newman. "Foster is almost certainly telling the truth, but there is absolutely no way that I'm going to be able to save him from being sentenced to die. Makes me sick to think that I chose to become part of a system that can so easily and arbitrarily decide to destroy a man for doing exactly what was right."

Newman caressed her cheek with the backs of his fingers. "You didn't make that choice, Abby," he said. "You just got handed the bag to hold. The problem is that your client, Foster, had the bad luck to be serving under a psychopath who happened to be the son of a powerful man. Sometimes, no matter how unfair it is, there's just no way to win."

"And how am I supposed to live with that? Can you tell me how I'm supposed to sleep at night, knowing that a good and innocent man went to death row because he did the right thing? Sergeant Foster shouldn't be standing court-martial, he should be given a medal." She sat forward suddenly, and spun to look him in the eye. "What if I went to the press? What if I leaked the story of how a congressman can railroad the man who stopped his son from committing even more horrible crimes in the future? Maybe I can get just enough public pressure to at least keep Foster out of the execution chamber."

Newman was shaking his head. "Abby, it won't work," he said. "First of all, Congressman Gibson stands a fair chance of being the next president, if he does decide to run. He's popular, and from what I've heard so far, all the speculation polls are finding him to be a very viable and likely candidate. The press is not going to go up against a man like that, not anybody who could get you serious attention, anyway. But even more than that, they would trace the leak back to you and you could be facing a court-martial of your own. If you decide to keep fighting for the Sergeant and end up losing your own career, well, you can console yourself by remembering that it's better to sacrifice your career than your soul." He pulled her hand up to his lips and kissed it. "Besides, you might decide you like being a stay-at-home mom, and I've never been all that excited about having a wife who works."

"Art, be serious! I've got to think this through, I can't just lay down on this."

"Abby, sweetheart, I'm being completely serious," Newman said. "You cannot win, that much is just true. No matter what you do, your Sergeant Foster is going to end up dead over this. Your CO knows it, Sergeant Foster knows it, and you know it. What you have got to do, if you're going to survive this at all, is detach yourself from it. Stop thinking of Foster as a client, and just think of him as a casualty of war."

Mathers leaned back against him again, and he could tell that she was crying softly. He had often wondered if she really had the hardness of heart that it took to be a good lawyer, and it seemed this case was going to be the one that broke her. Of that, he was absolutely certain, so he simply put his arms around her and let her cry.

Sometimes, that's just all a man can do. The following morning, she would be walking into that court-martial, and he wasn't sure whether she would even be the same person when she came back out. They ended up falling asleep right there on the couch, huddled together in Mathers' desperate need for human contact, and only woke when the sun came through the window to tell them that it was time, once more, to face the future.

The court-martial was a joke. The prosecution paraded its entire line of witnesses before the judge and members of the court, while Mathers had only Foster, himself, to put on the stand. She had done her best, cross-examining each witness and watching them squirm on the stand as she piled on all the pressure she could to try to break their stories, but they had obviously been well rehearsed. She could make them nervous, but she couldn't make them crack.

When it came time for the defense to make its case, she put Foster on the stand and simply let him tell the story in his own words. To her, they were the first words that sounded even slightly believable in the entire proceeding, but the prosecution turned his cross-examination into one of the most vitriolic attacks she had ever seen in a court.

Still, Foster could not be rattled. He kept his cool, never once becoming upset or angry, calmly answering every question. Some of them he answered over and over, always with the same response, until at last even the judge and panel got tired of hearing it all repeated. After, she rested her case, knowing she had done all of the little she could do, and knowing full well that it wasn't going to be enough.

"Sergeant Foster," she began, as the members of the court filed out to begin their deliberations. "I've been thinking, and—well, I want you to know that you won't be forgotten. We may still have a chance to save you on appeal, but no matter what happens, I want you to know that I'm not going to let this be swept under the rug. I've copied all of my notes in your case; I've got hours and hours of recordings from where you and I talked it over, so I know the whole story. We might not have a chance to win here in this court, but there's another court. I'm going to write a book about you and this case, so that people learn what really happened, and just how corrupt our system really is."

Foster sat there at the defense table and smiled at her. She knew, of course, that the smile was merely an affectation, that he had practiced it over and over until he could make it look genuine, but it still made her feel good.

"Lieutenant Mathers, I appreciate that. But do yourself a favor, and wait until Congressman Gibson retires."

The members of the court returned after only twenty-four minutes of deliberations, and their foreman stood to read the verdict. Noah was convicted on all counts, just as he had told her he would be.

"Sergeant Noah Foster," intoned the presiding officer, as Noah stood to hear the official pronouncement of the verdict. "The members of this court have found you guilty of multiple counts of murder and sedition. This court will now move to the sentencing phase, unless the defendant is in need of a recess."

Noah kept his eyes on the eyes of the judge. "I don't need a recess, Sir," he said. "I'd like to proceed."

Mathers leaned over and whispered into his ear. "Foster, are you sure? We can take a break, reconvene tomorrow."

Noah shook his head. "All that would do is give me one more day to second-guess what we could've done. Let's just get this over with. There's actually a lot of books I want to read before I die, so the sooner I get started, the better the chance I'll get to finish at least some of them."

Mathers looked up at the judge. "Defense is ready to proceed, Sir," she said.

Just like the court-martial itself, the sentencing phase was a farce. The presiding officer listened to statements about Foster's character from his commanding officer and several of the men who had already testified against him, painting him as a dangerous and psychotic individual. When it was her turn, she put Foster back on the stand and let him talk about his childhood, the things that had happened to him. She asked him about his psychological problems, and was quickly shut down by the judge.

By the time she finished, she was standing before the presiding officer with tears streaming down her cheeks.

And then it was time. "Sergeant Noah Foster," the judge said, "you have been convicted of murder and sedition, both of which are eligible for the death penalty under the Uniform Code of Military Justice, and this court has heard testimony from a number of your peers and superiors that makes me wonder how you ever managed to get into the Army in the first place. Men like you are not fit for military service, and it amazes me that it took so long for your flaws to become visible. It is therefore the order of this court that you shall be taken forthwith and transported back to the United States Disciplinary Barracks at Fort Leavenworth, Kansas, there to be executed by lethal injection at such time as may be ordered by the Commander-in-Chief of the United States of America."

There was no outburst. Foster stood silent as the sentence was pronounced, and the only sound in the room came from the soft sobbing of his defense attorney. He turned to her.

"Lieutenant," he said, "I want to thank you for all you've done, and all you tried to do. What's our next step?"

"I'll begin work on the first appeal immediately," she said. "Then we'll keep at it until we either get your sentence commuted, get your conviction overturned or—or we exhaust all possibilities. The way this usually works, they'll have you shipped back to the states within the next couple of weeks. They'll fly me back for each appeal hearing, so you'll see me again."

"Good, I'd like that. Looks like my ride is here," he said, indicating the two MPs who stood by the door waiting to take him back to his cell. "Try not to let this get you down, Lieutenant. Believe me when I tell you that I can see how hard you tried. Like I told you before, it's time you go and find someone you can save, and put all your effort into them."

He held his hands out for the MPs, and they put the cuffs and shackles back on him before leading him out the door. Mathers was alone in the courtroom, and for just a moment, she simply sat down at the defense table and let her tears flow.

Five minutes later, she walked out of the room with her head held high.

Things moved quite a bit faster than Mathers had expected, and Noah was shipped back to the states less than a week later. She had spent as much time with him as she could, in preparation for the appeal, but there were still numerous points she needed to discuss with him. She stormed into her commanding officer's office once again.

"At ease, Lieutenant," Captain Willis said. "You want to tell me what this is all about?"

"It's Sergeant Foster," she said. "I'm working on his first appeal, but I went over to the stockade this morning and they said he's been sent off to Leavenworth already. What's going on?"

Willis leaned back in his chair and ran a hand over his face. "Lieutenant Mathers, didn't we already have this conversation? Your client got the attention of some high-profile political power, remember? Don't expect the government to drag its feet on this case."

"He still has a right to his appeal," she said. "How am I supposed to properly prepare for the appeal, when I didn't get enough time to sit down with him and get all the information I need?"

Willis looked her in the eye and let out a sigh. "Look, Abby, I know how frustrating this is, and especially for someone young and idealistic like you. You've just got to accept that you've done the best you can do, and learn to live with it. If you still need to communicate with the Sergeant on his appeal, there's an email set up that you can use, and he'll be taken to a special computer where he can read your emails and reply to them."

Mathers stood there and stared at her CO for a long moment. "Sir, with all due respect, I've been here long enough to qualify for transfer back to the US. I'm going to apply for the transfer today, and I hope you approve it." She saluted, then executed another perfect about-face before walking out the door. Willis sat there and watched her go, knowing that there was nothing he could say or do to make her feel any better. *Damn it,* he thought, *most lawyers get at least a few years under their belts before all their ideals are ripped away from them. Maybe I should have kept that case for myself, instead of giving it to a newbie.*

FOUR

DEATH ROW AT the US Disciplinary Barracks, which was better known as "The Castle," didn't look like anything you'd see in movies. Noah wasn't placed into a cell with bars, but into an actual room. There was one bed, bolted to the floor and the wall, a table with one bench seat attached to the wall beside it, a set of shelves, a stainless steel combination sink and toilet unit, and a shower stall. He was allowed to make purchases from the commissary, including food, snacks and candy, pencils and stationery, playing cards, and personal hygiene items, and the prison library brought a book cart around three times a week. He would be allowed to select up to four books at a time to keep in his room.

For a man who had been sentenced to death, this almost seemed like easy street.

He'd been given a mattress, a pillow, sheets, blankets, towels and such just before he'd been escorted into his room, so the first thing he did was make up his bed. That occupied less than three minutes, and he didn't know when he might get a chance to get the books, but there was a small tablet of paper and a couple of pens on one of the shelves, so he sat down and began to write some letters.

During the time he'd been incarcerated in Iraq, Noah had not been permitted to write any letters to friends back in the states, on the theory that the situation made him a security risk. Now that he was back in America, though, he'd been told that he could write to anyone he wanted. He had very few friends, but he wanted those that he did have to know the truth of what had happened to him.

He picked up a pen and stared at the paper for a moment, trying to decide whom to write to, first. His grandparents had kept in touch with him over the years, but he wasn't sure that he was ready to tell them what was going on. His friends from the first foster home he lived in had remained loyal to him, especially Molly, but she was a genius, and would immediately start trying to figure out some way to help him. Considering her career in a government think tank, he didn't really think it would be a good idea for her to get involved in his problems.

Jerry, his best buddy from those days, had grown up to become a rocker. He was front man for one of the most popular rock groups going, named The Question. He was rarely anywhere near home, and the letter might take months to even get to him. Jimmy, the other boy he'd befriended back then, was doing time himself, after getting caught up in an investment scam that tried to hide money from the IRS. He had two more years to go on a five-year federal sentence, so Noah figured that his own sentence would probably be over before Jimmy got out.

The only one left to write letters to, then, would be Jerry's sister, Lizzie. Lizzie and Noah had exchanged a few letters over the years. Even though she was married, he knew that she still harbored a bit of a crush where he was concerned, but he also knew that she would make sure everyone else who needed to found out the truth. He sat there for a moment, and then began to write.

Lizzie,

First, let me apologize for not writing sooner. I've been in a situation where I wasn't allowed to write letters back home to anyone, until now, and I hope you understand and forgive me. Believe me, it wasn't my choice.

I'm afraid I've gotten myself into some trouble. It's a long story, and I'll tell you, but the gist of it is that I found myself in a position where I had to kill some of my own men. Please believe me when I say that it was absolutely necessary, and I saw no other choice.

However, when I reported the incident that led to it, other men who should have been prosecuted for their own crimes all concocted a story of their own, and laid all the blame on me. I have been court-martialed, convicted and sentenced to death. I'm filing an appeal, but there really isn't much hope that I can prove my innocence, or even prevent my own execution.

Noah went on to explain the whole story, including just who Lieutenant Gibson's father was. He cautioned her not to try to get involved, and to make sure she got that through to all of the others. There was nothing they could do to help him, and any attempt to do so would only blow up in their own faces. He didn't want that, and had already accepted the inevitability of his fate.

It took him a little over an hour to write the letter, and he folded it up and put it in the envelope, leaving it open as he was required to do. He slid it through the slot in his door, so that one of the guards could take it to the mailroom. Then he sat down at his table again and began thinking about what he should do next.

He'd only been there for a couple of minutes when he heard the keys outside, and his door opened.

"Noah Foster?" One of the guards stood there in the open doorway, just looking at him.

"Yes," he said. He hadn't expected anyone to come to talk to him just yet, so his senses were on high alert.

The guard nodded. "I'm Lieutenant Spencer," he said. "I'm in charge of this unit. I make it a point to come and meet everyone assigned here. You getting settled in okay?"

"Yes, Sir," Noah said, coming to attention, "and I apologize for my disrespect a moment ago. The way the light is set in here, I couldn't see your rank tabs."

The lieutenant smiled. "It's not a problem, we don't stand on a lot of ceremony in here. At ease. Have you got everything you need?"

Noah shrugged. "I don't know that I really need anything," he said, "but would you know offhand when the book cart might come around? Oh, and when do we get to order from the commissary?"

"Well, I can send the book cart down in just a few minutes, that's no problem, and you can go ahead and put in a commissary order whenever you like. You get it the next day after your order. There should be an order form in one of those tablets on the table."

Noah looked quickly, and sure enough, he found the form tucked into the back of the tablet he'd been using. "Thank you, Sir," he said. "I'll do my best not to cause you any headaches."

The lieutenant nodded again. "I've actually been going over your file, today, and from what I can see, you must have been a model soldier and a model prisoner. Never so much as a disciplinary action, until now. I'd just about bet that there's a lot more to your story than meets the eye, but I've been around here long enough to know that it probably doesn't matter a whole lot." He glanced down the hall to his right, then back at Noah. "We got a pretty good psychologist here, a lady named Doctor Oakes. She can't do squat about your case, but there's a very good chance she can help you cope with it better. Don't hesitate to put in a request to talk with her, when things start to get to you."

Noah smiled. "Thank you, Sir, but not a whole lot gets to me. I'll be fine. Of course, it'll help when I can get some books to read."

"Okay, then," the lieutenant said. "I'll see to it the book cart comes in just a few minutes. And if you feel the need to talk with me again, I run this unit on an open-door policy. You just tell one of the guards, and they'll let me know. I'll come to see you at my first opportunity."

The door closed, the keys rattled, and Noah was locked in again. He sat down at the table and began checking off things he wanted to purchase from the commissary. He ordered shampoo, soap, deodorant and an assortment of snack foods, and added a deck of playing cards for good measure. If he was going to be in solitary confinement, he might as well play a little solitaire.

Lieutenant Spencer was true to his word, and by the time Noah finished preparing his order, he heard keys rattling again, and the door swung open. A guard stood in the hall and watched as an inmate trusty pushed the book cart into the room.

"You allowed to keep four books in your room," the trusty said, in the down-home dialect of the South, "and after this time, you got to give me back a book to get a new one. If you tell me what kind of books you like, I'll try to pick some out the library and put on the cart for you."

Noah grinned at him. "I appreciate that," he said. "I like stories about history, especially stories that talk about how people did things a hundred years ago or two hundred or however long. Westerns are good, too, and if there aren't enough of those to go around, I like spy stories and stuff like that." He was looking through the books on the cart as he spoke, and pulled out a book about King Arthur, and another about magic. "These kinds of stories would be okay, too," he said, and the trusty nodded.

Noah chose his four books, and set them on one of the shelves. The trusty began to pull the cart back out the door. "Okay, I be back in a couple days, and I see what I can do for you. My name's Benny, you be seeing me a lot."

The guard closed the door as Benny left the room, and Noah sat down to begin reading. King Arthur was one of his favorite quasi-historical figures, and Noah enjoyed reading about his adventures, whether from the original legends or those written by later authors.

Life settled into a routine rather quickly, mostly involving reading, eating the occasional snack, working out in the room, and his once-daily, hour-long recreational break, which took place in a concrete square somewhere in the middle of the building. The top of the square, but for a double layer of chain-link fencing, was without a roof and open to the sky. Since the weather was warm, he enjoyed the sensation of being outdoors, even if he couldn't see a tree or blade of grass anywhere.

The rec yard, that concrete square, was just about fifty feet on a side, so Noah calculated that twenty-seven laps would constitute about a mile run. He ran for the full hour every time he got to the rec yard, averaging a mile every eight minutes, which gave him a little over seven miles a day.

In his room, he did push-ups, sit-ups, squats and jumping jacks, averaging three hours of PT every day. His shower stall had a solid rod across its door from which a curtain hung, and he began using it for chin-ups, inverted crunches and other workout exercises that he devised. He had always kept himself in good condition, but he was rapidly getting into the best shape of his life, even if only to escape the boredom of death row.

He had been there a month when Lieutenant Mathers turned up. He was in the middle of a workout when the door opened, and one of the guards told him that he had a visitor. Since he hadn't been expecting her, he had to go to the visiting room covered in sweat, and he was surprised when she rushed across the room to give him a hug.

"Sergeant Foster," she said excitedly. "I've been trying to get word to you for two weeks now that I got myself transferred back to the states. I'm actually in Missouri, at Fort Leonard Wood, but since I'm still officially assigned to your case I can come to visit you anytime you need me to. Sit down, sit down!"

She hurried around to her side of the table and took her chair, while Noah sat down in his own.

"So, how are you doing?" Mathers asked. "Anybody mistreating you in here? Any threats, beatings, anything like that?"

Noah shook his head. "No, nothing at all," he said. "I'm doing well. I get to read, work out, rest when I want to. This whole death row thing isn't all that bad, to be honest. Well, except for the fact that it comes to an unhappy ending."

Mathers rolled her eyes. "Do you ever take anything seriously? Listen, I've been working on the appeal, and I finally managed to get hold of your psychological records. The problem is that they don't show you having any serious troubling issues. This histrionic blunted affect disorder that it talks about, that's considered a high-functioning mental condition that doesn't prevent you from acting rationally, and even makes rational decision-making easier, because you naturally think in logical sequences."

Noah shrugged and grinned. "Sure, as long as I've got somebody to copy. Rational? I wonder if there's an accurate definition for that word. My real concern is that maybe I'm too rational, rather than irrational. To me, seeing what I saw when I got to the lieutenant and the platoon that day, I took what I considered to be rational action. I put a stop to the situation. Seems to me it's the rest of the world acting irrationally, by trying to eliminate me from the gene pool."

Mathers sighed, and shook her head. "I know, and I agree completely, but that doesn't help our appeal. If the judge would actually read what this says about you, he'd know that it's almost impossible for you to act in any manner other than rationally. That should be enough, at least, to commute your sentence to life."

They talked it over for a couple of hours, but every idea that Lieutenant Mathers put forth was shot down by Noah's logic. There simply didn't seem to be a feasible way to convince the court that Noah deserved to live, after he'd already been sentenced to death. Noah did his best to comfort his attorney, who was taking it all a lot harder than he was.

"Aren't you scared?" Mathers asked him. "Aren't you worried about the fact that they want to take you into that room, strap you down and inject chemicals in you that will make you go to sleep forever?"

Noah's eyebrows went up. "Why should that scare me? You know, my grandfather is a minister, and many years ago he led me through the process of becoming a Christian. If my grandfather is right, then death is only going to be a doorway from this world into Heaven. And if he's wrong, then it's simply going to be the end of my consciousness. I won't feel anything, I won't know that I'm dead, I will just come to an end. There won't be any pain, there won't be any sensations at all, because there won't be any *me*. So you tell me, what is there to fear in death?"

The lieutenant's eyes were wide. "What is there to fear? Maybe nothing, for you, but what about the people you leave behind? What about the people who will hurt and grieve because you're gone? Aren't there people out there who depend on you?"

"No, not really," Noah said. "I have very few friends, and my grandparents are the only family I have left. They claim to be happy to hear from me now and then, but they don't want to be close because I scare them. Being a minister, my grandfather simply can't understand someone who doesn't have the capacity to love inside him, so to him, I must seem like some sort of demon. Whatever the case, I'm pretty much alone in this world, and while those few friends might think it's sad that I'm gone, we're not so close that it would bother them for more than a couple of hours."

Mathers shook her head. "Sergeant Foster," she said, "it will bother me. I know, down deep inside my heart, I *know* that you are innocent of the things you were convicted of doing. I know that, while some people might think your psychological issues make you a problem, the truth is that you are probably one of the finest men I've ever met, so if these monsters manage to do what they want to do, and take you down the hall and execute you, then you can be certain that there will be at least one person out here who will mourn your passing." Mathers wiped furiously at her eyes, at the tears that were leaking out of them. She began gathering her notes. "Anyway—I'll be back in about two weeks, and hopefully I'll have some more ideas. If it's possible at all, I'm going to find a way to keep you alive."

Noah looked at her, and smiled. "Something I need you to understand," he said. "Just because I don't fear death, I don't want you to think that I welcome it. I still have a survival instinct, so if you come up with something that will work, then trust me, I'm all for it. Good luck, Lieutenant Mathers, for both our sakes."

Noah knocked on the door, and the guard escorted him back to his room. When he got there, he sat down and thought about Lieutenant Mathers and her determination to stop his execution. While a part of him hoped she would succeed, another part was fairly sure that she would not, and he realized that when that final day arrived and he took that last walk down the hall, it would be she who truly suffered, rather than himself.

Some people might have thought that he was being compassionate, concerned for her feelings. The truth, though, was that his mental programming, the logical progression of thoughts that he had forced upon himself since he was seven years old, required him to consider the best interests of the people he dealt with. In Iraq, that had led him to become an extremely efficient soldier, so that his enemies did not suffer unnecessarily. In this case, it meant that he felt he should lessen her grief as much as he could.

Noah decided to end his appeals. By doing so, he would clear the way for his own execution, which would relieve Lieutenant Mathers of her duties as his attorney and allow her to begin the grieving process while he was still alive, which he had read could sometimes make it easier to bear.

He sat down at his table and began composing a letter, telling her of his decision. He didn't explain that he was doing it primarily to make things easier for her, because he knew that would make her more resistant to his choice. Instead, he told her that he was beginning to feel a depression set in, and that since he had been without emotions for so many years, the sudden onslaught was just more than he could handle. He pointed out that there was no hope, not really, of any success in preventing his execution, so he would prefer to simply let it happen as soon as possible.

And then, he encouraged her in her plan to write his story. Perhaps, he said, his name might one day be cleared by her efforts, and he hoped that the attempt to tell his story truthfully would help to bring her peace.

Since the letter was to his attorney, he didn't have to leave it open for inspection. Noah sealed the envelope and added the address that she had given him during her visit, affixed a stamp, and pushed it through the slot.

Two days had passed since Lieutenant Mathers had come to visit, and Noah was back to his usual schedule, working out for an hour and a half in the morning before sitting down to read until lunchtime. After lunch, he would get his hour of rec time, running laps around the yard, and then would come back and read until dinner, after which he would work out again for an additional hour and a half. It was morning, and he had just finished his morning workout routine, before climbing into the shower to wash off the sweat.

He heard the keys over the sound of the water, reached up to turn it off quickly, and then peeked around the curtain. Lieutenant Spencer stood there, grinning at him.

"Foster," he said, "you got a visitor, a light colonel from the JAG Office. Better hustle it up, she doesn't look like one who wants to be kept waiting."

Noah's eyebrows shot up. "Yes, Sir, be right out." He hurriedly rinsed himself off, dried as quickly as he could, and climbed back into his brown jumpsuit. As soon as he was dressed, he knocked on the door, and he wasn't surprised when it opened immediately.

Lieutenant Spencer was still there, and personally escorted him down the hall to the interview room.

The lieutenant opened the door and let him step inside, to find a thin, graying woman he'd never seen before sitting at the table. As Spencer had said, she wore the insignia of a Lieutenant Colonel in the Army. She looked up at him and smiled, motioning for him to take the seat across from her.

"Sergeant Foster," she said, "I am Lieutenant Colonel Janice Hogan, from the Judge Advocate General's Office. I've been sent here to interview you prior to your execution."

Noah sat there and looked at the woman for a moment. "Wow, you guys don't waste any time, do you?"

The woman smiled. "Well, I try not to. On the other hand, contrary to what you might think at this moment, my purpose is not to hasten your execution. My interview is on another matter entirely, but since it wouldn't do me any good to try to interview you afterward, well, I thought it best to come on down and see you now."

Noah's eyebrows raised, and he cocked his head a little to one side in confusion. "I'll grant you it wouldn't do a whole lot of good to try to interview me after my date with the needles, but if you're not here as part of the process for getting ready for the execution, then can I ask what this is about?"

"It may well be about keeping you alive, Sergeant Foster," she said. "Assuming, of course, that's something that still interests you at all. Does it?"

Noah sat there for a moment and thought through what she had just said. "It does," he said, "depending on what it's going to cost me. Since I know what kind of pressure has been applied to make sure I keep that date, then I can only assume that you're not who you claim to be, and this meeting isn't anything like what you logged when you signed in here today. That tells me that there's a catch, and until I know what it is, I'm not going to make any agreements."

Hogan's eyebrows were the ones to go up this time. "Impressive," she said. "No one else has ever figured me out so fast. What tipped you off?"

Noah shrugged. "It's like I said," he said. "Congressman Gibson wants me dead, because I killed his son and because he doesn't want the reason his son died to ever come out publicly. Since he's on the fast track to the Republican nomination for president, and stands a decent chance of winning in the next election, I don't think there's anybody in the Army who is going to go up against him. That tells me you're not Army, so you must be with one of those alphabet soup groups that we hear all the legends about. Normally, I'd guess CIA, but Gibson is on their oversight committee. FBI doesn't have the kind of power it would take to get you in here like this, nor does DEA. If I had to gamble on it, I probably bet you have something to do with Homeland Security, am I right?"

Hogan smiled. "No, but you're closer than I would've thought you could get. That's some incredible deductive reasoning. I've seen reports about you and your ability to extrapolate facts from minor details, but I wouldn't have believed it if I hadn't seen it myself." She reached up and slipped both of her thumbs under what appeared to be her hairline, and lifted the gray wig to let Noah see the blonde hair underneath. "As you can see, you're very close to being right. I'm not who I claim to be, but this disguise makes it possible for me to move about in circles that I couldn't normally get into. Now, shall we continue this conversation?"

"Sure, we can continue," Noah said. "At least up until the point where I find out what the catch is."

Hogan smiled and inclined her head, a tacit admission that there was indeed a catch. "And if it's something you can live with?"

"Then I suppose we'll keep on talking," he said. "What's the chance we can just cut to the chase and you tell me what it is right now?"

The woman across the table from him laughed, and he

realized that she wasn't nearly as old as she appeared to be. "A very good chance, actually," she said. "I'll just come right out and say it. You're one of the most capable and efficient killers that the Army has ever seen. You lack any semblance of human emotion, and appear to be completely without conscience or morals, other than those you impose upon yourself. That makes you an absolutely ideal candidate for an opening in my organization. If you accept the job, then I make all of these troubles go away, set you up with a different identity, and train you to defend your country in ways you never dreamed of before. Your duties would be to act in the best interests of the United States, including the elimination of specific human targets when necessary."

"I'd be an assassin? Is that what you're saying?"

"That would be one of your job descriptions," she said with a grin. "You've seen all the superspy movies, the ones that make it seem like American agents are somehow beyond the normal human?"

Noah chuckled. "Yeah," he said, "but I could never suspend disbelief long enough to convince myself that Tom Cruise could be one of them. Are you trying to say that such agents actually exist?"

The grin got wider. "I'm trying to say that they will as soon as you agree to sign on." She leaned forward. "Sergeant Foster, there's no doubt in my mind that you were telling the truth in your court-martial, about what really happened out there. Now, you can sit here and await your execution, or you can accept my proposition and become even more important to the peace and security of this nation than you ever were as a soldier."

"And all I've gotta do is kill the people you tell me to kill, right? Well, let me ask a fairly serious question. Who decides who those targets might be?"

She smiled. "I do," she said, "but not arbitrarily. Other agencies submit a request for elimination, naming a target that they feel should be removed. Along with that request must be a complete and detailed file outlining the reasons behind the request. I was appointed by the president as an autonomous director of the organization I run, which is called E & E, and before you ask, that is short for Elimination and Eradication. I review the file, and if I can honestly tell myself that I agree that this person should be removed, then I will approve it and send the elimination order down to one of the teams that I run."

Noah tilted his head to the left. "Teams?"

She nodded. "Yes," she said. "I currently have seven agents, men and women who, for various reasons, came onto my radar as having the potential to be beneficial to my mission, just like you. Each of those agents has a support team, consisting of a transportation specialist, an intelligence specialist, and a capable thug, for when a little extra muscle is needed. If you come on board, you will have such a team, yourself. You'll be trained in a number of skills and disciplines, and when you go into the field, your team will answer to you and only you. You, in turn, will answer only to me."

Noah looked into her eyes for several seconds, and concluded that she was being completely honest with him. "Well, so far, the only problem I got with this whole plan is the idea that you get to decide who lives and who dies. Who decided that you are the one who gets to play God?"

"Our commander-in-chief," she said. "Up until I got this assignment, I was an intelligence analyst with another of those groups that you mentioned earlier. The president was intrigued by the fact that I would occasionally suggest that assassination might be an appropriate measure to take, and a few years ago he called me in for a private conversation. He told me that he had convinced the Joint Chiefs of Staff that it was time to create an organization along these lines, and that he had a candidate for its management, namely me. He offered me the job, and assured me that I would be completely autonomous and could never be ordered to sanction an assassination, so I took it."

"Just out of curiosity, do you have any trouble sleeping at night?" Noah asked.

"Not a bit," she said. "You'll find, if you accept my offer, that I never sanction an assassination lightly. I have to be absolutely certain that it's justified and warranted, or I'll disapprove the request. My decision is always final, and there's nobody above me to complain to. I can guarantee you, if you come aboard, you will never wonder whether your target deserves what you do to him. That's because I will make sure you know exactly why I have sanctioned that death, including giving you access to all of the information that led me to decide it needed to be done."

Noah sat there in silence for a full three minutes, just looking into the eyes of the woman across the table. He expected her to become impatient with him, to demand an answer, but she just sat there and looked straight back into his. At last, he spoke.

"So how would this work?" Noah asked her.

"Two days from now, you'll be found dead in your cell, hanging from the air vent, an apparent suicide. You'll be carried out and buried, a death certificate issued to serve as proof to anyone who ever wants to know that Sergeant Noah Foster died in prison by his own hand. Of course, the body that gets buried won't be yours. You'll be loaded into an ambulance and driven to a highly secret facility where your training will begin. Among the things you'll be taught will be your own new life history, and because we like to keep things simple, all we're going to do is change your last name, and we'll give you a history that will let you go out into the world as a free man. You'll also have your appearance slightly altered, not a lot, but just enough so that if you ever ran into someone who knew you before, they would go, 'Wow, that guy looks a little like someone I used to know, but it's not him.' It's not that we're really worried about you running into old friends, since we already know you don't have very many, but as you can imagine, the existence of E & E is something we don't want to let the world in on. Any other questions?"

Noah sat there for another minute, watching her eyes. He liked the fact that she didn't flinch, because most people couldn't play stare down with him. He suddenly smiled, and leaned forward with his hand extended.

"Noah Whoever-I-am, ready to report for duty. Just tell me what to do next."

"Well, the first thing I want you to do is to sit down and write as detailed a narrative as you can about your life. What I want is to know how you see yourself, who you believe you are. Just write it out in your own words, and keep it in your cell. We'll pick it up when we come to get you."

Noah's eyebrows went up slightly. "No problem, I can do that," he said. "Is it going to matter that you'll find out I'm nothing but a wolf in human clothing?"

FIVE

NOAH WAS ASLEEP when they came for him. His door opened, which woke him instantly, but he stayed on his bunk as if sleeping. A second later, he felt the light sting of a needle, and then he was asleep again.

He came back to consciousness slowly, and could tell that he was lying on something that was moving. He tried to open his eyes but they wouldn't, and when he tried to move his hands, he found that they were unresponsive as well.

He could hear, though, and the sounds coming through told him that he was in a vehicle. The steady hum beneath him was from tires on the surface of a road, of that he was sure. The purring noise was certainly from a well-tuned engine.

"Ma'am," he heard a voice say, "I believe he's awake. It'll take a few minutes for everything to wear off, but his breathing says he's conscious."

"Thank you, Marco," he heard, and he recognized the voice as Lieutenant Colonel Hogan. "Noah, just relax. We've gotten you out of the Castle, and we're well on the way to the training facility. The cocktail of drugs we gave you should wear off the rest of the way shortly, so don't fight it. You'll be able to sit up in just a few minutes."

Noah took her advice and relaxed, and a few seconds later he began to feel some of his muscles twitching. He tried again to open his eyes, and this time it worked. A quick glance around told him that he was in the back of an ambulance, and Hogan was sitting beside him along with a paramedic.

"Well, hello," Colonel Hogan said. "Welcome back to the land of the living. Oh, wait a minute—I spoke too soon. You're actually quite dead, just wait and I'll show you the news stories about it."

"No problem," Noah said. His voice sounded rough. "I'm not worried about the news of the past, just what's to come in the future."

"Well, that would spoil all my fun," she said. "It's really quite a story. It seems that this young sergeant, who was sentenced to die for killing his platoon leader and several of his men, had this horrible attack of conscience and hung himself in his cell. There was a faint heartbeat when he was found, so of course he was rushed out to the hospital, but unfortunately, he passed away in the ambulance. He'll be buried in the prison graveyard tomorrow morning. Pretty good story, don't you think?"

Noah, his muscles still weak and sluggish, struggled up to a sitting position. "I think I read a book with that plot, once. In the one I read, though, the hero got a second chance at life. Your story go anywhere like that?"

Hogan reached up and took off her wig, tossing it into a bag at her feet. A moment later, she scratched just in front of her left ear and Noah saw a flap of skin come loose. She tugged on it, and a rubber mask peeled off of her face. The woman who sat there in Hogan's uniform was suddenly blonde and twenty years younger.

She extended a hand. "I'm Allison Peterson," she said, and Noah shook hands with her. "I'm the administrator of E & E, and your new boss."

Noah grinned and nodded. "Pleased to meet you," he said, "for the second time. So, I gather everything worked the way you expected? I did as you said, didn't eat a thing all day and tried to act depressed."

"Like a charm," Allison said. "Fasting helps the drug work better, so it can slow your heart down to almost nothing. We needed the prison doctors to call for the ambulance. However, you've actually been out cold for almost thirty hours. Your death has already been certified, and your body has already been shipped back to the prison for burial. Fingerprint records have all been changed, dental records, everything; the body they got looks so much like you that even you might believe you're dead, if you saw it."

"I doubt it," Noah replied, still grinning. "I tend to disbelieve things that are obviously not true, and since I'm sitting here, well…So, what's next?"

She took a deep breath and let her smile relax a bit, even though it stayed in place. "Next is your initial training. We have a facility set up here in Colorado where you'll be instructed in new styles and techniques of martial arts, various new weapons, and lots of other super-spy-type stuff, and some of the most intense physical training you've ever experienced."

"Sounds cool," Noah said. "I've been involved in martial arts since I was eight years old. My grandfather thought it would be a good idea, something to help me focus my 'anger and other emotions.' I enjoyed it, because it had so much structure to it."

Allison watched him coolly. "I know," she said. "I also know that it was one of the things that caused your grandparents to send you back to the foster homes. They said you became violent and too intense, that you scared them."

He shrugged. "This man showed up at our house one day and started screaming at my grandmother," he said. "I thought he was threatening her, so I ran into the room and attacked. Turned out he wasn't actually screaming at her, he was a friend of theirs who was crying because his wife left him. That was the one that actually set them off, but it seemed like the more I got into the martial arts classes, the faster my reactions became. My instructor said I was a natural, but my grandmother thought there was something weird about me, because I was always working out anytime I didn't have something else to do."

"And what did your grandfather say?"

Noah chuckled. "He put me in the martial arts classes because he'd been a marine, years before. He naturally thought that being able to defend yourself was a skill every man should have, so he wanted me to be able to do so. He thought it was hilarious, though, six months into my training, when I began beating my instructor. Needless to say, he and I were not in the same weight class, so when he agreed to spar with me, it was more of a gag than anything else. Kinda surprised him when I began winning our little matches. Grandpa thought it was funny."

"What made him become scared of you?"

"A lot of the guys in my class were into lifting weights, so I talked him into buying me a weight bench. I started working out every day, and it really made me feel good, so Grandpa decided he'd work out with me, make it sort of an 'us guys' kind of thing. We were both benching about a hundred, hundred and ten pounds when we started, but a month later, I could press two twenty, and he was only up to about one forty. That was when Grandma started saying I was weird and unnatural, and he started pulling back from me. It was only a month or so later when he told me they'd have to put me back in foster care because of health problems."

Allison nodded. "Noah, you claim to have no emotions, and everything in your psych profile says that's completely true. Did you feel anything during that time? Any rejection, any sadness?"

Noah shook his head. "No. Like everything else in my life, I looked at it logically. It was obvious to me that he was lying about health problems, because he hadn't even been to see a doctor. Since he was lying, that meant he had other reasons for not wanting me living there anymore, and those reasons could only lead to them feeling resentment if they had to keep putting up with me. I told him it was okay, and that I would pray for him to get better, and I think that took away some of his guilt. For me, it just meant a change of scenery."

"Just another transition," Allison said. "You were sent to a foster home in the city where your grandparents lived, at first, but then you got transferred back to the one they took you out of. How did that happen?"

"You know, Ms. Peterson, all of this is in the memoir you had me write for you," Noah said. "It was lying on my table, did you get it?"

"We got it," Allison said with a grin. "I've even skimmed through it, but I haven't had the chance to read it in detail. That's why I'm asking you questions directly. How did you get yourself back to your original foster home?"

Noah grinned. "If I was going to be in the foster system, I wanted to be back around my friends, and back with the caseworker that I knew and trusted. The one they gave me that time was a man, and he had a mean streak as wide as he was. Seemed like no matter what his kids asked of him, he would do everything he could to make sure they didn't get what they wanted. One of the first things he did was take away my weight bench; he said I couldn't have it because it would make other kids jealous." He shrugged. "I cut school one day, and called Ms. Gamble, my original caseworker. I said this guy was making me uncomfortable, with the way he looked at me. Two days later, she got an order from the court to transfer me back to Mrs. Connors' house, and back to my few real friends."

Allison nodded approvingly. "Good," she said. "Deviousness can save your life, in our line of work. Among the things you'll be learning will be techniques for lying convincingly, beating a polygraph, acting and creative writing. You'll learn to use your imagination to create a character or scenario that will help you carry out a mission, and we'll develop your natural acting ability, this knack you have for making people think you're perfectly normal when you're not, so that you can become that character or act out that scenario."

Noah shifted himself around until he found a comfortable position. "You mentioned a support team," he said. "When do I get to meet them?"

"That depends on how well you do in training. Obviously, if it turns out we can't use you, then there won't be a need for a team. And incidentally, this isn't a pass or fail kind of course; it's more like pass or die, because if you flunk out, we simply eliminate you. Nothing personal, you understand, but we do everything we can to minimize the risk that E & E will ever be exposed."

"Of course," Noah said. "I was pretty sure that's how it would be, because it's just logical. Anyone you recruit who can't perform up to the standard you need would have to be eliminated. Nothing else would make sense."

"I expected you to see it that way. Okay, so to actually answer your question, assuming you make it through your basic training, we'll introduce you to your team sometime in the next few weeks. Normally, we don't even bother to recruit people for your team until we know whether we're going to need them, but I'm feeling pretty confident about you, so I've got people in mind."

"That also makes sense. I'm guessing you find them in the same kind of place you found me? Prisons, places like that?"

Allison nodded. "Prisons, county jails, juvenile detention centers and just about anywhere else our society uses as a dumping ground for people with some of the skills we need. For example, some of the transportation specialists we use are former car thieves, drug runners, bootleggers and such. Our intelligence specialists tend to be young and extremely bright, with a penchant for computer hacking."

"And the muscle tends to be just that, I bet, guys who have a tendency toward violence, and just need a little direction. Am I right?"

"Of course," she said. "If humankind were capable of being

completely honest with itself, it would probably be possible to find a way to properly use every skill and talent that people naturally turn to evil purposes. One of the things that has always amazed me is how many people will work harder at doing something criminal, something that will make some fast cash but have a high risk of ruining their lives, than they will at doing something that's perfectly legitimate and can keep them happy for the rest of their days. To me, that is what I call illogical."

"Ma'am?" the paramedic said. It was the first time he had spoken since Noah had awakened. "Driver says we'll be pulling into the compound in about fifteen minutes."

SIX

"THANK YOU, MARCO," she said. "Incidentally, Marco, this is Noah. Noah, meet Marco. Marco is one of our thugs, and he's proven himself enough times that we use him in a lot of different capacities. At times, he becomes the fifth man on a team, if a little extra muscle is needed."

Marco and Noah looked at each other. "Welcome to Neverland, Noah," Marco said. "If you make it, maybe I'll get to back you up one day."

Noah nodded at him. "Then let's hope I make it, so we get that chance." He turned to Allison. "Neverland?"

"An inside joke," she said. "Each of the teams is named after a place, person or thing from mythology or fairy tales. For example, if you make it through, you'll be heading up Team Camelot, since that's the next designation on my list."

Noah's eyebrows went up. "Interesting," he said, "especially in light of the fact that King Arthur is my own favorite historical character. Will that be my codename? King Arthur?"

Allison laughed, and Noah was surprised at how genuine and unpretentious it was. "No, I'm afraid not," she said. "If a codename is used for you, it will be simply Camelot, and each of your team members would be designated as Camelot One, Camelot Two, Camelot Three, etc. We don't usually resort to such theatrics, though. In this day and age, secure communication depends more on technology than it does on subterfuge. Each of our people has a phone that is capable of ultra-secure communication, anywhere in the world, due to some awesome encryption technology. I can call one of them up, give them detailed orders and instructions on their missions without ever once having to use a code, because my phone will scramble it into meaningless and indecipherable beeps and tones, while the recipient's phone contains the algorithm that will turn it back into the sound of my voice. Oh, and by the way, it's the confirmed voiceprint of the person I'm calling that activates that algorithm, so even if someone else gets hold of the phone, they'd never hear those orders."

Noah nodded. "Yeah, I can understand how that works. Pretty cool." He felt the ambulance slowing down. "Seems like we're about there."

"Yep," Allison said. "Listen, when you go to get out of the ambulance, be careful. The drugs we used might still make you a little groggy, so don't be afraid to hang on to Marco. He'll help you get into your room. You'll find clothing and just about anything you might need already there. Needless to say, it's not possible to bring personal effects with you, since you're officially dead. We don't use a uniform, so our procurement department has just stocked you up on an assortment of clothing for right now. You'll find that we know quite a bit about you, and so your preferences should be pretty well reflected in the choices we've made."

"Hey, just about anything would be better than the boxers they gave me in prison. Damn things feel like they're made of sandpaper." He could feel the ambulance maneuvering its way along an apparently twisting path. "Good-sized place you got here?"

"Actually, it is. We've got about ten thousand acres, a little over fifteen square miles. There are various obstacle courses and training structures. We've got mockups of different kinds of rural and urban environments, military installations, terrorist enclaves and compounds, you name it. We're right on the edge of some government facilities, so we're under a no-fly zone. The only aircraft that can get into our airspace are our own and, in some areas, the same holds true for vehicles. Nothing comes in, unless it's one of ours."

The ambulance stopped. Marco moved to open the back doors, and that's when Noah realized that it was daylight outside, early morning, apparently.

Allison reached into her pocket and withdrew a plastic card that she handed to Noah. "This is your temporary ID and debit card," she said. "You'll use it to pay for things, here. We'll get you set up with proper ID within a day or so, and actually on the payroll."

Noah glanced at the card, and saw that it was a simple debit card, without even a name on it. Allison went on. "I'm going to guess that you're probably hungry. Once we get you into your room, Marco will show you how to get to the nearest restaurant."

"Yeah, beats heck out of going to a chow hall," Marco said with a grin. "They treat us pretty good here, and the food is awesome. You'll like it."

Noah shrugged. "I could eat," he said.

Allison rose and stepped down onto the ground, which Noah could see consisted of a paved parking lot, while Marco reached down to help Noah up. They got him on his feet, and Noah realized that he actually was a bit on the dizzy side. Marco stepped down first, then held on to Noah, who was also holding on to the edge of the door until he got both feet planted firmly on the ground.

Noah looked around, and realized he was standing in the parking lot of what looked like a small motel. The lot was surrounded on three sides by a U-shaped building, and he counted about thirty doors facing into the center. Several of the doors had cars parked in front of them.

"This is our temporary housing unit, where we put new people for the first few days, until we get them sorted out. It used to be a motel, and that's what everyone calls it: the motel." Allison pointed at the door that was closest to him. "That one's yours," she said. She handed him a key on a plastic fob. It was marked with the number seven, and he saw the same number on the door. "There's a TV and computer in your room, and you're connected to the internet. Don't try to make contact with anyone from your past; that's a guaranteed failure and we've already discussed what that means. Get yourself settled in, and then Marco will walk you over for breakfast. Your first class starts at ten this morning, so you've got a couple of hours to get breakfast, take a shower and get dressed. You'll be seeing me around, don't worry, but I'm not one of your instructors. We'll talk now and then, though."

She turned and walked over to a car that was parked nearby and drove away. Noah looked at Marco, who was standing beside him. "Ready?" Noah asked, and Marco grinned. Noah walked carefully to the door, still a little shaky, and used the key to open it.

It looked like the kind of room you'd find in one of the better chain motels, with a few added features. There was a queen-sized bed, along with a dresser and what appeared to be a closet, a table with three chairs, and a desk with yet another chair and a laptop computer on top of it. Sitting on top of the dresser was a large, flat-panel TV, and he saw a small refrigerator, a microwave oven and a coffee maker set up on the counter back by the bathroom.

The bathroom itself was large, and he was surprised to see a jacuzzi tub. He glanced at Marco. "Nice place," he said.

"Yeah, they tend to pamper us just a little bit. Trust me when I tell you that you're going to work for it, and I mean work hard."

Noah shook his head. "Work don't scare me," he said. "Have I got time for a shower before breakfast?"

Marco grinned. "Come on, man, you don't smell that bad. Let's go grab some eggs and bacon, then I'm going to get a shower myself, after that. You can get one then."

Noah nodded, and followed Marco back out of the room,

locking it behind him. Marco turned right and went to the end of the row of rooms, then took another right when he reached it. They were on the right leg of the U, and Marco pointed at a brightly lit building just a few hundred yards away.

"That's the restaurant, dude," he said. "It works just like a regular one, and you can order anything off the menu. The food is good, that much I can tell you."

They entered the restaurant building, and Noah was surprised when an actual hostess seated them. As soon as she handed them their menus, a waitress appeared and poured coffee for each of them, then waited to take their breakfast orders. Noah chose the eggs and bacon that Marco had mentioned, because they just sounded appealing. Marco followed suit, and the waitress walked away.

Noah added sugar to his coffee, then took a sip. "Now, that is good," he said. "Trust me, the stuff they give you on death row is probably the cheapest generic crap you can buy anywhere. This is good coffee."

"I told you, the food here is great. Wait 'til you taste the bacon, I've never been able to find any out in the world that was half as good."

Noah took another sip of coffee, then set the cup on the table. "So what's on the agenda for me today?"

"Well, this morning you've got to go see Doc Parker. He's the shrink that decides where to place all the new recruits who come in. He'll decide whether you're actually an assassin, or if you belong in a support team. He'll keep you busy until lunchtime, and we'll come back here for that, then you've got two hours of PT. After that, you get a half-hour break so you can grab a shower, then they got you scheduled for weapons class. You'll like that one, it's pretty cool. You learn to use every kind of weapon you can imagine, and probably a thousand things you'd never think of on your own. Our boss lady works on the philosophy that absolutely anything can be used as a weapon, and she likes to make sure we all understand what that means."

"So, even the support teams go through this training?"

"Well, at least some of it," Marco said. "Let's face it, there's always the possibility that you and your team could be out on a mission, and something happens to you. That doesn't necessarily mean the mission is over, and there's a good possibility that your support team will be ordered to complete it. They need to know how to use the weapons, too."

Noah shrugged. "I guess that makes sense," he said. The waitress brought their plates, and the two men enjoyed their breakfast, chatting about inconsequential things as they ate.

When breakfast was over, they went back to the motel, and Noah stepped into his room. "I'm going to go grab a shower, myself," Marco said, "and I'll be back over here as soon as I'm done. You're supposed to be at Doc Parker's office by ten, so we got a little over an hour. See you in a bit."

Noah waved. He started rummaging through the dresser of the closet to find some clean clothes to put on after his shower, then turned on the water. A quick glance around the bathroom showed his own favorite brands of soap, shampoo, shaving cream and even razors, and he had to grin. He thought for a moment about climbing into the jacuzzi, but then decided to just settle for a shower.

Twenty minutes later, he stepped out of the bathroom feeling more refreshed and alive than he could remember feeling in several months. The dresser held clean socks and underwear, and he found jeans and polo shirts in other drawers. There were nicer clothes hanging in the closet, including a couple of business suits, but no one had told him to get dressed up, so he decided to go casual.

He peeked out the door but saw no sign of Marco, so he lay back on the bed and picked up the TV remote. He clicked the TV on, and started flipping through channels, mostly just curious about what kind of programming would be available in a place like this, but then he stumbled across a news program and saw an announcer talking right next to a photograph of his own face. He turned up the volume to listen.

The announcer was talking about how Sergeant Noah Foster, who had recently been convicted of multiple murders in Iraq, had committed suicide in his cell at Leavenworth. Apparently, Sergeant Foster had left behind a suicide note in which he recanted his earlier claims that he had been innocent.

Reporters had interviewed the sergeant's family, who declined to appear on camera, but said that he had always been a troubled young man. His grandfather was quoted as saying that he hoped Noah had made peace with God before he hung himself.

Noah shook his head. He wasn't a bit surprised that his grandparents wanted to distance themselves from him, and a part of him understood and respected their feelings.

The reporter also interviewed his attorney, Lieutenant Mathers. She was shown on camera, loudly insisting that there was something fishy about his death. "Let me tell you something," she said to the reporter. "We were preparing an appeal, an appeal that had a very good chance of overturning Sergeant Foster's conviction, and there is no way, let me repeat that, there is no way that I will ever believe that man took his own life."

The reporter went back to talking about the suicide note, and Noah turned off the TV. He wished there were a way he could let Lieutenant Mathers know that things had worked out for him, but there wasn't. He was allowed no contact with anyone from the past, and that would include her. Hopefully, she would figure out that there was no way she could win before it destroyed her completely.

There was a tap on the door, and Noah called out, "Come in." Marco stuck his head in.

"Ready to go?" Marco asked, and Noah rose from the bed, clicking off the TV as he did so.

"All set," he said, and stepped outside, locking the door behind him. He followed Marco to a fairly new Ford Mustang, and climbed into the passenger seat as Marco got behind the wheel.

"Okay, we're off to see the wizard, a.k.a. Doc Parker," Marco said. "When we get there, I'm going to let you go on inside, and I'll just wait out here in the car." He held up a paperback novel. "Brought my own entertainment with me, so don't worry about trying to hurry things along. I'll be sitting outside when you get done."

"No problem," Noah said.

SEVEN

DOC PARKER WAS a small man who appeared to be in his late 70s, maybe even early 80s. He had an office that sat in a little building all by itself, and he had been waiting for Noah when he arrived.

"Come in, come in," he said. "You're late, young man. You were supposed to be here three minutes ago. One thing you need to learn here, if you learn nothing else, is to be prompt. If you can't keep to a schedule, how can those working with you be sure that you can do your part, when the time comes?"

Noah's eyebrows shot up. "My apologies, Sir," he said. "I'm new here, just arrived this morning."

"What's that got to do with anything? There will be a lot of times, if you live long enough, when you will arrive in the morning at some new destination and have to kill five people before you can even have breakfast. Now, imagine if there are other people depending on you to do your part, so that they can then do theirs—should they have to wait for you to acclimate yourself? Should they have to hope that you show up on time? Bear in mind, if you don't show up on time and do your part, there's a pretty good chance that some of them are going to die. Promptness, my boy, promptness is important, and don't you forget it."

Noah dipped his head once. "Understood, Sir. It won't happen again."

"You're damned right it won't, because if it does, it will be the last time." The old man pointed at a chair. "Put your ass right there," he said, "and pucker your lips as tightly shut as your asshole is."

Noah took the seat, and sat there in silence as the old man sat down behind the desk in front of him. He waited for a couple of minutes, as Parker seemed to be looking for something in the papers scattered across the top of the desk.

Suddenly, the old fellow looked him in the eye. "Well, I'll be damned," he said. "If I didn't know better, I'd think you knew how to follow orders." He paused and looked at Noah for several seconds, then broke into a huge grin. "That's two tests you passed in as many minutes. Most newbies get tired of waiting for me to stop digging through my papers, and speak up to get my attention, which means they fail. Those who don't fall for that one usually grin and start talking after I act surprised that they didn't, which means they fail. About one in fifty are smart enough sit there and say nothing, like you just did. You wanna tell me who tipped you off?"

Noah grinned, but didn't open his mouth, and the old man burst out laughing. "Oh, my goodness, you're going to be the best one I've had in years, I can feel it already. Listen up, youngster, from here on out, if I ask a question it means you can answer it. You already proved you could keep your mouth shut when you need to, and that's pretty important. Got that?"

"Got it, Sir," Noah said, and then closed his mouth again.

The old man nodded his head, his smile wide and genuine. "Okay, then," he said. "My job today is to try to give you an idea of why our organization exists, and why it must exist. Do you have any opinion on that subject, before I get started?"

Noah looked at the old fellow for a moment, then nodded. "I know from personal experience, Sir, that there are people in this world who make it a much more dangerous place for everyone else. Sometimes, they might be enemy combatants of one sort or another, sometimes they may be proponents of organized crime, sometimes they may just be people whose views or purposes create a risk for our country, but whatever the reason, the only solution is to remove them from whatever equation they may be part of. In some cases, it's simply not possible to remove them through the use of normal legal means, so other methods will have to be employed. That means it's necessary for those other methods to exist, and that's where we come in."

Doc Parker nodded. "Very good," he said. "And do you approve of those other methods?"

"I do," Noah said, "because no matter how much we want to believe that our world is just and fair, it isn't. At least in some cases, the only way to have justice is to leave fairness at the door on the way in."

The old man picked up a file on the desk in front of him and flipped it open. "I see that you have been known to take steps that might be considered leaving fairness at the door, yourself. I've read through your entire file, so I know your story. There's enough glaring truth in it to make me personally think that we should send one of you guys after the officers who sat on your court-martial. They weren't looking for truth or justice; they were trying to find a big enough rug to sweep you under. Of course, that had a lot to do with a certain politician. Had my way, we'd send one of you boys after him, too. Sadly, they don't let me have my way."

Noah didn't say anything, but the old man saw the look in his eyes. "Speak up, youngster, if you got something to say."

"The only thing I want to say, Sir, is that the congressman was only acting to protect the memory and name of his son. While I may not approve of how he went about it, he did act within what I consider normal human behavior. I can't really be angry at him for that, so I cannot agree that we should send someone to do him harm."

"That's because you think too logically," Parker said. "You don't have access to that part of your brain that allows you to feel and experience and utilize emotions, so your thinking is too clear for most people to even understand. That will be an asset for you around here, but you can't let your understanding of human behavior convince you not to eliminate someone whose normal human behavior creates a danger. Understand?"

"Understood, Sir."

Parker tossed the file back on his desk. "Noah—you don't mind if I call you Noah, do you?"

"Not at all, Sir."

"Good. Noah, you did a good job of answering my question about why our organization should exist, but you didn't quite come up with the right answer. You see, E & E is the first organization of its kind in the United States. While there have been organizations in the past that have indulged in assassination at times, they have all been under the direct oversight of one of the intelligence agencies, or the president of the United States. What that means is that there was no one to keep hold of their leash, so when our current president conceived the idea for E & E, he was smart enough—and don't ask me how, when he's been so stupid on everything else—to make sure that the only person who could give the order to use that most efficient tool of diplomacy would be completely unknown to any of those agencies, and not subject to the orders of any of them, including the commander-in-chief. He created this agency, chose an incredibly insightful intelligence analyst to run it, transferred an enormous amount of money that would allow it to remain autonomous for many years, and then created a secure channel through which any agency that wanted to use this tool would have to submit a request. That request is reviewed by our administrator, and then she sends back her determination, whether to approve or deny the request. If it's approved, she simply hands the mission over to one of her people. If it's denied, then the same request cannot be made by the same agency again."

The old man paused, and Noah nodded. "Yes, sir," he said. "This has all been explained to me."

"Who cares? I'm just doing my job, and my job says I have to explain it to you all over again, so sit there and be quiet. Now, where was I? Oh, yeah, well, anyway, not even the president can order our administrator to approve a request. From what I understand, that was the one rule that she asked for, and he agreed to it without argument. What that means is that no one can ever force her to order anyone's death. And, since nobody outside this organization except the president knows who the administrator is, nobody can put pressure on her to do so." Parker leaned forward and put his elbows on the desk, his hands folded neatly in front of him. "That's the big difference between this agency and any other one that's ever existed, in this country or anywhere else. It's also the reason why this agency has been so successful at making a difference in this world. Now, can you tell me what makes you think you belong in this organization?"

Noah felt a moment's surprise at the question. "I can't say that I think I do belong here," he said. "I simply defer to the administrator, who apparently does think so."

"That was an excellent answer," Parker said. "Then why do you think she chose you?"

"It's been established that I have no normal emotions, and an apparently limited or nonexistent conscience. From what I understand, that gives me a bit of an edge, because I don't have to second-guess myself before I take a shot."

"Another great answer. You keep this up, and I may have to put your picture up on my wall, something to point at to show other idiots who come through here what they could have been. You were chosen, Noah, because you've proven that you will take action when action must be taken. You don't agonize over it, you simply decide whether action needs to be taken, and then you act on that decision. That's something we spend incredible amounts of time and money trying to teach to our students, and here you come along with it already hardwired into your Cybernet. If I could figure out what makes you tick, I'd be doing all I could to program the rest of our boys and girls to think just like you. Unfortunately, the root cause of your incredible, unique existence is probably found in the tragedy you suffered as a child, and without a time machine, I can't go back and put any of my other students through similar experiences."

"Apparently you're not the only one, Sir," Noah said. "Over the past few years, I've read about a number of experiments that have been conducted, psychological experiments that were designed to turn off emotions in certain people. I've never been able to get access to any of their actual results, but some of the psychology behind the experiments sounded at least somewhat valid."

Parker nodded, but waved off the suggestions. "I know about some of those experiments, and frankly, I disapprove. They're nothing like what happened to you, in any event. Your emotional shutdown came at a moment when you were probably being assaulted by some of the most painful emotions possible. Your psyche, in order to protect itself, simply flipped a switch and turned those emotions off. This is a defense mechanism, a way in which the subconscious acts to protect the individual. Tell me, have you ever been to see a psychotherapist about this?"

"Yes, a couple of times. My grandparents sent me to one, and during the time I was in the foster care system, I was ordered by a court into psychoanalysis. In both cases, I simply kept up my act and managed to convince both psychiatrists that I was a fairly normal kid who had been through a rough time. If you're asking whether I ever cooperated, then the answer would be no. I don't feel emotion, so I have no concerns over whether there's anything wrong with me. Because of that, I just couldn't see any reason to cooperate with someone who wanted to take away the very thing that, to me, makes me feel comfortable with myself."

Parker laughed. "We sent some people to actually interview some of the folks who knew you when you were younger," he said, "on the pretense that the interview was related to a possible pardon, or commutation of your sentence. There was one woman who said that she compared you to Mr. Spock, from *Star Trek*. According to her, you are probably as close to a true Vulcan as the world has ever seen. Do you think she's right?"

Noah grinned. "You're talking about Molly," he said. "I remember when she started calling me that; it was a long time ago, when we were kids. On the other hand, she got me started watching that show in reruns, and the more I saw Mr. Spock, the more I felt a kinship with him. Over the years, every time there was a new *Star Trek* show, I looked at the Vulcans to see if I could feel that same kinship, and I usually did. I found it with Mr. Data, too. He was another one who was always trying to figure out how to be human, just like me."

Parker was nodding his head. "And of course, he thought in terms of logic. He had to, since he was essentially a robot, and I'm certain that's exactly how you've felt for most of your life."

"Like a robot?" Noah asked. "Of course I do. I've literally spent an incredible amount of time sort of meditating, thinking: if this happens, then I must do that. I took a course in computer programming, and a lot of what I've done over the years to try to make myself appear normal could be compared to writing software. I just kept repeating it over and over to myself, until it became automatic."

The conversation went on for a couple of hours, until Parker finally glanced at the clock. "Well, youngster, I would have to say that this has been one of the most rewarding sessions I've had yet. You're an incredible fellow, and I do wish we could find a way to distill you down into a liquid and pump you into the veins of all the rest of them. However, since we can't do that, I'm going to pass along my recommendation that we do everything we possibly can to get you through the course and into the field as soon as possible." The old man picked up a pen and scribbled something on to a slip of paper, which he then folded and handed to Noah. "Someone will ask you for this, sometime today. Guard it with your life, because at my age, I could drop dead, and if you don't have that when you're asked for it, then there would be no way to prove that I endorsed you. Without my endorsement, you go before the firing squad, so you really don't want to let that get out of your sight." Parker sat there and looked at him for another moment, then flicked his fingers as if telling Noah to go. "It's lunchtime," he said, "and I suspect your escort is waiting impatiently outside for you. Don't keep the poor fellow waiting, he's probably starving. Go get some lunch. We're done."

Noah grinned, then got up out of the chair. "Thank you, Sir," he said, and then turned and walked out the door. Marco was waiting in the car, with the door open and one leg propped up on it as he read his book. He pulled his leg in and dog-eared the book as Noah climbed into the passenger seat.

"He give you a pass?" Marco asked.

Noah patted his pocket. "Said he did. Am I supposed to give it to you?"

Marco's eyes went wide. "No way, man, not me. Somebody big will ask you for it, maybe even at lunch. That's when they got mine."

Noah grinned. "You could've warned me about his little games he likes to play. Lucky for me, I know when to shut up."

Marco backed the car out of the parking space, and pointed it back toward the restaurant. "Not allowed. I couldn't give you any heads up. If I did, and the dragon lady ever found out, they'd be using me for target practice next week. I like you and all, you seem okay, but I like my ass a whole lot better."

Noah chuckled, and they rode the rest of the way in silence.

It was while they were sitting in the restaurant and having lunch that a short man walked over to their table.

"Marco," the man said, "why don't you introduce me to your friend?"

Marco had looked up as the man approached them, and grinned. "Sure, Mr. Jefferson. This is Noah, he's new here. Noah, I want you to meet Mr. Jefferson. He works at admin, with the boss lady."

Noah stood and extended a hand. "Mr. Jefferson, good to meet you," he said.

"You, too, Noah," said Jefferson. "I believe Doctor Parker may have given you a note for me?"

Noah glanced at Marco, who nodded once, then took the slip of paper from his pocket and handed it to Jefferson. The man unfolded the paper and glanced at what Parker had written, then looked up at Noah with a big smile.

"Have you looked at what he wrote?" Jefferson asked, but Noah shook his head.

"No, Sir," he said. "I was curious, but it was handed to me folded shut and I was not told that I was allowed to look at it."

Jefferson laughed. "That explains a lot. Here, take a look," he said, holding the paper up so that Noah could read it.

This man Noah will be our Superstar.

Noah glanced up at Jefferson. "Thank you, Sir," he said.

Jefferson clapped him on the shoulder and walked away without another word, so Noah sat down and resumed eating his roast beef sandwich and fries. He saw Marco looking at him, and shrugged.

"I couldn't help glancing up and seeing what Parker wrote," Marco said. "He gave you a lot to live up to. Superstar? That's heavy."

"I don't have a clue what it's supposed to mean," Noah said. "Didn't really make any sense, to me. How could I be a superstar, and of what?"

Marco paused in the middle of taking a bite of his own sandwich. "Noah, you do know what we do here, right? Our boys and girls kill people, or sometimes they just make people disappear. Seems like Doc Parker thinks you might be the best one yet."

Noah ate in silence for a moment, then looked up at Marco again. "So, how did you get here? Were you on death row, too?"

"No, but close," Marcus said. "Third-time loser in California, got my third strike on a breaking and entering charge. Automatic life in prison, and I was only twenty-four. The dragon lady sent somebody in to make me an offer, a chance to have a life again and put my street skills to work doing something good for my country. All it was gonna cost me was everyone I ever loved, but since I was never getting out again any other way, I decided I had really already lost them, anyhow. So I took the deal." He took a bite and chewed for a moment, as if he was thinking. "I almost flunked out, the first month. I came within a split second of picking up a phone and calling my mother, just to let her know I didn't really die in the riot at the prison. I was sitting in an office, another interview, and the guy got up and walked out. He left me alone in there, and there was a phone on his desk. I thought about it for a few seconds, then picked up the phone and started dialing Mom's number. I got to the last number, and froze up with my finger on the button. Stood there like that for I don't know how long—then I just hung up the phone. A few minutes later, Mr. Jefferson, there, walked in and told me that if I ever tried that again, I'd be eliminated. It was a test, of course, and I almost failed it."

"I'm glad you didn't," Noah said. "You seem like a guy I'd like to have covering my back. Maybe we'll get to work together someday."

EIGHT

WHEN LUNCH WAS over, Marco drove Noah to the PT field, which was about half a mile from the area where the motel was, which Marco called Alley Town. He introduced Noah to several of the other people there, including the instructor, who was known only as Jackson.

"You gotta watch out for Jackson," Marco said. "He's one of the most sadistic SOBs you'll ever meet, anywhere, bar none."

Jackson, who was standing right there as Marco made his evaluation, laughed and clapped him on the shoulder. "That's what makes me so good at what I do, Marco," he said. "If I recall correctly, you were a skinny beanpole when you got here, but look at you now. You can run ten miles in just over an hour, bench three hundred pounds, and climb a fifty-foot rope with nothing but your hands in under thirty seconds. Think maybe my stubbornness and cruelty have paid off a bit?"

Marco grinned. "I never said you weren't good at what you do, I just said you were a son of a bitch." He looked at Noah. "If anybody can get you in shape, Jackson can."

"I enjoy a good workout," Noah said. "What's the focus here, on this one? General calisthenics?"

Marco burst out laughing, then turned and walked away, leaving Noah with Jackson and a couple of others who were standing around watching the new guy. Jackson smiled.

"Ever heard of parkour?" Jackson asked, and Noah nodded.

"Yeah," he said, "that's the stunts you see on YouTube, right? People running up walls and stuff like that?"

"That's close enough for the moment," Jackson said. "Parkour is about moving from point A to point B as quickly as possible, while using any obstacles in your path to increase the efficiency of your travel. It began as *Parcours du combattant*, which is French for 'the Path of the Warrior,' and was originally developed as training for French special forces." He looked Noah up and down. "A lot of the new ones we get here have had little or no physical training at all, but I can tell that is not the case with you. Ex-military, right?"

Noah nodded again. "Army, Ranger. Some of our obstacle course training is probably similar."

"Okay, then," Jackson said, "just bear this in mind. A lot of the stuff you see on YouTube that's called Parkour really isn't. It's not about flips and stunts, it's about what I said, getting from point A to point B as quickly and efficiently as you can, by using the obstacles in your path as tools to help you reach your objective. I can sum it up really easily, like this. The whole time you're moving, imagine that you're being chased by an invisible creature that makes Freddy Krueger look like one of the Care Bears. If it catches you, you're dead, so it can't catch you. Got it?"

Noah had a huge grin spread across his face. "I got a feeling this is gonna be fun," he said. "When do we start?"

"Right now," Jackson said. "Follow me." He led Noah toward a building that stood beside the field, a two-story concrete structure that might have been some sort of warehouse, and pointed at it. "There are flags hidden somewhere around that building. They could be inside, outside, on top, out behind the building—they could literally be anywhere." He motioned to one of the other students who were still following along, a young woman. "This is Angie," he said. "Angie, show Noah how quickly you can bring me one of those flags."

The girl didn't so much as nod, but suddenly took off running toward the building. She veered off to the right, and for a second, Noah thought she was going to run around it, but then he spotted her true intent. There was a car parked up close to the building on that side, and when she got to it, a single leap took her onto its roof, where she spun suddenly to the left and leaped again. Her hands caught a protruding brick, while her feet contacted the wall for a split second, and then hands and feet worked together to fling her upward. She caught the top ledge of the building, and somersaulted over it, disappearing from view.

Jackson was looking at a stopwatch in his hand. "Twenty-four seconds, and she's on the roof. I think that's her best time yet."

One of the others, a guy who looked like he might have been all of fifteen, nodded his head. "I think you're right," he said. "She got mad when I beat her yesterday, so I figured she was gonna try to show me up today."

Without even looking at the boy who had spoken, Jackson said, "Noah, meet Gary. Gary tends to set the bar on this course."

Noah was concentrating on the building. Whatever was going on here, he wanted to make sure he was going to develop the necessary skills and muscle tone, so he didn't let himself be distracted, and that's why he saw the flicker of motion through the window on the second floor. "She's inside," he said. "Second floor, that window." He pointed at the one he meant.

"Yes, she's working from the top down. Going to the roof first meant that she would have gravity to help her as she moved downward through the building itself. Besides, if there had been opposition inside the building, that would increase the element of surprise for her. Keep watching."

Noah watched, and a few seconds later he saw another flash of motion, and realized that Angie had literally flown out of a ground floor window at the rear corner of the building. She rolled and came to her feet, still running, and he saw a scrap of yellow fabric in her hand.

Jackson clicked the stopwatch as she slid to a stop in front of him, the yellow flag held out in front of her. "One minute and fifty-nine seconds," he said. "That was an outstanding time, Angie. Good job." He turned and looked at Noah. "Noah, there are two more flags somewhere in the building. Do you think you can get one of them as fast as Angie did?"

Noah spun and launched himself into a run, choosing to follow the same path to the roof that Angie had taken. Like her, he leapt to the roof of the car and used it to throw himself at the wall, and caught the same protruding brick that she had used. When he threw himself upward, though, he didn't have quite the momentum that she had enjoyed, and only one hand managed to catch the upper ledge.

For a split second, he thought he was going to lose his grip and fall, but his right foot found purchase on another brick, and he was able to transfer some of his weight to it. That let him bring his other hand up and get a grip on the edge, after which he swung his legs until he got his left foot on the ledge, and then rolled over the top. He landed on his back on the roof, but didn't allow himself to rest. He rolled to his feet, looking around to see how Angie had gotten into the building.

There was no access door on the roof, nothing that could lead down into the building, but he saw what looked like a flagpole on the far edge. There was a sturdy rope hanging down from it, and it was swinging slightly, as if someone had moved it not long before. He ran to it and looked over the edge to see an open window directly below the pole, so he grabbed the rope and threw himself over the edge. His momentum caused the rope to crack like a whip, and then it swung him directly to and through the window opening.

He landed on his feet, ran quickly to the door he saw in the opposite wall, then through it and into a hallway. His eyes were scanning the entire time, and he ran quickly through the hall, looking into every room for the yellow flag. He was just about to move toward the stairs at the end of the hall when he saw a tiny bit of yellow protruding from what looked like a cabinet in one of the rooms.

Into the room and to the cabinet he ran, and as he snatched it open, he saw the yellow flag flutter toward the floor. He caught it in midair, then spotted the open window across the room. He checked his memory of the building, and decided that the window ledge was about eighteen feet above the ground, but he had made bigger jumps than that in the past. He threw himself through the window and spun in the air so that he landed on his feet, still running forward, then didn't slow until he got back to Jackson and the others.

Jackson clicked the stopwatch, and Noah saw Gary and the others all staring at it with their eyes wide.

"One minute," Jackson said, "and twenty-two seconds. Noah, you just set a new record for this course. I was planning to put you with a beginner group, let you just follow some of them around for a few days, but you just blew that one, Buddy. If you can come up with moves like that your first time, then you belong with this bunch."

Noah was breathing hard, but he managed to smile. "Get used to it," he said. "If there's one thing I just can't stand, it's second place."

Jackson grinned. "Good," he said, and hooked a thumb at Gary. "This punk needs some competition." He turned and looked at the kid he'd just called a punk, and grinned. "Gary, why don't you set the pace today. Don't overdo it, remember that not everyone can quite keep up with you, but make sure they get a workout." He glanced at a wristwatch. "You got eighty minutes, let 'em have it."

Gary nodded, and threw Jackson a grin of his own. "You got it," he said, looking at the others and letting his eyes come to rest on Noah. "Try to stay close, okay?"

Gary took off at a fast jog, and Noah was easily able to keep up. Angie and Marco were right beside him, and the rest of the group was strung out over twenty feet or so, making for an interesting game of follow the leader.

Noah had expected them to go back toward the little concrete building, but Gary took off in an entirely different direction, back toward Alley Town. Noah had noticed several different buildings along the road, but hadn't paid a lot of attention to them. Suddenly, he wished he had.

It wasn't all about buildings, though, which Noah quickly discovered. Gary took off from the road onto a path through the woods, and soon they were leaping over fallen trees, bouncing off of rocks, even swinging on vines as they made their way through the patch of wilderness, but it soon opened up into a cleared area with a number of structures. Many of the buildings in this region were several stories tall, reminding Noah of some downtown district in a typical American city. People were moving about the streets and sidewalks, and there was a considerable amount of vehicular traffic, as well.

"What's this?" Noah asked, and it was Angie who spoke up first to answer.

"Urban sprawl," she said. "This is the administrative area, where all the offices and such are. A lot of the big shots from Washington come in here, so that's why there's a big hotel and all these office buildings."

"Yeah," Marco said, "and it also gives us an urban-type training area. We run mission scenarios here, where we have to deal with opposition by city cops and such."

Gary suddenly picked up the pace, and Noah and the others had to pour on the speed in order to keep up. They all followed as he climbed over a dumpster onto a semi trailer, then jumped from it onto a window ledge. One by one, they jumped and climbed from one ledge to the one above it, until they were all on top of the building, more than five stories above the ground.

Gary didn't slow. As soon as everyone was on top, he took off again, running straight to the far edge of the building and throwing himself into the air. Noah was third in line, with Angie just ahead of him, and when she also flew off the building, Noah simply followed. He pushed off at the last second with everything he had, and then realized that he had just made a leap that had to carry him more than fifty feet forward, even as he dropped down two full stories to the roof of the building across the street.

A split second ahead of him, he saw Angie hit and roll, and followed suit. The parachute training he received in the Army came in handy, for he knew how to take the hit on his feet, then roll it out and come back up on to them. They were still moving, and he didn't let himself slow down. He just kept following the girl in front of him.

Gary snatched open a door and disappeared down a flight of stairs, with Angie and Noah hot on his tail. Noah didn't look back to see where Marco was, assuming that he would be there, somewhere. He was too busy concentrating on following and keeping up.

Angie leapt up onto the railing beside the stairs and slid down, but when Noah tried it, he ended up rolling down the steps themselves. A few bruises on his backside told him that he would need more practice for some of these moves, so he got to his feet as quickly as he could when he hit the landing, then ran down the steps three and four at a time after that.

Gary veered off on the third floor, opening the stairwell door and flying down the hallway. He went through an office where several people were working at computers, literally flying directly over some of them to get to a window across the room. When he reached it, he threw himself through it but caught the window ledge with a hand and swung himself downward.

Angie hesitated, and Noah passed her, flying through the window just as Gary had done, and using the ledge to stop his forward momentum and drop to a balcony just below. Gary was already inside, back through the window beside the balcony and running like mad through another office full of computer terminals. Noah dived through the window and rolled to his feet just as Angie hit the balcony behind him, but he didn't wait to see if she followed.

The shortest route to the door Gary had disappeared through was diagonal, so Noah jumped up to run right across the tops of several desks. The people sitting at them were screaming and yelling, and sliding themselves away from their desks, and Noah realized that he had stepped on and broken at least one keyboard, but simply yelled, "Sorry!" as he ran out the door.

Gary went into another room, this one apparently just for storage, and Noah got to the door just in time to see him going out the window on the far side. Noah followed, of course, and found himself once more on top of a trailer, but then they ran down the cab of the truck and onto its hood, sliding off onto the road in front of it and continuing their run.

Up this, over that, leap here, run there—for more than an hour, Gary kept them moving, but finally, they were back at the exercise yard. Noah estimated that they had run a good twelve miles, and he didn't even want to think about how many of those miles might have been vertical. The entire group collapsed onto the grass of the field, breathing heavily and gratefully accepting the bottles of water that were being passed around.

"So," Noah heard Jackson's voice, "how did that feel?"

Noah looked up at the man, and managed a very feeble grin. "At the moment, the stitch in my side feels a lot like I've been shot, but I think that will pass. We do this every day?"

Jackson nodded. "Five days a week," he said. "We've found that there is absolutely nothing that can keep a man in better shape, as well as keeping you ready to move on a split second's notice. You get good at this, and you'll find that you'll see escape routes that no one else would believe, or ways to reach a target that anyone else would think was untouchable. This discipline is a lot more than just exercise and fun; it changes your entire way of thinking. Where other people will see obstacles, even blank walls, you'll soon start to see pathways you can use to get where you want to go. It's awesome."

Noah nodded. "Like I said in the beginning," he said. "This is gonna be fun."

NINE

"I'LL LET YOU get to your room and get a shower," Marco said, "while I go grab one myself. Soon as you're done, come on out by the car, because you've got weapons class next. I'll drive you over, but I got something else to do after that. Someone else will show you how to get back."

Noah nodded, and as soon as the car was parked, he got out and jogged over to his door. He opened it quickly and slipped inside, stripping off the sweaty clothes he was wearing as he walked toward the bathroom. Fifteen minutes later, quickly showered and dressed, he pulled the door shut behind him once again.

He was sitting on the hood of the car when Marco came out of his own room, and they got in without saying a word. Both of them were still feeling the effects of their workout, and Noah was honest enough with himself to admit that he wished he had time for a nap. He leaned back in the seat as Marco drove, but the ride was far too short for any real rest. The car pulled up in front of a large brick building, and Marco pointed at the door.

"That's where you go," he said. "Your instructor in there is Daniel, and you'll know him because of his German accent. He's a good guy, and if there's any kind of weapon he isn't an expert with, I'll guarantee you it's not one you've ever heard of. I've gotta get to a class of my own, so I may not see you again today. Take it easy, and we'll probably see each other tomorrow."

"Later," was all Noah could manage, as he got out of the car and walked toward the door. He opened it and walked inside, and immediately realized that he must be late. There were quite a few people seated at long tables, all of them facing toward the front of the room where a tall, dark-haired man was pointing at a projection screen.

"Well, it seems we have a visitor," the man said, and the accent told Noah that this must be Daniel. "You would be Noah, then?" Daniel asked.

"I am, Sir," Noah replied. "I apologize for being late."

Daniel pointed at an empty seat at the front table. "Please sit there," he said, and Noah moved to take the seat indicated, on the right side of the center aisle. The seats were benches, wide enough for two people, and Noah's seatmate was a young black man. The fellow nodded at him, but didn't say a word as he took his seat.

Daniel tapped the screen with a finger to draw everyone's attention back up to it. Noah looked up to see a diagram of what appeared to be a Bowie knife.

"We're starting today with our section on knives," Daniel said. "With all of the high-powered, high-tech weaponry that is now available in this world, it may seem strange to you that we put such emphasis on something as simple as the knife, but you should not find it so. When everything else you might use can fail you, the knife is a tool that is easily concealed, easily maintained and easily used." He pointed at the diagram. "It was an American who created what is still considered to be one of the finest designs for the knife, and we all know it as the Bowie knife. By giving the full length of the blade a single edge, rather than the double edge of most knives throughout history, the majority of the blade was much stronger due to its thicker back edge. The dipped and curved point of the blade, the edge of which was also sharp, allowed the knife to pierce more easily, and could be used as a skinning edge for those who carried this knife when hunting. In addition, this narrowing groove that runs the length of the blade allows blood to flow past the knife when it is used for stabbing, hastening death as the victim can bleed out more quickly."

Daniel turned back to face his students, and clicked a remote to turn off the projector. At the same time, the lights came up so that everyone could see him clearly. "There are two very important things you must remember about your knife. The first is to never leave your knife in your victim, and there are two reasons for this. Reason number one is quite obvious, in that the knife would leave a clue that someone could use to identify you as the killer. Reason number two should be even more obvious, but for some of you idiots I have to make sure you understand it. You do not leave a knife behind in your victim, because a good knife is very difficult to find. Once you have found one, don't let it go."

There was a ripple of laughter through the room, and Daniel's grin said that he was expecting it. "The second thing you must remember about your knife is to keep it well sharpened and maintained. While it may seem to you that a knife is so simple that it does not require much in the way of maintenance, you should be aware that many things can affect how well a knife serves you. If an edge becomes nicked, for instance, it may drag when used for cutting, and slow you down. A deep nick of the blade can catch on bone, preventing you from removing the knife from the target." He clicked the remote again, and the lights went down as the projector came back on, showing a new image of a knife with a rough and chipped blade edge. "Flaws like these can cause the knife to hang up even in softer tissues, so it is always important to maintain a smooth, very sharp edge." He clicked again, and a new knife appeared on the screen. At first glance, it seemed slightly misshapen, but Daniel pointed at its grip. "If the hilt of your knife becomes loose, then the tip of the blade is no longer where you expect it to be. With every motion of the hilt inside the grip, the tip is moved away from the centerline of the knife, which is where you have always expected it to be. While it may seem to be only a slight difference, that slight difference can cause you to miss a critical organ or artery, meaning your target does not die. In addition, a loose grip can throw off the balance of the knife, affecting how you handle it in many ways. This is unacceptable."

He clicked again, and a third knife appeared on the screen. This one was rusty and dull. "This knife is one you would only want to use if it were the only possible option. The two damaged knives we have already looked at would be preferable to this one, and can anyone tell me why?"

Daniel waited for a couple of seconds, but no one raised a hand or spoke up. He looked around the room, and his eyes settled on Noah. "Perhaps, Mr. Noah, you would like to make a guess as to why this knife would be the last resort?"

Noah looked at the picture on the screen, and folded his hands in front of himself. "The edge of that knife is very dull, which means it's not going to be very effective if I have to fight. Since it's so rusty, I have to assume that the owner hasn't bothered with any kind of maintenance, and in fact it's probable that, if I've got that knife at all, it's because I stumbled across it somewhere. That means I have absolutely no sense of its balance or weight, so the only possible value it could have to me would be if I could use it for stabbing. Also, rust can cover up cracks and breaks in steel, so it's even possible that the knife has been damaged to the point that I can't trust it even for that."

Daniel nodded at Noah, and smiled broadly. "I've been hearing good things about you, today," he said, "and waiting my chance to form my own opinion. I must admit that you have made a very valid assessment, but you missed one thing. Would you care to try again?"

Noah looked again at the picture on the screen, letting his eyes roll over the knife from its tip all the way to the top of the hilt. He saw again that the edge was dull, and that the knife had not been cared for, but if there was something else he should've seen, it was escaping him. He was about to say so when a thought struck him.

"Well, the only thing I can see that I haven't said already is that, if that was my knife, then I probably shouldn't be trying to use it at all. If a warrior can't take care of his weapons, he doesn't deserve them."

Daniel laughed. "That is another very valid point, but it wasn't what I was looking for," he said. "Look very closely at the photo. Can you see the gap between the grip and the finger guard? What that means is that the hilt is not only loose, it is actually detached. It is quite possible that if this knife were used to stab your target or opponent, when you tried to draw it out you would find yourself holding only the grip, while the blade remained where you had put it."

Noah nodded, seeing the gap Daniel mentioned. He wondered if he should've seen it without it being pointed out, but the gap was very small. He had been looking at the blade, which he considered the effective part of a knife, and hadn't considered the overall condition as well as he should have.

Daniel continued his lecture on knives, and how they should be maintained and cared for. At one point, he opened the box and began distributing Bowie knives to each of the students, along with sharpening stones and oil, and then began teaching them how to put a razor edge onto such a thick piece of steel. Noah, who had loved knives since he was a child, was quite adept at sharpening, and so were several of the others. After a few minutes, those who knew what they were doing were urged by Daniel to help their classmates.

The class continued this way for a couple of hours, and Noah got to know a few of his fellow students. When everything was winding down, and they were putting away the knives and stones, Daniel called Noah aside.

"I told you that I had been hearing good things about you," he said. "That is true. However, what you should know is that not everyone is convinced that you are all that you're expected to be. There is something about you, and none of us knows quite what it is, that has convinced our administrator and psychologist that you are going to be something special." He smiled. "Do not be so surprised; even in a place like this, rumors abound. It is impossible to completely keep a secret when there are so many hundreds of people around, but all of us are committed to this organization, so it's not a matter of a threat, so much as a matter of trust. Some of us do not trust you, and are reluctant to see so many of our superiors putting such hope in you."

Noah looked at Daniel for a long moment, and then smiled. The smile had no emotion behind it, but was meant only to disarm any concerns the German instructor might have.

"I don't know what you mean, about people putting hope into me," he said. "I'm here because I was offered a chance to become part of this organization, and since the alternative meant having a permanent address in the local cemetery, I was kind of glad the offer came along. Other than that, though, I'm not out to impress anyone, I'm not out to show off—I'm just here to do a job. As long as I can believe it's a job that needs to be done, I'm in." He turned and walked toward the exit.

The man who had shared his seat tapped him on the shoulder, and Noah turned to look into his face. "I'm Roger," the man said. "I know you're new here. Have you had permanent quarters assigned yet?"

Noah shook his head. "They got me staying in some little motel," he said, "over in Alley Town."

Roger nodded, and grinned. "That's what I figured," he said. "Need a ride? It takes them a few days to get wheels assigned."

"Yeah, thanks," Noah said. "I appreciate it, if it's not taking you out of your way."

Roger started toward the door, and chuckled. "It is," he said, "but it's okay. By the way, you do know that's not the only restaurant here, right? We got several on the compound, including some good old burger joints."

Noah laughed. "Seriously? Where are they, I could stand a nice thick burger and fries."

They stepped into the parking lot and Roger pointed at a pickup truck. It was a small one, and looked like it had probably seen better days. "Hop in," he said. "Burger and fries, coming right up."

Noah climbed into the little truck, as Roger got behind the wheel and put the key in the ignition. He turned it, and Roger realized that the truck's appearance was deceptive. The engine that started up ran quite smoothly, and when Roger put it in gear, it was obvious that it had quite a lot of power.

"This truck seems to have a bit more motor in it than normal," Noah said. "You build it yourself?"

"No," Roger said. "This was assigned to me, because I've always been a country boy who loved pickup trucks. Just about everything they give us to drive is pretty well built, you'll see. I think a lot of them come from what the government confiscates, you know, like from drug dealers and such. Somebody went to a lot of work to shove a big block under the hood of this thing."

Roger drove the truck toward the urban setting where they had had their workout earlier, and Noah paid attention to the landmarks. "This is kind of ingenious," he said. "It's like we've got samples of just about every different kind of environment here. Small-town, big-city, countryside—I even saw a stretch that looks like desert. Only thing I haven't seen so far is water, and I'd be willing to bet there's a lake here, somewhere."

"You'd be right," Roger said. "Southwest edge opens up on a lake that can get pretty treacherous at times. It's fresh water, but other than that you could swear you were out on the ocean, in spots."

"So the idea, I gather, is to let us run practice missions in all these different environments?"

"Oh, that's part of it," Roger admitted. "There's a lot more to it than that, though. Part of it is the workouts, to let us get used to running courses of all kinds. Then there's the fact that a lot of our people have been locked up for years, so they need to get used to being in the world again, and this is how they do it. To be honest, I think that's pretty much one of the more important reasons for it, but there's probably other reasons I don't even know about."

Noah was surprised to see a typical fast food restaurant appear ahead of them. "That's wild, I didn't see that when we were here earlier. I wonder what else there is around here that I didn't see."

Roger shrugged his shoulders. "Well, unless you're starving, let's take a cruise and see." He drove past the burger place, and cruised through the urban section, going from street to street, and Noah realized that the section seemed to be made up of about thirty-six city blocks, a six-block by six-block grid. He saw office buildings, banks, apartment buildings, a large hotel, a shopping center with several stores, a couple of theaters and several different restaurants. There was a school complex that seemed to have everything from kindergarten through high school, and an impressive hospital that looked like it was ready for just about anything. Roger took another turn, and then they cruised through a few smaller streets that were lined with houses.

"Good grief," he said, "I've seen towns that weren't this big, including the one I was born in. I see gas stations, convenience stores—are those real, or just simulations for training?"

"Oh, they're real, that's for sure," Roger said. "And one thing you need to know, right now, is that not everyone here even knows what goes on. This area shows up on maps as an honest-to-goodness town called Kirtland. One thing you never, ever do, is mention our real purpose in front of anyone you aren't certain is part of it."

"Well," Noah said, "in that case, I'm awfully glad you told me. I wish somebody had told me this sooner, in fact."

Roger laughed. "Chill, dude," he said. "It's all good. You ready for that burger?"

Noah managed a grin. "Yeah, I guess so. So, where do you fit in with this organization? Or is that one of those questions you can answer, but then you gotta kill me?"

"It isn't quite that bad," Roger said. "I got myself into a mess, where I owed a bunch of people some money, and let's just say they were pretty serious about trying to collect it. They made a couple of threats against my family, so I decided to make, shall we say, a preemptive strike."

"You killed them?"

"I did," Roger said. "Unfortunately, I wasn't nearly as smart as I thought I was, and left a trail of clues behind that just about any amateur cop could've followed. I was arrested less than twenty-four hours later, and because there were seven victims, I couldn't even plead out. The case was too good against me, so the prosecutors wouldn't deal and said I had to go to trial. A conviction would've meant the death penalty, so when I got a visit from a lawyer who offered to give me another chance, here, I took it."

Noah watched his face as he was talking, and could tell that Roger had regrets about the killings. "So, what's your job assignment? Are they planning to use you as an assassin?"

Roger shook his head. "No, I lucked out on that," he said. "They tell me I'm just going to be somebody's muscle, kind of a backup. I still have to have the training, just in case I ever have to, you know, complete a mission—but I hope I don't. You know, sometimes you do what you gotta do, but that doesn't always mean it's easy to live with."

Noah looked at this young man, and wondered what it would be like to feel remorse over someone you killed, or over anything you did. "Yeah," he said, "I know just what you mean."

TEN

NOAH BIT INTO the triple-decked burger, and moaned in epicurean delight. "Oh, man," he said. "Oh, that's delicious. Can't you just taste all the triglycerides?"

Roger laughed and looked over at him. "Not me," he said. "I can't get past the flavor of the MSG. At least they don't try to shove health food down our throats, here. If there's anything in the world that truly signifies the American way, it's just plain got to be the fast food burger. Let's face it, all those soldiers over there in the war, that's what they're really fighting for. Burgers and fries, and I am not referring to the French variety."

Noah shrugged, but he was chuckling at the same time. "Hey, I was over there," he said. "Not all of us dreamed about burgers, there were some of us over there who thought about girls, instead."

Roger looked at him sideways. "You're gonna sit there and moan about how good that burger is, and try to tell me that wasn't one of the things you thought about while you were in that desert?"

Noah winked at him. "Hey, I said *some* of us thought about girls. I didn't say I was always one of them. A lot of times, I was focused on burgers and pizza. As far as I'm concerned, burgers and pizza are the two primary food groups, with fried chicken making a good show of coming in third." Noah took another bite. "How old are you, Roger?"

Roger leaned his head back against the headrest, and grimaced. "I'll be twenty in two weeks," he said. "I confess this wasn't how I planned on spending my twentieth birthday, but at least I'm getting to have one. The way things were going, I wasn't likely to have had the chance."

"Things moved that fast? I mean, I'd think it would take them a while to get around to a trial."

Roger nodded. "It did," he said. "I sat in the jail cells for three years, while my public defenders kept trying everything they could think of to stall."

"Three years? Then, I take it you were only sixteen at the time of the murders?"

"Yep," Roger said. "Because of the number of victims, and what the prosecutor called the 'animal ferocity' of the way I killed them, the judge decided that I should be tried as an adult. We tried every possible way to get that decision thrown out, but it didn't work."

Noah shook his head in sympathy. "Man, I'm sorry. Nobody should have to deal with things like that in their teens."

"Oh, I did it to myself," Roger said. "I told you I was a country boy, but I didn't tell you that I had a cousin who was a drug dealer in the city. He came to me with this plan for us to make a bunch of money, by bringing some of his product to the little towns around where I lived. It sounded like fun, and quick bucks, so I went along with it. The trouble was, his end of the business wasn't doing so well, and he was losing money. He was taking some of the money I was bringing in and covering his own ass with it, and then he pointed a finger at me when things came up short. His boss paid me a visit, and explained the situation. He made it clear that my mother and little sister would suffer if I didn't come up with the money, and there was no way I could, so after he left, I stuck a gun in my cousin's face and made him show me where to find him." He took a bite of his burger, and chewed it up slowly before he went on. "Ten o'clock in the morning,

I showed up at his front door and started blasting away with a 12-gauge and a Glock. Once I started, I just couldn't stop, and I killed our supplier, his wife and all five of his kids."

Noah saw the tears that were running down Roger's face. "Well, I know how terrible that must look to other people, but from what I know about the drug business, it tends to run in families. You may have saved lives fifty years into the future, and it's a safe bet that a lot of innocent people have already died because of that supplier. Your solution might not be the one that's politically correct, but it's probably the only one that could ever really eliminate the drug problem." Noah paused for a moment. "It may be hard for you to understand that, because you're looking at the deaths of those children as nothing but murder. The thing is, while it may be tragic that they had to die, if they carried on the family business then they would eventually be responsible for hundreds, possibly thousands more deaths. Sometimes you have to look at the greater good, no matter what the consequences to yourself might be."

Roger quickly wiped away his tears and grinned sheepishly at Noah. "Yeah, well, other people told me that, too, even Doc Parker. That doesn't make it any easier to live with, though."

Noah thought quickly about the men he had killed, the ones that had led to the murder charges, and tried to feel any remorse, anything that might be considered sadness. With each one, though, all he could sense was the necessity of the shots that he fired. He had felt no desire to harm or kill those men, nor any hatred or animosity, not even anger; the situation had forced his hand, and he had done what had to be done. To Noah, everything came down to a simple black or white. In order to feel remorse, there had to be a gray area, some part of the situation that made you uncertain of your choices.

Noah was never uncertain, so he had no clear idea of how to help Roger deal with his own guilt. All he could do was mouth the same platitudes he'd heard others use in Iraq and the 'Stan, when they were trying to comfort the new guys after their first kills.

"Sometimes," he said, "you're faced with a choice. You can kill, or you can die, and in this case you had the threats against your family, too. Roger, it sounds to me like you did what you had to do. All you gotta do now is learn how to live with it."

They finished eating and tossed their trash into one of the nearby cans, and Roger started the truck for the drive back to Alley Town. He stayed quiet all the way to the motel, and just waved as Noah got out. A moment later, the truck turned the corner and was out of sight.

Noah fished the key to his room out of his pocket, and let himself in. Like in every motel room, there was a telephone beside the bed, something he hadn't even paid attention to before, but now it had a red light blinking on it. In motels, he knew that meant there was a message, so he picked up the phone and dialed zero for the operator.

A computerized voice said, "Room seven has one new message," and then he heard, "Noah, this is Allison. You made it through your first day, and I'm glad to say I've had nothing but good reports. Tomorrow, we're going to go ahead and schedule you in for intake and ID, so someone will pick you up at your room at about eight AM. For tonight, kick back and relax. If you need anything, Marco should be around, so you can get him to drive you wherever you need to go."

Noah hung up the phone and walked over to open the mini fridge. As he suspected, there was nothing in it, so a moment later he walked out the door and over to Marco's room. He knocked, and Marco opened the door a moment later.

"Hey, Noah," Marco said. "How's it going?"

"Well, the dragon lady left me a message that she's had good reports, so I'm guessing I'm doing okay in that regard," he said. "I got to see the exciting town of Kirtland today, and I was wondering if I might talk you into a ride over to one of the stores. I'd like to pick up some snacks and stuff."

Marco grinned. "Settling right in, aren't you? Sure, give me a second to grab my keys."

Noah walked over to Marco's car and waited, but it was only as few seconds before his friend came out and got behind the wheel. He hit the lock button, and Noah climbed in; then he fired up the car and they were on the way.

"You want a convenience store," Marco asked, "or something bigger?"

"Convenience store will do just fine. I just want to grab some chips and pop, stuff like that."

It turned out there was a convenience store not too far away, and Noah took only a few minutes to grab the snacks he wanted. There were a lot of things to choose from, and he paused to look at the coolers full of beer.

"You can have some, if you want," Marco said. "Or if you prefer, there's a bar down the road. We can stop in for a cold one, if you want to."

Noah grinned, and carried his purchases to the register. The girl there rang them up quickly, and smiled at him as he swiped his card. A moment later, she handed him his receipt and two bags containing chips, candy bars and a couple of six-packs of root beer.

They got back into the car, and Noah put his purchases into the backseat. "A beer sounds good," he said, and Marco smiled as he put the car back in gear. A moment later, he parked in front of a little building with a flickering neon sign that read, "Charlie's."

"Something I forgot to tell you earlier," Marco said, "is that not everybody here is in on the secret behind this place. We don't talk about anything to do with the organization except with people we're certain are part of it themselves."

"Yeah," Noah said, "I got lucky and someone else filled me in on that. It would've been nice to have known that a little earlier, but luckily, I didn't run into a situation where it could blow up in my face." He grinned and knuckled Marco on the shoulder. "It's okay, come on," he said. "I'm ready for a cold beer."

They walked inside, and Noah felt like he had walked into a typical bar in any town in the country. The lights were dim, the fixtures were old, and the air-conditioning was set way too high. Marco led the way to the bar, and they climbed up on a couple stools. An old man, presumably Charlie, walked over to them and grinned, showing all four of his bottom teeth.

"Evenin', boys," he said. "What can I do you for?"

Noah started to speak, but Marco held up a hand to stop him. "Two beers, in the bottle, no glasses," Marco said.

The old man chuckled, then turned around and pulled two bottles of Budweiser out of the cooler, popped the caps and set them on the bar. "Four fifty," he said, and Marco threw a five-dollar bill onto the bar.

"Keep the change," Marco said, and the old fellow chuckled again as he walked away. Marco turned to Noah. "Yeah, I forgot to tell you, it's always best to stick with bottles, here. The draft stuff seems to be watered down, or maybe it's just that nasty."

They clinked their bottles together and each took a sip. Noah grinned. "That's good," he said. "It's been a long time."

Marco eyed him. "How long were you locked up?"

"About three months," Noah said. "They didn't waste any time getting me to trial, but our boss lady came and made her pitch before they got around to carrying out my sentence. Since I was just hanging around there, waiting for my chance to be next in line for execution, her offer struck me as a good one."

Marco nodded. "Yeah, it usually does." He took a long pull on his bottle. "Although, I have heard that a few people have turned it down. Seems pretty stupid, to me, but then you never know."

Noah shrugged. "I think it would depend on what the person thought of himself," he said. "I can see where someone might decide they didn't deserve a second chance. Of course, that wouldn't be me, and obviously it wasn't you, either."

"Not my problem," Marco said. "I was just glad I made it through the first few days after I got here."

Another man walked in and sat down at the bar, only a couple of stools away, so Noah and Marco began to guard what they were saying. They talked about casual things, like Marco's car, and Marco told Noah about some of the more interesting parts of the town of Kirtland. The conversation sounded like one between a couple of old friends, one of whom was local and entertaining the other on a visit.

They ordered a second beer, this time on Noah. The old bartender took his card and swiped it for him, then passed it back without a word. They continued to sit at the bar while they finished them off, and by then, Noah was ready to go back to his room.

"I guess I got a big day ahead of me, tomorrow," he said as they got back into the car. "Something about going through intake?"

Marco nodded. "Intake isn't too bad," he said. "By the time you get the offer made to you, they already know more about you than you know about yourself, so it's not like you've got to fill out a lot of paperwork, or anything like that. It's more about them telling you the rules, the basic rules you got to remember and stick to. Then they'll give you your permanent ID, driver's license and all that stuff, and put you officially on the payroll."

"Yeah? And is the pay any good?"

Marco glanced over at Noah, and then burst out laughing. "It's not bad," he said. "I'm not sure what your pay grade gets, but I'm making more money each year than I thought I'd ever see in my life. Not trying to brag, but I pull down a little over a hundred thousand a year. That's not bad for being a leg breaker."

Noah whistled. "Not bad at all," he said. "The only question left, then, is what in the world can you do with it?"

"Pretty much anything you want to," Marco said. "Not all of us live here. I don't, but when I'm helping out with a newbie, like you, I get to stay at the motel for free, instead of having to pay for a hotel room downtown."

"Really? So where do you live?"

Marco grinned. "Middle of nowhere, in Louisiana. I got a little place on the Bayou, where nobody bothers me. I like it that way. Once you've been with the organization for a while, you can apply to live anywhere you want to. They give you a cover job to explain your income, so you can live right out in the open. Me, they got me listed as a truck driver. Every now and then, I really do drive a truck, but it just makes a convenient excuse for why I'm out and gone a lot, so the few neighbors I've got don't get suspicious of anything."

They got back to the motel, and Noah carried his bags into his room. He put the soft drinks into the refrigerator, then opened the bag of chips and lay back on the bed to watch some TV.

ELEVEN

NOAH HAD GOTTEN into the habit of waking at five thirty in the morning, the usual time when the lights came on at the prison. His eyes opened, and he rolled over on the big bed, instantly remembering how his circumstances had changed. He sat up, and a moment later he climbed out of the bed and staggered toward the bathroom. A couple of minutes later, he came out and grabbed some clean clothes, then went back in to get a shower and shave.

Allison's message had said that someone would pick him up at around eight, so he had plenty of time for breakfast. He slipped out the door, glancing over at Marco's room to see that there were no lights on yet, and then walked to the restaurant alone. He had just gotten his coffee when he heard his name, and turned around.

Allison was walking toward him, and sat down in the chair opposite his. She smiled at him, and he returned it out of habit.

"I thought I'd just come and collect you myself this morning," she said, "and I figured you'd be over here early for breakfast, so I decided to join you. I haven't eaten here in a while, but I know how good it is so I thought it was well past time to pay a visit."

Noah picked up his cup and saluted her with it. "Glad to

have the company," he said. "Anything I need to know about today, before we get started?"

A waitress hurried over and took Allison's order, and Noah waited until she was gone before he looked expectantly at his boss.

"Nothing specific," she said. "We'll be going over some rules and regulations that are in place, and getting your new identity all set up. A lot of it's already been done, but there are some simple things we need to go over."

Noah nodded. "It occurs to me that I haven't actually thanked you," he said. "Your intervention has saved my life, and I do appreciate it."

She grinned at him. "Well, considering the alternative, I'm sure you do," she said. "The thing you gotta remember, though, is that you earned the opportunity. You demonstrated some incredible abilities, and those are abilities that we need in this organization. It simply made sense for me to do everything I could to recruit you."

"Then here's hoping I prove to be worth all your effort."

Allison smiled. "There's something special about you, Noah," she said. "Doctor Parker says he wishes we could figure out a way to boil you down to your essence, so that we could just inject it into people. Luckily for you, he hasn't found a way to do that, so we can't produce dozens of you. You get to stay unique, and everyone who's gotten to know you so far is convinced that your uniqueness is going to pay off for us in many ways."

"Because I don't have feelings?" Noah asked.

"That's certainly part of it," she said. "The significance of your lack of emotions is that you don't suffer from guilt or remorse, so that you effectively have no conscience."

"I know," he replied. "That's why I had to develop a sort of moral programming code, something to let me know when I was overstepping the bounds of propriety. It's my own sense of right and wrong."

Allison nodded. "Yes, and it seems to be an effective one,

because you've gone this long without ending up in trouble. From what I've been able to determine through my own research and Doctor Parker's, most people who suffer from conditions like yours can't even function properly in society. I think your success in doing so probably goes back to the fact that you had an extremely intelligent friend who could help you understand what was happening to you when you were a child."

"Molly," Noah said. "If it hadn't been for her, I probably would have lost my mind way back then, or at least found myself lost and confused among all you humans."

Allison gave him a curious look. "You speak as if you don't consider yourself to be one of us," she said. "I've heard you say that before, that you don't think of yourself as being a human at all. Is that really how you feel?"

"I suppose it is," he said. "Humans have emotions, they have feelings, and a lot of their actions and decisions are guided by those feelings. Those are specific attributes of the human animal, and some other animals as well, but I don't have them. That leaves me thinking that I'm a lot more like a robot than a person. Wouldn't you agree?"

"As a matter of fact, I do," she said, "and that's specifically why you're so valuable to us. You have the ability to act without having to agonize over a decision. You can evaluate a situation and decide, almost instantly, based on that evaluation, the best action to take. This makes you the best possible candidate for one of our operatives, because you won't ever second-guess yourself. That's gotten more of our people killed than anything else."

Noah looked at her. "You're right about that," he said. "I don't need to think something through over and over, I just need to know the circumstances that I'm dealing with. That lets me make a decision, and I can live with any decision I've made."

Allison paused as the waitress brought their plates, then picked up her glass of orange juice and took a drink before continuing. "You know, I read your file. There are some interesting things in it."

Noah nodded, and grinned. "I'm sure there are," he said, "especially for someone reading it from your perspective. I'm going to guess that you're referring to the incident that happened outside Kandahar, am I right?"

Allison cocked her head to the right, and smiled. "When you were ordered to guard the road and make sure no one drove up it, you didn't hesitate to open fire on a carload of civilians who tried to force their way around you. When your men tried to file reports accusing you of murder in that case, you just stood on the fact that you were following the orders you were given. However, in the matter with Lieutenant Gibson, when you could have used the same defense to look the other way, you chose to stand up for what you believed was right. What was the difference?"

"The difference was simple, to me," he said. "When my unit was assigned to guard the Kandahar Road, we were specifically given orders to prevent any vehicular traffic passing a certain point. If that meant that we had to open fire, then we were in fact ordered to do so, even if it meant firing on local civilians. In the other situation, we were supposed to be on patrol looking for possible terrorist encampments. Our orders did not include engaging or killing any civilians, under any circumstances, and certainly did not include clearly criminal actions like rape. By engaging in the activities that I reported, Lieutenant Gibson not only committed rape and murder, but he also violated the spirit of the orders he had been given. His actions could not be condoned, and required me to make a full report."

"I'm curious, Noah," Allison said. "You stand pretty firmly on orders, and what they mean. What if Lieutenant Gibson had simply ordered you to participate? Would you have obeyed?"

Noah shook his head. "No, Ma'am, I would not have. You see, to me, orders from a superior help me to establish what I need to be doing. However, I'm still fully aware that the people giving those orders are humans, and humans are often guided more by emotion than I am. If I'm given an order that clearly violates a superseding order or the prevailing moral code, then I am going to resort to my own understanding of right versus wrong. That's what happened in this case; the situation was so far outside what I perceived as right that I was forced to take action."

Allison smiled at him, and reached across to pat his hand. "And that's what I'm talking about," she said. "You just explained the very reason why we need you. Noah, we've lost several teams over the past few years, simply because the team leader hesitated. That's one thing I will never have to worry about, with you, because hesitation is not your weakness. When the time comes to take the shot, I know that you'll take it."

Noah didn't reply, but simply began eating his breakfast. On that morning, he had opted for a waffle with bacon on the side, and it was every bit as good as he'd expected it to be.

Allison dug into her own breakfast, and the two of them ate in silence. Noah finished first, and waited, sipping on a second cup of coffee until she was done.

"Oh, that was good," Allison said. "I think I could almost sit here and order another plate, but duty calls. Shall we go?"

Noah followed her out the door, stopping at the register to pay his tab, and then walked with her to her car. He got into the passenger side as she slid behind the wheel, and a moment later they were on the way to Kirtland.

The administrative office turned out to be on the top floor of one of the big office buildings in town, putting them more than ten stories above the street level. The elevator was smooth and fast, and required a special key. It opened directly into the administrative office complex, and Allison led the way to her office.

A secretary looked up and smiled as they walked past, and Allison told her to hold any calls or messages until further notice. She went directly to her desk, pointing at the chair in front of it for Noah, then picked up a large envelope and handed it to him before she went around to take her own chair.

"Go ahead and open it up," she said, and he did so. Several items slid out of it into his hand. "You'll find a cell phone, a Colorado driver's license, a birth certificate, a Social Security card, a passport and a few different credit cards, all of them in the name of Noah Wolf. I got the idea for your new last name from that comment you made the other day, about feeling like a wolf in man's clothing, hope you don't mind. Oh, and you're a year older, now, with a different birthday. Instead of being born in Illinois, you were originally born in California, but your parents moved to Iowa when you were only a year old. You grew up there, living in a small town, and you were taught at home. Your mother didn't trust public schools, and your father left decisions about your education to her. Your parents died when you were twenty, in an auto accident. You have no siblings, no other living relatives."

Noah studied the documents in his hand, and then looked up at Allison. "Doesn't sound all that different," he said.

"It actually doesn't take a lot of difference," she replied. "We're not out to make you an entirely different person, just slightly different, so that no one would mistake you for someone that they used to know. Oh, and incidentally, you have an appointment with our cosmetic surgeon next Monday, eight AM. Nothing too serious, a little work on your nose and cheekbones, and as you can see, the photos on those documents already reflect those changes. Amazing what computers can do these days, isn't it? Oh, and incidentally, that cell phone is very special and very expensive, so don't lose it! It doesn't have to use a cell tower; it's capable of going direct to satellite. You could be on a ship in the middle of the ocean, and you could still make a call on that phone."

"Cool," Noah said, and then he grinned. "I saw the difference in the photos, and I was going to ask about it," he said, then held up a key ring. "Okay, scanning through these things, my address is on a rural route out of Kirtland?"

"Yes," she said. "We usually put our assassins into something relatively private, while others get apartments or houses in town. Yours is a refurbished farmhouse on sixty acres, just off Temple Lake Road." She stood and walked over to a map that hung on the wall, motioning him to approach. She pointed at a spot on the map, and said, "This is where we are now. If you follow this street out to where it meets Temple Lake Road, then turn right, you'll be headed in the right direction. Your house is actually on County Road 640, right here. Turn right onto the gravel, and it's about half a mile down the road on the left. I'm a little bit on the jealous side, because you actually have about eight hundred feet of lakeshore, with your own dock and a boat and everything." She went back to her desk and sat, and Noah reclaimed his chair as well. "The house has four bedrooms, three bathrooms, a nice kitchen and living room, and a two-car attached garage. You've also got some other buildings, including a barn, a couple of workshops and a mobile home that's actually pretty nice. Doctor Parker chose this place for you, based on some of your history. I gather you like living out in the country?"

Noah put on a light smile, and nodded. "My last foster home," he said, "I lived with this older couple who raised goats and had this massive garden. I was with them for four years, right up until the old man died, and then their kids decided to put their mother in a nursing home. Since I was already almost 17, they just stuck me in a group home for the rest of my time, but I actually missed living on the farm."

Allison grinned. "Well, you can raise goats if you want to, but I'd suggest you hire yourself a farmhand. You can probably get someone cheap, if you throw in that mobile home as part of the pay package. As you can see from some of the other documents there, you are a security consultant who works with many different companies around the world to establish physical and digital security for their business operations. As such, you're occasionally called out on a moment's notice and may be gone for weeks at a time. Of course, it also explains how you can afford such a nice place."

"I think I'll leave farming to the farmers. Fishing, however, I do enjoy."

"Well, you can do plenty of it from your back yard," Allison said, "since it overlooks the lake. I'm told our lake has the best fishing in the whole state, but I haven't had time to go and try it, yet. Let me know if it's really that good, and I'll come out sometime and give it a try." She looked down at her desk. "Okay, now let's move on to other matters. By the way, you'll note that there are a number of keys on the key ring. You're going to need a car, and because you're a young, single, successful guy, Doctor Parker said we needed something expensive and powerful, so he chose a '72 Corvette. The car has been rebuilt from the frame up, and is extremely powerful. He says you can handle it, so don't prove him wrong and kill yourself in it, okay? You also have a pickup truck, but from what I understand, it's an older Ford that just sort of came with the house."

Noah shook his head. "That old couple I lived with? They had this old Ford truck, it was like a 1969, I think, and it looked like crap, but it would outrun everything around there. They used to let me drive it to school and around town, and I always felt like that truck and I were a lot alike. Neither of us was what we seemed to be, but we were both ready for whatever the world threw at us."

Allison looked at him for a moment. "Just when I think I'm beginning to understand you, Noah, you throw me a curve ball." She looked back at her desk, and then back up at his face. She leaned back in her chair. "Noah, after the reports I got on you yesterday, I've decided to accelerate your training. Mr. Jackson says you can keep up with his best, and only need some good workouts to help you build some stamina, and you're already quite proficient in most of what we teach our people here. I'm comfortable that you can handle what we do, and you're probably going to be better at it than anyone else we've ever had."

Noah looked at her, his face blank. "You're the boss," he said, and she smiled.

"How do you feel about it?" she asked, but then she started laughing. "Right, I should know better than to ask that, shouldn't I? Even I haven't actually come to grips with your—I don't know what to call it. What I'm actually trying to ask is whether you'd be willing to meet your team, today, since it's a foregone conclusion that you're going to pass and end up in the field."

Noah blinked. "Are they already here? Here at the facility, I mean?"

"Oh, yes," she said. "I hand-picked them from our current crop as soon as I knew we had you locked in. They're the best we've had in each of their specialties, and in my personal opinion, they are the ideal team for you. I think there could be some advantages in having you go through some of your training together."

Noah got up and walked over to the window, and looked out over the cityscape outside. In the distance, he could see mountains and forests, even though the terrain closer in wasn't quite so rough. There were also storm clouds in the distance, and he wondered if they might be some sort of sign for himself. His grandfather had been a minister, and had tried very hard to instill in Noah the belief that God was always in control.

Well, God, he thought to himself, *have you got storms headed for me?*

"Let's do it," Noah said.

TWELVE

"GOOD," ALLISON SAID. "Come with me." She rose from her desk and walked out of her office, shushing her secretary who was trying to catch her attention. "Not right now, Jenny," she said. "I'll be back in a bit, and you can grouch at me then." She kept on walking to the elevator with Noah on her heels.

She pushed the button for the basement, which was the garage area. "Incidentally, your Corvette is parked here and waiting for you. You can pick it up when we get done today. Right now, we're going to go over to another office, and get you officially assigned to your team and introduced to them. And just so you know, most of our people don't meet their teams for at least three months. That give you an idea of how much confidence we've got in you? Not that we want to add any pressure, of course."

"No problem," Noah said. "I still haven't quite figured out what pressure is."

They got back into her car, and she drove out of the garage and across a large part of the downtown district, parking on the street in front of another office building. She got out of the car and Noah followed her through the front door, and to yet another elevator. This one only went to the fifth floor, and he followed her down the hallway to a door marked Davis and Johnson, Accountants.

"We're here to see Mr. Johnson," Allison said to the secretary, who looked absolutely terrified when she walked in. The woman was heavyset, and Noah wondered for a moment if she was going to have a heart attack as she fumbled with the phone to tell Mr. Johnson that he had a visitor. A moment later, she managed to stammer out that Mr. Johnson would be happy to see them if they would just go through the door to the right. Allison smiled, and Noah wondered why the secretary looked even more frightened.

Allison led the way through the door, and a tall, balding man appeared in the hall ahead, obviously waiting for them. He ushered them into what appeared to be a conference room, with a large table and many chairs.

Allison pointed at Noah. "This is him, Russell," she said. "Noah Wolf."

Johnson let his eyebrows go up a bit as he looked Noah over. "Mr. Wolf," he said. "I have heard so much about you, sir. Some of it, I've got to say, is downright unbelievable."

Noah looked him in the eye. "Then don't believe it," he said. "After all, that's your choice."

Johnson smiled, and looked at Allison. "Okay, so he's every bit as brassy as you said he was. What are we up to, today?"

Allison had seated herself in one of the chairs around the table, and she leaned back and locked her fingers across her stomach. "Russell, I'm going to speed up Noah's training. He doesn't need all this crap—he's ready to go just about anytime. Let's go ahead and set up his team, now. Bring them in so he can meet them."

For a moment, Noah thought Johnson was going to argue, but he seemed to think better of it before any of the words that were forming behind his forehead could make it out of his mouth. "Certainly," he said, and then he got up and walked out of the room.

Noah looked at Allison, and his left eyebrow managed to

go up half an inch above the right. "He doesn't seem too happy about your plan," he said.

"Of course not," Allison said. "He's a bean counter. His job is to make sure that everything we do here pays off. That doesn't just mean monetarily, since we don't actually make any kind of profits, but every expenditure we make has to be justified, and that's his job. If I overrule him and say you're ready to go when his bookkeeping doesn't show that he's gotten his money's worth on your training, then it leaves open the possibility that something could jump up and bite him in the butt. That scares a bean counter, trust me on that."

Noah shrugged. "I'm just here to do what you tell me," he said. "If I have to listen to him, or anyone else, then you're going to have to point that out to me. One of the first things I learned when I began taking jobs was to find out who the boss is, and then do what the boss told me to do. As far as I can tell, you're the boss, so if there are any other bosses around here I need to know about, please make sure I do."

Allison laughed. "No, I'm your boss," she said. "That's not anything you gotta worry about. Johnson just likes to make sure his own ass is covered, that's all. He does his job, though, which is why he's still here."

Johnson returned a few moments later, and announced that Team Camelot would be assembled in the conference room within a few minutes. "Do you need me to stick around for this introduction?" he asked Allison.

"Not particularly," she said. "This is out of the ordinary, I know, but it's the way I want to do things in this case. They all know me, so I can handle this."

Johnson nodded, then turned around and left the room. A moment later, a tall, thin young man stuck his head into the room.

"Ma'am? I was told to report here?"

Allison smiled at him. "Yes, Neil, come on in. We're having a little get together, and you're part of it."

The young man came in and took a seat, and Noah looked him over. He barely looked old enough to be out of high school, and was probably a star on his high school basketball team, to judge from his height. Noah guessed him at around six foot five, but he was thin enough that a best guess of his weight put him around one fifty.

Neil was looking him over, as well. Noah wondered if the kid knew that he was looking at his new team leader.

Another man suddenly opened the door and poked his head inside. This one was not as tall, but he was definitely bulkier. He saw Allison, grinned and walked in. "Well, it looks like I'm in the right place," he said. "Johnson called and said I was supposed to be here, like ten minutes ago." His eyes flicked to Noah, but then he looked back at Allison.

"Yes, Mr. Conway," Allison said. "Please come in and have a seat; we're waiting for one more person."

The man she'd called Mr. Conway sat down, and nodded at the skinny kid named Neil. Noah took note that they obviously knew each other, and suspected from this that they were both guessing he was to be the new member of their team. Neither of them said a word to Noah, or to each other, for that matter. They seemed content to just wait quietly for whatever Allison had in store.

"Is this where I'm—oh, I guess it is," said a young woman at the door, just before she stepped inside. She nodded at Allison, then at the other two men, and took a seat.

Allison sat forward and smiled. "I'm doing something that breaks our usual protocols," she said, "because we're dealing with an extremely unusual situation." She indicated Noah with a flick of her head. "I want you all to meet Noah Wolf, who is going to be your team leader. Noah, let me introduce you to Sarah Child, who is your transportation specialist. Sarah came to us about eight months ago, right after she and her father were arrested for running one of the biggest chop shops in the Dallas area. Don't let her small size and pretty face fool you—she can drive anything that has wheels and can probably tear it apart and rebuild it even while it's moving down the road. When you're out on a mission, it will be her job to make sure you get where you're going, and hopefully back again."

Noah leaned over and extended a hand, and Sarah shook it. "Nice to meet you," he said, and the girl rolled her eyes.

"Yeah, charmed, I'm sure," she said.

Allison pointed at the tall, skinny kid. "This is Neil Blessing," she said. "Neil is one of the most accomplished computer hackers we've ever run across, and he was so good that we recruited him straight out of high school. Of course, that had a little bit to do with the fact that he was going to complete his senior year at the Chicago Youth Authority Special Education Division. Like you, Neil is an orphan who spent the majority of his teens in foster care, and he seemed to like the offer we made him."

"Yes, I did," Neil said. "Especially since she's leaving out the part about how I was to be transferred to a federal prison on my eighteenth birthday, to begin serving a sixty-year sentence without possibility of parole, just for making some minor adjustments to, oh, well, my bank account. Let's see, sixty years in prison, or work for the government and help them kill people? Hmm, not that hard a choice."

Noah leaned forward again, and shook hands with Neil Blessing. "I completely understand," Noah said. "Good to meet you."

He looked at Allison, who flicked her eyes at the other man. "This big lug is Moose Conway. Moose will be your muscle, the backup man. Like you, he's got a military background, and just barely failed to make the cut for Navy SEALs. He's been here for about a year and a half, now, and actually graduated, but he asked to be recycled and go through all the training again. Since we didn't have a team to assign him to at that moment, I agreed, and he's probably the best possible man to have in that position on your team."

Noah extended a hand to Moose, but the big guy just looked at it. "You may be the team leader, and I may have to take orders from you, but that doesn't mean I have to like you," Moose said. "I know who you are—I read all about you in *The Army Times*. I don't know how anyone can give you a second chance after you killed your own men and even your platoon leader. You keep your hands to yourself, understand? I'll do my job, and you can count on me to do it, but don't ever expect me to sit down and have a beer with you. You're a mad dog, and you should have been put down."

"Mr. Conway," Allison said, "you will stand down, right now. As it happens, there is a large mountain of evidence that proves that Noah was completely justified in the actions he took. You of all people should know that things are not always as they seem, and this is one of those cases. I'm not going to bother trying to explain it all to you, but get this through your head. Noah Wolf acted honorably when he killed Lieutenant Gibson and the other men who died that day. If he hadn't, he would not be sitting here, right now, because I would agree with your assessment. Do I make myself clear?"

Moose nodded once. "Yes, Ma'am," he said. "I'll just keep my opinions to myself."

Noah stood up. "Allison, if Mr. Conway does not feel comfortable being on my team, then I believe you should release him from it. I cannot count on a man who harbors animosity toward me."

Allison looked at him and grinned. "Then, if I were you, I would find a way to eliminate that animosity. He stays on your team, because he's the best man I've got for the job." She looked at all four of them. "You four will make up our newest team, which will be Team Camelot. Camelot—that's Noah—will be going through an abbreviated training course, and you'll be going through some of it with him. It's quite possible that you may find yourselves out on your first mission within just a few months. Keep yourselves sharp, and stay ready. At this point, I don't know what your first mission will be, so I can't give you any tips on how to prepare for it. Just be ready, because you'll probably have to move quickly when it comes." She looked at each of their faces in turn. "Any questions?"

Sarah raised a hand. "I have one," she said. When Allison nodded at her, she looked at Noah. "All I want to know is are you going to get us all killed?"

Noah's left eyebrow popped up. "I'm certainly not planning to," he said. "Can I ask what prompted that question?"

Sarah looked at him for a minute, then shrugged her shoulders. "A friend of mine says he knows who you are," she said. "He says you don't think like a normal person, that the things most of us worry about don't seem to mean much to you. Is that true?"

Allison started to interrupt, but Noah put a hand on her arm. "According to a small army of psychiatrists, I suffer from an unusual form of PTSD that leaves me without emotions. I don't get angry, I don't get scared, I don't love and I don't hate. I've spent almost all of my life pretending to be normal, but you four deserve to know the truth. If you tell me a joke, I may not realize it unless somebody else starts laughing. If you share some bad news with me, I'm going to offer sympathy, not because I feel it, but because I've learned that's what you're supposed to do in that situation. I've spent my entire life studying how humans act, so that I can pretend to be one of you. That's the reality I live in." He took a deep breath. "As to the value I place on things like human life? Let me put it this way. The reason I have bothered to study the way humans act is so that I can do what other people would consider the right thing, when it's time to do it. Sometimes, however, I have to do what I believe is right, and that may not be exactly what everyone else wants. Instead, it will be based not on fear or anger or any other emotion, but solely on a logical conclusion drawn from available facts. Now, what that should mean to each of you is that I'm going to naturally want to do whatever I can to protect you. However, if protecting you means the failure of the mission, then I'm going to put the mission first. Does any of that make sense to you?"

Sarah sat there and just stared at him, and Moose busied himself with looking at the ceiling, but Neil leaned forward, put his head in his hands and muttered, "Oh, God help us, we're all going to die."

THIRTEEN

"**D**ON'T LET MOOSE get to you," Allison said. "He comes from a long line of soldiers and sailors, and if he had his choice, he'd still be in the Navy."

"Then why isn't he?" Noah asked.

"Remember I said he just barely failed to make Navy SEALs? Well, after he was notified that he was not selected, especially after going through such intense training just to find out if he was good enough, he sort of snapped. The captain who told him the bad news ended up with a shiner, and Moose ended up with a BCD."

"Bad Conduct Discharge?" Noah asked. "He's probably lucky that's all he got. Assaulting an officer, without reason? Really bad idea."

Allison grinned at him. "Yes, well, Moose figured that out the hard way. Anyway, that's how he turned up on my radar, and I couldn't see any sense in letting all that training go to waste."

Noah looked at her sideways. "With that kind of training, I'm surprised you didn't make him a team leader himself. An assassin."

She shook her head. "No way. Moose isn't a man who can inspire others to follow him; he's not a natural leader. And except for that one lapse in judgment, he has always been dedicated to following the orders of those in command. You figure out a way to make a friend out of him, or at least get his animosity under control, and you'll have the most loyal man you could ever hope for on your side."

Noah nodded. "Speaking of loyalties," he said, "tell me about Neil Blessing. Is he always that sarcastic?"

"He is, yes. It's a defense mechanism with him. Neil was always the nerdy kid, and as tall as he is, it turned out he was far too clumsy for any type of athletics. Academically, intellectually, he's a genius, and if he hadn't been stupid enough to brag on Facebook and twitter about hacking into the bank's computers, he probably would've gotten away with it. It seems that there's always little fractions of a cent in the daily interest calculations that get swept into some digital limbo, and Neil created some way to collect all those fractions and add them together in his own bank account. Fifteen thousandths of a cent at a time doesn't sound like much money, until you realize that his bank is a national corporation with several million clients. This kid was racking up almost eleven thousand dollars a day, and not one cent of it was ever detected as missing from anywhere else."

Noah blinked. "If he was dumb enough to brag about what he'd accomplished, then I'm not sure why you're still calling him a genius."

"Stop and think, Noah," Allison said. "Genius is the ability to see past the limitations that most of us are faced with, and accomplish the impossible. That's what he did, without a doubt. However, it is possible to be a genius and still be rather stupid, like that guy who created the internet security software that made him a billionaire, then ran off with his secretary and murdered her husband so no one would find them. Pretty stupid, wasn't he?"

"Okay, I guess I see your point. Can I at least hope that Neil has learned his lesson about boasting?"

Allison laughed. "I suspect you could actually bet on that."

They pulled into the underground garage of Allison's building, and this time she pulled up behind a black-and-silver

Corvette. Pointing at it, she said, "That's your car. Like I said, don't go wrapping it around any trees, or I might decide to shoot you myself."

Noah grinned and got out, but she called him back just before he got into the Corvette. "Don't forget to gather your things from the motel," she said. "Those clothes are yours, along with the computer. Take them out to your house with you." She waved once, and drove away.

Noah got into the Corvette and slipped the key into the ignition. He pushed in the clutch and started the car, found reverse on the four-speed and backed it out of its slot. A moment later, he was turning out of the garage onto the street, and making his way back toward the motel.

Marco stuck his head out of his room as Noah pulled in, and came jogging over a moment later to eyeball the Corvette. "Holy cow," he said, "what a ride! How did you swing this?"

Noah shrugged. "The dragon lady said Doc Parker picked it for me. Can't say I'm too upset about it, though. It's a sweet set of wheels."

Marco whistled. "I'll just bet." Without asking, he reached down to the grill and pulled the hood release, then tilted the hood up and whistled again. "Man, I haven't seen that much chrome in forever," he said. "Looks like a four fifty-four big block, but I'd bet there's nothing stock about it. Want my guess? It'll pass everything except a gas station."

Noah grinned. "Good thing they give me a gas allowance, then, isn't it? Listen, I just came to grab my clothes and such, they got me in a house out by the lake already."

"Yeah, I knew that," Marco said. "I'll only be here a couple more days myself, just getting in some refresher training. Not that I need it, you understand, but it never hurts to keep yourself on top of your game."

Noah nodded, and opened his door. "Hey, by the way, how

do I check out of the motel? I mean, there isn't an office or anything. Where do I leave the key?"

"Just leave it in the room," Marco said. "Somebody comes around to clean up after we leave, they'll take care of it. Just make sure you take all your stuff with you, because once you leave the key, you can't get back in." Marco waved, and wandered back toward his own room.

Noah quickly gathered up the clothes that had been bought for him, carrying them out carefully and laying them on the passenger seat of the car. When he was done with that chore, he went back to get the computer and found that it had a satchel it fit into, so he packed it carefully and carried it out as well. The only things left were the snacks and pop he had bought the night before, and he was glad he hadn't thrown away the plastic bags he'd carried them home in. They went back into the bags, and then into the floorboard of the car.

A quick glance around the room told him he hadn't left anything behind, so he dropped the key onto the dresser and started out the door. At the last second, he went back and checked the bathroom, gathering the shampoo, soaps and razors, and taking those as well. He closed the door behind him and got into the Corvette, fired it up, then began following the map Allison had given him to find his new home.

Even though the compound wasn't all that large, the drive out to his new house took almost 20 minutes, mostly because Temple Lake Road was full of twists and turns. He found County Road 640 with no trouble, turned onto it, and found the house only a couple of minutes later.

It was bigger than he'd expected. When Allison had said it was a refurbished farmhouse, he had thought of something like the one he had stayed in as a teenager, an old, rickety two-story that looked like a refugee from Green Acres. The house he found, however, was probably twice the size of the one he remembered from back then, and quite beautiful. It appeared to have been built from cedar, and he could see that it had undergone some extensive remodeling in the not-too-distant past.

He parked in front of the garage, then walked over to the door and opened it with the key. The sky was overcast, so he found the light switch inside the door and was amazed when he saw the expanses of oak that greeted his eyes. It took him more than fifteen minutes just to walk through the house, looking at all of the different decors that were used inside, and he couldn't help wondering if it weren't all lost on a man who didn't even know how to appreciate such beauty.

He went out to the garage and found the button to open the garage door, then walked out and pulled the Corvette inside. He closed the garage and began carrying all of his things into the house. Snacks went into the kitchen, root beer into the refrigerator, and then he had to decide which of the four bedrooms he wanted to claim. In the end, simple logic won out, and he took the one on the ground floor that had the big master bathroom attached to it.

Allison had told him that he didn't have anything scheduled for the rest of the day, so he gave himself a chance to look the place over. Once he had explored the house for the third or fourth time, he walked outside and began looking at the rest of his little estate.

The first thing to catch his eye was the barn, and he wandered over to it and pulled the big door open. A musty smell greeted him, the old scent of horses and cattle that always seems to be present in one of these buildings. It reminded him briefly of the farm he had lived on as a teenager, and he remembered some of his adventures in the loft of the barn back then. A quick look around showed him the ladder that led up to the loft in this one, and he climbed up it just to look around.

The loft had a lot of old hay bales in it, and there were quite a few boxes full of old dishes, knickknacks and other things that the previous owners had probably left behind. Curiosity, while it's not an emotion, was something that did plague Noah at times, and he found himself rummaging through the discards. There were figurines and collectibles of different kinds, none of which, he was sure, had any true value, but some of them just appealed to him, even if he couldn't say why. He emptied one box, and then began putting into it things he wanted to keep, like the many figurines of cats. Cats, he had decided years before, were a lot like himself. They didn't operate on emotion, but rather on logic, and when they were done with you, they were simply done. A cat said goodbye by simply sticking its tail in the air and walking away. Noah thought that was a wonderful example, and tried to follow it whenever he felt like saying goodbye.

He carried the box down carefully, climbing one-handed until he got back to the ground, then took it inside the house and set it on the kitchen counter. Everything in it would need to be cleaned before it could be set out, but he would save that chore for later. He went back outside and began exploring the rest of the little farm.

He found the mobile home that came with it, and saw that Allison was right about it being in surprisingly good shape. It occurred to him again that he could rent it out, but then he decided he didn't really want neighbors that close to him. He wandered over to one of the two workshop buildings, a fairly large one with overhead doors that was big enough to pull a truck into, and the pickup he'd been told about was sitting inside it at that moment, a Ford from the mid-nineties. The building was obviously intended for mechanical work. It still held a lot of old tools, and there was quite a workbench along one wall. Noah enjoyed tinkering with vehicles and machinery, and he could think of several ways to put this building to use.

The other workshop was smaller, and there were some old woodworking tools stacked up all around it. Some of them were older power tools, but there were a lot of hand tools, as well. The discovery appealed to him, since he'd always wanted to try his hand at woodworking but had never had the time.

A path led down to the lake, and Noah followed it. There was a dock at the bottom of the flight of wooden stairs, with a small boat house attached to it. Allison had told him that he had a boat, so he walked over to the boat house and found the key that would open the door so that he could look inside.

There it was. Noah was looking at what he guessed to be a twenty-four-foot cabin cruiser, an inboard outboard that looked like it had been very well maintained. He climbed onto the boat and peeked into the cabin, which was basically nothing but a bed and a very small bathroom. There was a tiny refrigerator and a microwave oven that he guessed would pass for a galley, but there was nowhere to sit down there. Up on the deck, however, there were four bucket seats and a couple of bench seats with a table between them, and a folding top that would probably protect passengers from the elements. It was a nice boat, and he was looking forward to getting it out on the lake sometime soon. He locked up the boathouse again as he left.

He made his way back to the house, and started trying to settle in. The place was fully furnished, and everything seemed to be either antique or of very high quality, so he suspected that the furnishings may have come from the previous owners. The only things that truly seemed new were all the kitchen appliances and the big flat-panel TV in the living room.

Every room was furnished, including the extra bedrooms upstairs and the room full of bookcases that was downstairs. There were hundreds of books on the shelves. Noah glanced at a few of the titles, but most of them he'd never heard of. Still, he did enjoy reading, so he hoped to get time to check them out sometime soon.

He rummaged through a few of the closets, and found a decent stock of bath towels, sheets and blankets. Except for the fact that the dressers and clothes closets were empty, it almost looked like the owners had simply stepped out for a few minutes. The kitchen cabinets held dishes, pots and pans, silverware and everything else he could possibly need. The only thing that was necessary for him to do was make a trip to the grocery store.

That thought made him wonder about his finances, and he reached into a pocket to pull out the envelope Allison had given him earlier. He found the paper that described his bank accounts, of which there were four. Each of them could be checked online, so he grabbed the computer, set it on the kitchen table and turned it on. The house seemed to be wired for Wi-Fi, and the computer already set up for it, because a moment later it told him that he was logged on securely.

Following the instructions on the bank paperwork, he discovered that he had a fairly large amount of money available. Allison had told him that he would be receiving a bonus for coming on board, and apparently it was a doozy. He'd have no trouble stocking up on groceries, that was for sure.

That was also when he discovered that there was a hefty mortgage on the farm, one that he was apparently expected to make the payments on. The mortgage came from one of the same banks he had an account in, so he went ahead and set up an automatic payment. That way he wouldn't have to wonder if it was paid when he was out on a mission.

Noah sat back in his chair and looked around at his new home. Only a few days before, he would have found it impossible to believe that he could ever have any kind of life for himself, but now he had a beautiful home, a fantastic car and the opportunity to serve his country once again.

FOURTEEN

NOAH HAD A life, all right, and it revolved around some of the most intense training he had ever received. While Allison had told him she was going to speed up his training schedule, she had also made it clear that there were certain things he couldn't skip, including working with Jackson on PT and Daniel on weapons, and a special class taught by an actual college professor on the Law of Nations, in particular where it pertained to espionage and assassination.

Physical training, for Noah, was mostly just fun. By the time he'd been in the organization for a month, everyone was trying to keep up with him on their daily runs, and he was finding new obstacle courses to put them through every day.

Weapons class was almost as enjoyable, especially since Daniel was running them through various types of specialty firearms. Noah had never realized that there had been so many different types of guns invented strictly for the purpose of getting them past any kind of security so that they could be used for assassination. There were guns that looked like ink pens, smoking pipes, walking canes and umbrellas, the types that were sometimes seen in spy movies, but there were also other kinds that Noah doubted most people had ever heard of. Those were the ones that were built into coffee mugs, spray cans, cell phones, and dozens of other things that no one would ever expect.

There was one that looked like a beer can, and had a single-shot straight barrel concealed within it. It was to be offered to the intended target, who could open it and tip it up to take a drink. The act of opening it would release a spring inside, so that when it was tipped up the first time the hammer inside would be cocked. When it was tipped a second time, however, a weight would release the hammer, and a forty-five-caliber bullet would be fired straight through the brain of the target. Noah enjoyed the logical ingenuity behind all of these devices, and was already thinking of ways to design some of his own.

Equally fascinating were the amazing number of guns that could be carried right past even the most sophisticated metal detectors, and even be missed by gun-sniffing dogs. Some of them were made of high-strength ceramics, others of plastic, but it was the ammunition that was so surprising. One of Noah's favorites was a revolver that was essentially a miniature rocket launcher, because the slugs that left its barrel were propelled by a chemical reaction involving hydrogen peroxide and iron. Peroxide rockets had long been used in special cars going after the land speed record, cars that weighed many tons. These little rockets propelled a slug that weighed only a few ounces, and at speeds that outclassed many conventional bullets.

On the firing range, Noah displayed the same incredible talent that had amazed his military instructors, hitting the targets perfectly after only a couple of preliminary shots to get the feel of the weapon. Once he knew the gun, there was almost nothing he couldn't hit with it, and his ability to move from target to target, seemingly without even looking at them, caused rumors to make their way through the ranks of his classmates. His own personal favorite was the one that said he was an android, a machine designed to look like a human. He thought that was so close to the truth that when a terrified classmate finally asked him about it, he simply smiled and walked away.

The one class he didn't care a lot for, however, was the one

Allison told him was most important. This was the law class, where he learned about all of the ramifications of what he would be doing, and what would happen if he were ever caught. He had always thought that line about how Tom Cruise and his secret agents would be disavowed if they were caught had been just a part of the script, but he knew now that it wasn't. If he or any of his team should be captured while on foreign soil, there would be no rescue. They were all expendable, despite the fact that small fortunes had been spent on training them, because if the government ever acknowledged sending such people into another country, it would start a war.

Professor McCarty was widely touted as one of the leading experts on the Law of Nations, and he had been engaged over the years to speak at schools all over the world. Noah would've been more than happy to let him go back to any of them, preferably somewhere on the other side of the planet, so that Noah wouldn't have to listen to him anymore. Unfortunately, he was teaching in a small classroom there on the compound, and there was no way out of it.

"One of the most famous cases," the professor said, "was that of Francis Gary Powers, the pilot of the U2 plane that was shot down over Russia. Mr. Powers was charged with spying, and it took all of the efforts of the State Department and diplomatic corps years to convince the Russian government that the plane had merely strayed off course. Mr. Powers was imprisoned in Russia for almost two years, subjected to intense interrogation that included various kinds of torture, and he eventually confessed to being a spy. In the end, he did finally get to come home, but it should be understood that this is the exception, and not the rule. Had Mr. Powers been captured on the ground, without his U2 spy plane being involved, it is highly doubtful that our government would've expended any effort whatsoever on his behalf. You see, it wasn't Mr. Powers that they were trying to protect. It was the fact that his plane had been shot down exactly where it was, because that's exactly where they had told him to be. If we had ever admitted that, Russia could have claimed that sending the plane to photograph their cities and military installations constituted espionage, and therefore was an act of war."

For three hours each day, Noah had to listen to Professor McCarty drone on and on and on. The only benefit was that, as a side effect of his PTSD condition, he had an exceptionally good memory. Almost everything he heard, he could remember at any time he chose. That, at least, saved him from the tedium of having to take notes.

There were other classes he found quite fascinating, however. One of those was the class in chemistry, which was so far beyond the things he had learned in his high school chemistry class that it was like being in another world entirely. While there was some foundation in what he had learned back then, the chemistry he was involved with now revolved around an entirely different kind of chemical reactions. He learned a great deal about how to make explosives, sometimes from common household items, as well as the creation of, uses for and ways to survive an incredible range of poisons.

Then there were the martial arts classes. Some of the things he was learning would have seemed impossible to him not that long before, but the physical training that he was getting was toning and strengthening muscles he hadn't even known he possessed. If anyone had told him, back when he was a kid in MMA classes, that he would one day be capable of doing a back flip and kicking three separate opponents before landing back on his feet, he would've laughed. Suddenly, though, it was a move that he was practicing every day, along with dozens of others he never would have dreamed of.

This training schedule had been rearranged to allow the insertion of his team. Sarah, Neil and Moose were with him in most of his classes, although Neil was excused from the PT class. Being tall, clumsy and skinny, the administrators had decided that his value was in his computer expertise, making them reluctant to risk him suffering any injuries.

Both Moose and Sarah performed well in PT, and Moose managed to stay close to Noah on their daily runs. All three of his teammates were proficient with many weapons, and did well in the weapons class and on the firing ranges, but they simply put in appearances in the chemistry and law classes.

For Noah's part, he was amazed at the quantity of information that was being crammed into his head. Once again, his almost photographic memory came in handy, because he had to memorize quite a list of poisons and their antidotes, as well as recipes for making them on the fly. He learned tricks and techniques for deploying poisons, including orally, in the air, and through the skin, and was taught which were most effective in various scenarios.

So many things were changing in his life. He had gone to see the cosmetic surgeon, just as he'd been ordered to do, and now the face that looked back at him in the mirror seemed somewhat unfamiliar. Noah was adaptable, though, and within a very short time, he was able to visualize his new face as easily as he had always done with his old one.

Allison had been right. The changes were subtle, but sufficient. If he ran into someone who had known him before, it was highly doubtful that they would recognize him, though they might feel that they saw a resemblance to someone they used to know. Ironically, they probably wouldn't even be able to remember who it was this stranger reminded them of.

Noah was drilled in his new history. If asked where he was born, he would instantly reply that it had been in Torrance, California, but that he had grown up on a farm outside of Paxton, Iowa. He had been homeschooled, but received a diploma through an accredited online high school, with exceptional grades. He had gone into the Army not long after, planning to use the G.I. Bill to finance his further education after his term of service.

In the Army, however, he had become an expert in security technologies, both physical and digital. Upon his discharge, he had been recruited by a consulting firm out of Washington, DC, and now traveled the world as a security issue troubleshooter.

Everything was documented; everything was backed up in databases all over the country. His school record, military record, birth certificate, even the death certificates of his parents who died in a tragic accident while he was serving his country—all would stand up to any scrutiny.

Besides training time, and at Allison's urging, he had begun spending personal time with the other members of his team, actually inviting them to his home on a couple of occasions. They showed up when they were supposed to, but it seemed to Noah that the only one he got along with was Neil. The skinny kid seemed to enjoy his company, and Noah began to suspect it was because he could get away with being even more sarcastic than usual, since Noah didn't always realize what was being said to him.

Sarah would occasionally join in on some of the banter, but he could tell there was something reserved about her, some reason she didn't want to open up to him or anyone else. He didn't care that much, because he wasn't interested in any kind of relationship with her other than a professional one. His only concern was that the distance might cause her to be untrustworthy when he needed her.

Moose, on the other hand, would sit there and refuse to even join in the conversations. Unless he was asked a point-blank question that pertained to his position in the team, he had nothing to say. Noah recalled Allison telling him that he needed to find a way to break through that wall, but so far, he didn't have any ideas along that line. Moose didn't like him—that was obvious. Noah didn't know what to do about it.

The boat occupied some of his days off. It had a big Mercury V-8 engine tucked into its stern, and would move along at a pretty good clip. Noah had learned to waterski a few years earlier, and began thinking about buying a set. All he needed to do was find someone to drive the boat for him, but so far, he wasn't having any luck in that regard.

Some evenings he spent alone, but occasionally he would wander down to Charlie's for a beer. He wouldn't let himself drink much, because he didn't trust himself not to get into trouble. A couple of early experiences in drinking, as a teenager, had showed him that he had as little common sense when he was drinking as he had emotion when he was sober.

Charlie, despite his near-toothless appearance, had turned out to be quite an intelligent person. He and Noah had several very interesting conversations, ranging on everything from politics to religion to the debate over which pile of crap might be best to put into the White House for the next term. So far, they hadn't come to any real conclusions on that one, but the debate was still ongoing.

To sum it all up, Noah was slowly going stir crazy. It was time for Allison to either put up or shut up, in his opinion—either give them a mission and let him determine whether his team could properly function, or else split the team up and reassign everyone. He had done everything he could think of to try to win them all over, but as far as he could tell, they were just as raw and fragmented as they had been the day they met.

He sat down at the bar, and Charlie set a bottle in front of him automatically. "Hey, kid," Charlie said, his habitual greeting.

Noah smiled. "Hey, Charlie, how goes it tonight?"

The two of them talked about the usual things for a few minutes, but then Noah got more serious. "Charlie," he said, "I've got a question for you. Let's say you've got this group you got to work with, people that are assigned to you, so that you're their boss. One of them seems to like you, one acts like she's afraid to let you get too close, and the third one just plain hates your guts. How in the world can you turn them into a team?"

Charlie grinned his toothless grin. "Oh, come on, kid, ask me a hard one," he said. "That's easy. First, you get the one that likes you to tell the others to knock off their crap. Then you get the girl who's afraid of you into what looks like a position where you can take advantage of her, but you don't. You walk her out the door, and let her go. Then you find the guy who hates you, get him alone, and challenge him. Tell him that if he can kick your ass, then you'll do everything you can to make sure he doesn't have to put up with you anymore. On the other hand, if you kick his, then he's got to shut up and back you up a hundred percent. Then you make damn sure you kick his ass all the way up to his forehead!"

Noah sat there and thought through what Charlie had said, and came to the conclusion that it warranted a chuckle. "That's a good one, Charlie," he said.

"Now, I wasn't kidding," Charlie said. "If there's one thing I learned the hard way in my years, it's that sometimes, the only way to get a man to be your friend is to whip him in a fair fight. The trick is to make sure the fight is more fair for you than it is for him, and I suspect you might be the kind of guy who could figure out a way to do that. Am I right?"

Noah grinned. "You might be."

Charlie went to help another customer, and Noah thought about what he'd said. When he left a half hour later, he was already thinking of ways to put the old man's plan into action.

FIFTEEN

HE DECIDED TO try to settle the issue all at once, and called all three of his team members that night. He told them that he needed to meet with them the following evening, and invited them over for dinner. All three agreed to come, but he could sense that Sarah and Moose were not happy about it.

Neil was, because the boy could put away more food than Noah had ever seen anyone eat! If there was one thing he knew was always going to get Neil's attention, it was free food.

Noah had bought a grill, and he was quite good at using one, so he grilled beef kabobs and put beer and soft drinks on ice, then set up a picnic table he'd bought and strung up some lights. The dinner was set for seven, but Neil showed up at six, and Noah took the opportunity to talk to him.

"So, Neil," he began, "tell me what you think about our team. Be straight with me, dude, I want to hear what you got to say."

Neil smiled. "Well, I'm not sure exactly what to say about you," he said. "I mean, even by your own admission, you're an enigma. A man with no emotions? That's almost scary, except that in this situation, I think it makes you the right guy to have in charge. Then you got me—I'm just the computer hacker who has to try to figure out what it is you need to do before you have to do it. There, again, I'm the right guy for that job." He took a drink of his root beer. "Now we get to the little hottie with the lead foot. Sarah's got some kind of issue with you, and I'm not sure what it is. She almost acts like she knows you, but I've dug deeply into her past, and I'm pretty sure there's no connections between the two of you anywhere. Maybe it's just that you remind her of someone, and if I had to guess, I'd say it's her father. From what I've been able to gather about him, he wasn't always the nicest man to be around, and I don't think he cared a lot about her feelings. If he wanted something done, she had to drop whatever she wanted to make sure it got done."

"Really? That could explain a lot," Noah said. "If you run across anything else, let me know, would you?"

"Of course, my King," Neil said. "Now we got to look at the real pain in the ass, the guy with the stupid name. Who on earth names their kid Moose, for crying out loud?" He waved a hand. "Yeah, yeah, I know, it's just a nickname. Once again, I did a little digging and found out that his real name is Milton. What kind of parent does that to a kid, either, now that I think about it? Anyway, Moose has got it in for you because of what happened to you in Iraq. He wants to pretend he's some kind of super soldier, but the reality is that he punched out his commanding officer over something stupid. It's a wonder he didn't end up in Leavenworth, with you. Anyway, he didn't, and now he's been assigned to us. If there was one thing that Queen Allison did to us to really give us the shaft, he would be it."

Noah nodded. "Okay, he doesn't like me, we know that. How do you get along with the other two?"

Neil shrugged, waving his bottle around in the air. "We all seem to get along fairly well, or at least we have on the few occasions when we've been together. Although, to be honest, it seems to be a little better when you're not around."

"Yeah, I'll bet. Let me ask you a question, and I want a straight answer. Do you think it would do any good if you told them to back it down?"

Neil's eyes went wide, and he began to laugh. "Okay, now you're starting to worry me because you sound a lot like an idiot. Noah, they think of me as just some kid who happens to be good with the computer. They're not going to listen to anything I have to say."

Noah grinned at him. "Okay, okay, it was worth a shot. I'm just trying to pull this team together, make it work like a unit. With Sarah acting like she's scared of me, and Moose wishing he could bury an ax in my forehead, I'm finding it pretty hard to do. Can't blame me for grasping at straws, can you?"

A car pulled in, and Noah looked around to see Sarah and her new Camaro. So far, the only time she'd even given him a smile was the first time he'd had them all to the house. He had opened up the garage and let her see the Corvette, and for a few minutes, he had seen an entirely different person. She definitely loved cars, and that one caught her eye. Unfortunately, it hadn't lasted. She had gone back to being her quiet, unfriendly self just moments after he closed the garage again.

She got out of her car and made her way over to where he and Neil were sitting near the grill. "Am I too early?"

Noah shook his head, and pointed to the cooler full of pop, beer and ice. "Nope," he said. "You're right on time as far as I'm concerned. Grab a bottle, join us guys. We're contemplating the secrets of the universe over here."

Sarah reached for a bottle, and Neil took advantage of the moment to lean close to Noah's ear. "Did you catch the eye roll?" the boy asked, and Noah tossed in a chuckle, right on cue. Sarah came over and sat down in another chair.

"So," she said, "secrets of the universe, huh? I'm gonna go out on a limb and say that I think that was probably a pretty short conversation. Am I right?"

"Ouch!" Neil said. "Do you always have to keep your claws out and sharp? Has it ever occurred to you that some of us might just want to be friendly?"

Sarah glanced at Neil, then flicked her eyes to Noah. "Sorry, Neil," she said. "That wasn't necessarily directed at you."

Noah looked her dead in the eye. "Okay, so what is it that I did to you in a past life that makes you so determined not to be friends with me in this one? Any chance you can let me in on the secret?"

Sarah shrugged and looked away. "Let's just say I know your type, and my experience has not always been a good one."

"What's that got to do with me?" Noah asked her. "Just because someone else has done you wrong doesn't mean I would. And if this is some sort of relationship problem, let me make something very clear. I'm not in the market for a relationship, not of any kind. I don't mind being friendly, but my focus here is for us to be able to work together. That's all."

Sarah looked at him, and Noah suspected that if eyeballs had laser beams, he'd have a couple of holes bored through him at that moment. "This isn't any kind of relationship problem, because this isn't any kind of relationship. As you say, we have to work together. I can assure you, right now, that's all it will ever be."

Noah shook his head. He didn't have the slightest idea what he might say to make things better, so he decided to say nothing at all. After a moment, Neil spoke up just to fill up the silence, and he and Sarah began a lighthearted conversation.

Moose showed up at seven, right on time. He parked his car and walked over to the table, grabbed a bottle of beer, spun the top off of it, and took a long pull. He glanced at Noah, then pulled up the chair beside Sarah.

"So, great leader," he said. "What made this meeting so all-fired important?"

Noah shook his head again, and leaned on the table as he looked at Moose. "Actually, I was hoping we could try to work out some of our differences. I've got a feeling we're gonna be looking at a mission sometime in the not-too-distant future, and

I'd really like to get some of this crap out of the way before we end up out in the field ready to cut each other's throats."

Moose glared at him. "Let me tell you something, Mr. Team Leader," he said. "I do not like you, and I don't have any problem with you knowing that. On the other hand, I, unlike you, know how to follow orders and respect the command I'm under. You don't have to worry about me cutting your throat, because I'm quite sure you'll find a way to do that yourself before too long."

Noah looked at him for a moment, and then got to his feet. "Moose, let me explain this to you. One of the standing orders that every soldier in Iraq or Afghanistan or anywhere else like that is given is the order to avoid any assault upon a civilian, because such an assault can be taken as an act of war. My platoon leader, who was supposed to be on a routine patrol, stumbled across five young girls and decided that he and his men should have some fun with them. Unfortunately, that would mean that there were five young girls who could talk about what they did, so he then decided that these girls should also become casualties, and he ordered them all shot. I had been assigned as cover fire, a sniper position on a hill some distance away, and when he finally called me down to let me know what was going on, only one of those girls was still alive. Lieutenant Gibson asked me if I wanted to join in the fun, and I declined, so he shot that girl and killed her, right in front of me. Now, you tell me which one of us was actually obeying orders that day, would you?"

Moose sat there for a moment, and then took another drink from his bottle. "That's the story you told when they court-martialed you," he said. "How come the story never came out before you were arrested and charged?"

"It did," Neil said. "If you could use a computer half as well as you can drink that beer, you could go right online and read the original transcripts of Noah's case. He actually made that report the very day it happened, but his commanding officer decided to ignore the evidence and go along with a few men who told other, conflicting stories that made our illustrious team leader out to be the bad guy. Since Lieutenant Gibson's daddy happens to be a congressman who's being groomed for the next presidential election, a lot of pretty powerful people decided that our boy here needed to be swept under a big rug. Imagine how it would've looked for the congressman if the truth had come out."

Moose sat there for a long moment without saying a word. When he finally did speak, he wouldn't look at Noah. "So maybe you got the shaft," he said. "If so, then I'm sorry. Just don't expect me to suddenly become your best buddy. No matter what your reason, you still shot your commanding officer."

"Oh, and you only punched yours in the eye," Neil blurted out. Moose spun around, glaring at the kid, and started to get to his feet.

"You don't know anything about it," Moose said, taking an ominous step toward Neil. "I got passed over, despite the fact that my scores were higher than three of the men who were accepted. The captain knew damned well what he was doing, and there was no excuse for him to pass me over. All I did was ask him why, and the next thing I knew, I had two guys holding my arms. I didn't swing at the captain, I was just trying to get myself loose from them, and he got in the way."

Noah had stepped in between the two of them, and held up a hand to ask for a truce.

"Okay, look, Moose," he said. "It sounds a lot like maybe there's been a big misunderstanding on both ends, here. What do you say we just put this behind us, and start over, right now?"

Moose shook his head. "I told you, don't expect me to be your friend." He suddenly threw down his bottle, shattering it on the flagstones of the patio, and turned toward his car.

"Stop right there," Noah said. "Moose, we cannot have this kind of problem between us. There's only one way I can see to fix this, so I'm going to give you one chance. You and me, right now, man-to-man. You kick my ass, I'll go to Queen Allison and ask her to transfer you away from me. I kick yours, you knock off this crap and back me up, show me you know how to be a loyal soldier. Deal?"

Moose stood there and stared at him for a long moment, and then he nodded. "Deal," he said.

Noah nodded, and walked over into the grass. "Whenever you're ready, then," he said, and he had no more than gotten the words out before Moose lowered his head and charged at him like a raging bull.

Noah waited until he was only two feet away, then spun to his left. Moose sailed right by, but Noah continued to spin and planted his boot in Moose's butt as he skidded to a stop. Neil burst out laughing, and Noah thought he heard a giggle out of Sarah, but he didn't have time to check. Moose was in a rage, and swung at him in a roundhouse that would have taken his head off, had it connected.

Noah ducked under it, and came back up with a fist into Moose's solar plexus, knocking the wind out of him with a single punch. The big man fell back, but he wasn't down for the count. He managed to suck in enough air to let him come after Noah again, this time more cautiously.

The two of them began striking at each other, and so skilled were they both that it began to look like a high-speed film from an old kung fu movie. They swung, struck, flipped and kicked like a pair of wild warriors, and soon each of them was marked and bleeding in spots. The fight went on for several minutes, but then Moose began to slow. Noah continued to block him more than strike at him, and then Moose left an opening that was too good to pass up, and Noah delivered a punch directly to the point of his chin. Moose went down, and didn't move at all.

Noah, gasping for breath, stumbled to his chair and sat while Neil and Sarah went to check on Moose. "Oh, good," Neil said, "he's just gone to sleepy land. I sure hope he'll be in a better mood when he wakes up."

"He'd better be," Noah said. "I'm not going to put up with a whole lot more of his attitude, if he isn't."

Moose groaned a moment later, and managed to sit up a minute after that. He was quiet, and so Noah got up and walked over to him. He extended a hand, and Moose reached up and took it. Noah pulled, and Moose made it to his feet.

"That settle it?" Noah asked.

Moose looked at him, and then reached up to rub his jaw. "It's settled, Sir," he said. "You'll get no more static out of me."

"That's good," Allison said, and they all spun to see her sitting on Noah's back steps. No one had heard a car pull up, nor any footsteps, but she was there and had watched the whole thing. "It's about time you got your ducks in a row, Camelot. And not a day too soon, either. I'm going to give you a couple of days to recuperate, and then you'll begin specialized training for your first mission. We've got some detailed briefings planned and very special simulations set up to help you work it all out, but I'd say we're looking at a go within a couple of months. And don't ask, because I'm not giving you any details, tonight." She got up and walked over toward the picnic table, as Moose came back to the others. "Now, somebody tell me, I've been hearing about these incredible kebabs. Please tell me there's enough that I can join in on this feast."

Noah grinned and pointed at a chair. "There's plenty," he said. "With Neil around, I've learned to make sure there's lots of food available."

SIXTEEN

TRUE TO HER word, Allison gave Noah and his team two days to let themselves prepare mentally for going out on their first mission. Ironically, they spent most of that time together, talking and gradually forming themselves into a unit.

It began the same evening as Allison's announcement. After the fight, Moose was making an obvious effort to be friendly, but Noah could tell that it wasn't easy for him, and so could the others.

"My God, Moose," Neil said, "you don't have to kiss Noah's ass just because he kicked yours. He just wanted you to knock off the bullshit, not become his new BFF."

Sarah giggled at Neil's comment, but looked at Moose. "He's right, Moose, lighten up a bit. If you stop being a surly asshole, no one will believe you're you."

Moose shrugged. "What, all I'm doing is being part of the team," he said. "And I'm going to tell you something else, just so you know, but anybody who can kick my butt the way he just did, that's somebody I want as a friend. Plain and simple."

"As long as we can put whatever differences we had behind us," Noah said, "then we're good. I think that the best thing that could happen here is for the four of us to become as close as we can. Granted, I'm not the greatest in the friendship department, myself, but I can tell you that I'm one of the most loyal friends you can ever have. The one thing you can be certain of is that I'll never deliberately let you down."

The others looked at him for a moment, but Allison smiled. "I was a little surprised," she said, "to see you two duking it out when I got here, but whatever method you had in your madness, Noah, it seems to be working. I gotta commend you for pulling it off, even while I want to reprimand you for risking damage to two of my assets."

"There wasn't much risk," Noah said. "I wasn't going to let Moose hurt me, and I wasn't about to do him any serious harm. It didn't take me long to figure out that we belong to E & E, which means you'd take a dim view of us breaking each other's bones in a recreational setting. This was more of a psychological exercise, getting the power struggle between me and Moose out of the way so that we can focus on our missions as they come."

"Wait a minute, hold up," Moose said. "I just want to go on record that there's nothing psychological about the swelling around my eye. Can I get a witness?"

"Hear, hear," Neil said. "That looked pretty damn physical to me!"

Allison tipped back her beer bottle and took a long pull. "Whatever it was, it seems to have solved a major problem, so you get a pat on the back, this time." Another drink finished off the bottle, and she tossed it into the trashcan behind her, then got to her feet. "Okay, children, it's getting late and I got a busy day tomorrow. I'm going home, but I'm going to put the word out tomorrow morning that you've all got the next two days off. I strongly suggest you use it to make sure that any other differences between you are worked out as effectively as this one has been. As I said earlier, I decided on your first mission, and you're going to need each other." She turned without another word, and walked off toward her car. The rest of them waved and called their goodbyes, but all they got in response was a wave of her fingers over her shoulder. Her car started a moment later, and she was gone.

It was Sarah who broke the silence. "Okay, all BS aside, would you really have let Moose go if he had kicked your butt?"

Noah nodded solemnly. "You all heard me, that was the deal I offered." He looked at Moose. "Don't misunderstand me—it wasn't that I wanted to get rid of you, because I didn't. One thing I've already figured out about the Dragon Lady is that she's pretty sharp, so if she decided you're the best man for my team, then I've got to figure she's right. This whole thing tonight wasn't about trying to get you off my team, it was about trying to make you want to be a part of it."

Moose stared at him for a good thirty seconds before he said a word. "Couple of things happened here tonight," he said. "First off, Neil kind of got to me when he said he found proof that you told the same story all the way through, about what happened back in Iraq. From the articles that I read, it sounded like you only came up with that story after you were court-martialed, so that made me feel a little better about you." He took a drink out of his bottle of beer. "Then, you made me your offer. If you had made that offer before I heard what Neil had to say, I probably would've tried even harder to whip your ass, but after that, I wouldn't have quit the team even if I had won the fight. Just the fact that you gave me that chance, that said a whole lot about you. I'm with you, now."

Neil waved a hand in the air. "Hey, just to make sure nobody has the wrong idea, I have been on your side the whole time, Noah. You don't need to beat the snot out of me, we good on that?"

All three of the others laughed. "We're good," Noah said. "No problem."

"If we're going to have a little confession time, here," Sarah said, "I should probably get in on it, too. I've been a little less than enthusiastic about having you for a team leader, Noah, because like everyone else, I heard about your—emotional issues?" She shrugged her shoulders. "I don't think it was the same kind of thing, but I grew up with a father who had absolutely no idea how to show emotion. It was like being raised by a machine, and that can really mess with a girl's self-esteem. I had some issues, especially back in my early teens, but I loved the old sonofabitch. When I heard about your problems, I was scared to death that it was going to be like going back home, again."

Noah smiled. "I think there's a big difference between not feeling any emotion, and just not being able to show it. You see me smiling, joking, laughing—sometimes you see me acting sad—what you all need to understand, if this is going to work and we're going to become a real team, is that all of that is an act. There is no emotion behind it, there's no feeling of any kind." He let the smile slide away. "I don't think like one of you. Here's how my thought processes go on our team. I'm looking at three people sitting here with me, and I know that each of you brings talents and abilities to the team that will make it far more likely that we can succeed in whatever mission we're sent out on. That makes each and every one of you extremely important to me, and in a normal setting that would mean that I considered you each to be my close friends. For me, what that means is that keeping you safe is the most important thing on my mind, second only to completing the mission. When it comes to the mission, we are soldiers, just like the ones I served with in Iraq, just like the ones Moose served with in the Navy, and the sad fact is that soldiers are sometimes expendable. I will always, and I mean always, do everything I can think of to keep each and every one of you safe and healthy, so that we all come home from the missions. That I can promise you."

The three of them sat there at the table and looked at him for a moment, and then Moose raised his bottle into the air. "To the team," he said. "Let's make it the best one there is."

Sarah clinked his bottle with her own. "To the team," she said.

Neil let out a long sigh, then sat forward and clinked as well. "To the team."

Noah raised his own bottle and they all toasted again. "To the team," he said. "We've all got to have each other's backs, every minute when we're out there. Are we all on the same page?"

All three agreed that they were, and they drank to their new union. When the bottles were back on the table, Sarah looked at Noah.

"So, I'm just curious, but if you don't have emotions, have you ever had a girlfriend?"

Noah nodded. "Yes, a couple. I dated some in my teens, and I had a couple of girlfriends even since I joined the Army. I'm good enough that my human act keeps them happy for a while, but I don't ever let anyone get too close. Wouldn't be fair to them."

Neil winked at Noah. "Sounds like Sarah might want to apply for the job," he said, and a moment later Sarah pushed him out of his chair on to the ground.

"No, I don't! God, Neil, why do you have to be such an ass?"

Neil laughed as he got back up to his chair. "Excuse me, but have you seen me? I'm a stretched-out beanpole with zits! Being a smart ass, and you can take that any way you want, is all I've got going for me."

They sat and talked for another hour, and by that time, each of them had consumed enough alcohol that Noah wasn't happy about them driving. With Moose backing him up, he managed to convince them all to simply go upstairs in his house and choose a guestroom for the night.

He went to his own room, took a quick shower and dried himself off, then walked naked out of his bathroom. He stopped just past the doorway, when he realized that Sarah was sitting at the foot of his bed.

"Sarah? Did you need something?"

She didn't answer, but simply stood up and looked at him.

She hooked her thumbs into the waistband of her shirt and pulled it off over her head, dropping it onto the floor. The rest of her clothes quickly followed, and she walked over and put her arms up and around his neck. She pulled gently, and he leaned his head down so that their lips met.

When the kiss ended, Noah pulled back and looked into her eyes. "Are you sure you want to do this?"

Sarah looked into his eyes for a moment, then said, "I do. You know we're not allowed to have any real relationships, right? I figure we need to find ways to help each other out. Sometimes, I just need a little intimacy, just to be close to someone, but the last thing in the world I want right now is to have any real romantic feelings involved. That makes you the safest game in town. As long as you don't mind being used that way, we can have a little fun, now and then."

Noah put on a friendly grin. "Sounds like you thought that out logically," he said. "My only concern might be that the other guys would get jealous. Should we keep this quiet, just between us?"

She shook her head, then kissed him again. "Moose is into big women, and he's just not my type, anyway. I prefer a man with a brain, but Neil is just a kid. You might not consider yourself human, but at least you are intelligent, and a man."

Noah lowered his eyebrows, squinting at her. "According to the dossiers they gave me on each of you, you're only two years older than Neil. There's a bigger age difference between us than that."

Sarah giggled. "I wasn't referring to his age, I'm talking about his whole attitude, the way he acts. He reminds me of a twelve-year-old boy who lived next door to us a couple years ago. He's just too much of a kid for me, but the whole point of that was that I don't think we need to keep any secrets."

Noah shrugged, and kissed her once more, then took her by

the hand and led her to the bed. He tossed back the covers and pushed her gently onto the mattress, then slid in beside her.

Like always, Noah woke at five thirty, this time to find himself tangled around the blonde girl in his bed. He managed to extricate himself without waking her, then quietly got out clean clothes and went to take another shower. When he came out of the bathroom fifteen minutes later, Sarah was still sleeping, so he woke her gently.

"Hey, it's morning," he said when her eyes were opened and focused on him. "I'm going down to the kitchen to make breakfast, but I wanted to wake you up before I start yelling up the stairs at the guys."

She yawned, stretched and then smiled at him. "Sounds good," she said. "Can I use your shower?"

Noah pointed toward the bathroom. "Right in there, help yourself. I'm gonna go make some coffee."

He went down the hall to the kitchen, and started a pot of coffee, then went to the base of the stairs. "Hey, in case you haven't noticed, it's morning time," he shouted. "Breakfast will be ready in thirty minutes. Anybody who isn't here then doesn't get to eat!"

He went back to the kitchen, opened his refrigerator and took out a dozen eggs and a package of sausage links, and set about making breakfast for his guests.

Neil and Moose found their way to the kitchen ten minutes later, and Sarah joined them ten minutes after that. Neil's eyebrows shot up when he saw Sarah, because she was wearing one of Noah's polo shirts, and possibly nothing else.

"But you're not the least bit interested in being Noah's girlfriend, right? I mean, that's why I got tossed on the ground last night, isn't it?"

Sarah smiled sweetly at him, then pointed at the tile floor under the stool he was sitting on. "That would hurt worse than the ground did," she said. "We all know we can't ever have a real relationship, so don't give me any shit about this."

Neil glanced down at the floor, then smiled at Sarah. "Point taken," he said, then turned back to the cup of coffee sitting in front of him.

Noah's kitchen featured a bar that was big enough for several people, and had six stools. Since it was close to the coffee maker, everyone had gravitated to it. Noah set a cup of coffee in front of the stool Sarah had taken, then poured a second cup for himself as he cooked. His range had a large griddle right in the center, which made frying a dozen eggs at once pretty easy, while the sausage was sizzling in a skillet.

"Anything I can do to help?" Sarah asked.

Noah looked up at her and grinned. "Plates are up in that cabinet," he said, pointing, "if you wouldn't mind getting them down. This is almost ready." The toaster popped as he was speaking, and he quickly buttered four more slices of bread.

Sarah got the plates and set one in front of each of their stools, then got lucky and opened the silverware drawer on the first try. She got out forks and knives for each of them, and set them near the plates. "Nice kitchen," she said.

"Yeah, all this was here when I moved in," Noah said. "Looked like it was all brand new, too."

She nodded. "Yeah, they gave me an apartment in Kirtland, and it was the same way, looked like it was all set up just for me. Even the colors and furniture were the kind I like."

"Me, too," Moose said. "I got a house in Kirtland, and it's all set up the way I'd want it, as if I had chosen it myself. They do seem to know a lot about us, don't they?"

"It's called quantitative psychology," Neil said. "It allows them to create mathematical models of human attitudes and psychology, even down to preferences and emotional behaviors." He looked at Noah. "I bet you're driving them crazy. Somehow, I can't see them being able to predict you all that well."

Noah shrugged. "I'm not real picky about most things," he said, "but they did manage to get me the kind of clothes I like to wear, and they knew what kind of razors and shampoo and such I like. As for the house, I think it's probably beautiful, but I can't really say that it appeals to me aesthetically. As long as it's functional, I'm content."

"Content?" Neil asked. "Wouldn't that be an emotional response?"

Noah shook his head. "No. Contentedness comes from an awareness of security. As long as you're not in danger, and there's no immediate situation that threatens your security or causes you discomfort, then you should be content. And speaking of content, breakfast is ready."

Sarah got up and handed him each of their plates, so that he could load them down with eggs and sausage and toast, and then she passed them back. She gave Moose his plate first, then Neil, then took her own and sat down. Noah joined them at the bar a few seconds later.

"Man," Moose said around a mouthful of egg and sausage, "this is really good. Thanks."

"Yeah, thanks," Neil said, the same way.

"Hey, no problem," Noah said. "Gotta keep my team healthy and fed."

"This is a good start," Sarah said. "These really are good."

They finished breakfast, and Noah made a second pot of coffee so that they could sit and talk for a bit.

"So," he said. "The dragon lady says we're looking at a mission in the not-too-distant future. Does anybody know anything about how they train for a specific mission, here?"

Moose nodded. "I got some friends who have been out already," he said. "Somewhere on this huge compound, they got a place they call Hollywood. They set up whole neighborhoods or mockups of specific buildings, so that we can literally practice whatever plan you come up with."

"I guess that's what she meant when she mentioned simulations," Noah said.

"Yeah, that would be it. They actually run through missions with people playing the parts of the bad guys, using special paintball guns that look and feel real, but shoot those little pellets that go splat."

"I heard a rumor a couple of days ago," Sarah said, "that they were building a set, you know, like a movie set. Something about Mexico, but that's all I've heard."

Noah pursed his lips in thought. "If it's Mexico, then we're probably talking about something to do with a drug cartel."

Neil was shaking his head. "Bet not," he said. "Maybe you guys don't pay enough attention to the news, but Mexico has been known for a while now as the conduit of choice for terror organizations to get their people and materials into the US. They use the same coyotes that the Mexican nationals use to sneak into the country, so I guess those guys don't care whose money they take. My guess is they got a line on somebody who's facilitating, and want you to take him out."

"Either way," Noah said with a shrug, "it's not a mission I'd have a problem with. Once we get our briefing, I'll probably want to sit down and get some input from you guys before I decide on the plan."

Neil made a face. "Oh, and here, I thought you were going to be the decisive leader, the dictator who tells us what to do and expects us to do or die. You're actually going to ask our opinions? That could be a little bit on the frightening side, just so you know."

Noah looked at him, his face blank. "One of the things I learned in the Army is that everyone sees things from a different perspective. If I get your opinions on this mission, it may give me another way of looking at something that could make the mission more successful, or at least help save our lives in the process. Trust me, I'm quite capable of making the decisions, and when I give an order I will expect it to be followed completely and without hesitation. Is that understood?"

Neil's eyes were wide. "Perfectly," he said. "You don't even need to tell me what the penalty is for hesitation."

Moose laughed. "One of the things about our fearless leader that I like is the fact that if one of us goes rogue, or puts the rest in danger, he isn't going to hesitate to take that one out." He looked pointedly at Sarah. "Even if he's sleeping with her."

Sarah glared at him. "Jealous much? For the record, where I sleep, or who with, is none of your business. And trust me, that part of him that you like is the very reason I'm dressed this way this morning. Great sex and no entanglements."

Moose laughed again, but this time he softened it with a genuine smile. "I wasn't being jealous, Sarah," he said. "You're sweet, but you're not my type. I was actually being a bit protective, because I've come to look at you like a little sister. I just didn't want to see you getting hurt, or getting so complacent about being close to the boss that you might make a mistake. Mistakes get people killed, and I don't want see you in a body bag."

Noah nodded. "Moose, you've made a good point. You're right, and if I ever feel that one of you is a danger to the team or to the mission, I wouldn't hesitate. That's just the way I am, and you all need to understand that. It would never be anything personal."

"And you'd never feel even a moment's regret, would you?" Neil asked.

"No, I wouldn't. Once again, that's just the way I'm built. It's not something I chose, and it's nothing I can change. On the other hand, it's the same ability that will allow me to act without hesitation to protect one of you. I won't have to stop and think about whether I should shoot the bastard who's pointing a gun at you, because it will be obvious to me. I'll shoot."

"Well, that's at least a little comforting," Sarah said.

SEVENTEEN

THE TEAM SPENT the rest of the day at Noah's place, and he took them on a tour, showing them the barn and other buildings. Sarah loved the mechanical shop, where Noah had already removed the non-running engine from the old truck and was preparing to rebuild it.

"Not bad," she said, looking over the tools that were there. "Been a while since I've seen a private shop that was so well equipped. You know what you're doing?"

Noah shrugged. "I lived on a farm for a while as a teenager, and got to help overhaul cars, trucks, tractors, you name it. I'm pretty good, but I'm smart enough to keep a Chilton manual around."

Sarah gave him a scoffing look. "Chilton manuals are old school," she said. "Nowadays, if there's something you don't know how to do, just Google it. I guarantee you there's a YouTube video to show you how it's done. I've seen one with a seven-year-old kid teaching people to do basic mechanical repairs. Just amazing."

"A mechanical prodigy?" Neil asked. "Somehow, I suspect you were probably one of those, yourself."

"Maybe," Sarah said. "I rebuilt an old Honda ninety cc trail bike when I was nine. Found it in my dad's junk pile and asked him if I could have it. He said I could, if I could get it running, so I went to Google. Two months later, I was riding it around the yard, and that's when he started teaching me about cars and such.

He said I had a knack for it, but I didn't realize back then what was going on."

"What do you mean?" Noah asked.

"Well, every once in a while, Dad would fix a car for someone, but most of the time all we did was take them apart. Everything went into these semi trailers, and I really got a kick out of taking a whole car and reducing it down to nothing. I was fourteen by the time I figured out that we were running a chop shop. The cars were stolen, and we were shipping all the parts to really big parts yards in different cities. I learned later that most of those parts were sold even before we got them into the trailers."

Noah nodded. "That's how you ended up in trouble, right?"

Sarah laughed, but it was a bitter laugh. "Some of the guys who used to bring us the boosted cars decided to retire, or maybe they just got too smart to keep doing it as cars got more and more sophisticated. When I was sixteen, my dad started taking me out on roundups, which is what he called it when we went out and stole cars. I got away with it for years, but last year I got caught, chased into a trap by a cop, so there was no way to escape. They got my dad that night too, and we were both looking at federal sentences, since we were selling parts across state lines. We would've gotten thirty years or more, which would've been a life sentence for my dad, but then this lawyer came to talk to me and said if I would be willing to join E & E, and let my dad and everyone else I knew think I killed myself in my cell, then I'd get a whole new life and my dad would get a more lenient sentence, only five years, with the chance to learn how to run a real shop when he got out." She shrugged. "I love my dad, but I was tired of living under his thumb, and I sure didn't want to be in prison for the next thirty years. I took it."

"That's understandable," Noah said. "Well, anytime you get an itch to get your hands greasy again, come on out. Once I get really settled in here, in the organization, I mean, I'm probably going to buy an old car now and then, one to fix up like a hobby. You'll always be welcome."

She smiled at him, and he realized it was the first time she had let him see her real smile. "I'd like that," she said. "Maybe this weekend, if we're off?"

Noah nodded. "Sounds perfect," he said, and then he led them all toward the lake. They ended up passing the mobile home, so he showed it to them as well. It was an older single wide, but it was in incredibly good condition. The furniture was not new, but it was all in perfect shape, and even the kitchen appliances looked like they belonged in a showroom.

"Holy crap," Neil said. "Who lives here?"

"Nobody. It's just an extra place. I thought about renting it out, but I'm not sure I'd want anybody that close to me."

Neil turned to look at him. "What if it was one of us? Dude, I grew up in a trailer just like this, till I was twelve. That's when my mom took off, and I ended up in foster homes. I'd rent this from you, if you'd be willing."

Noah looked at the kid for a minute, then grinned. "We can do that," he said. "We'll work out the details later, but you can move in whenever you want. Just tell me how much rent you think it's worth, and that'll be fine with me."

Neil seemed ecstatic, and spent a couple of minutes exploring the trailer. Noah gave him a key as they all went on down to the boathouse, and the kid left shortly thereafter to start moving. Noah took out his phone and called Allison, just to make sure this deal was okay with her, and she gave her blessing.

Noah, Sarah and Moose took the boat out for a couple of hours, then went back to the house and spent the rest of the day just hanging out, and talking. Sarah went into the kitchen and dug through Noah's freezer and pantry, then made a pizza for them for lunch. It was surprisingly good, and Noah said so.

"I had a boyfriend who ran a pizzeria," she said, "and he taught me. I'm really not much of a cook, but I can make pretty good pizza, and a few other Italian meals. My lasagna? To *die* for! Treat me nice, and I'll make it sometime."

"I love lasagna," Moose said. "Treat her real nice, boss."

They ate at the table, but then wandered into the living room and watched a movie. Noah wasn't terribly surprised when Sarah sat down beside him on the sofa, or when she moved closer and pulled his arm around her shoulders. He smiled, and she returned it, but he could see in her eyes that she was fully aware that the smile was strictly for her benefit.

"You don't have to do that, you know," she said. "I would imagine that it's been hard, all these years, not to be able to just be yourself. You don't have to pretend with us. We know you don't really feel anything. You don't have to fake it."

Moose nodded his head. "She's got a good point," he said. "With us, it's okay to just be—well, whoever you really are. We know the score, so if you don't laugh, or you don't smile, we're not gonna get upset."

Noah looked from one to the other, then nodded his head. "Thank you," he said. "I haven't had anyone who really knew about me since I was a kid, or at least no one who would just accept it. I think it would be nice to be able to let my guard down, here at home anyway."

Sarah smiled, genuinely this time, and turned to watch the movie. That movie led to another one, and then to a third. Like Noah, Sarah and Moose were enjoying the opportunity to just relax.

It was almost six in the evening by the time they were sick of watching movies, and Moose was making noises about being hungry again. Noah offered to cook dinner, but Moose suggested they go out, instead. There was a restaurant that he knew of that was only a few miles away on Temple Lake Road, actually a little ways off the compound, but they weren't restricted.

"Come on," Moose said, "it's my treat. Maybe I'm beginning to realize you're not that bad a guy, and maybe I'm beginning to think I shouldn't have said that about us never being friends. Let me buy dinner, I promise you're gonna love this place."

Noah got to his feet, and pulled Sarah up behind him. "It isn't that often somebody offers to buy me dinner," he said. "I'm not about to turn that down."

They followed Moose out to his car, a surprisingly sedate-looking Chevrolet sedan. Noah looked at him. "I would have figured you for the sports car type."

Moose shook his head. "Not really, not me," he said. "That would've been my kid brother, but he wrapped himself around a tree a couple years ago. He's alive, but he's in a wheelchair, now. That sort of put an end to any hot rodding ideas, for both of us."

Noah felt his eyebrows shoot up. "You have a brother? I thought we weren't supposed to have any living relatives."

Moose grinned. "My brother is convinced that I'm dead, and that he actually went to my funeral. I was killed in a fiery car crash, so it was a closed coffin. They didn't have to go to a lot of trouble to come up with a body, in my case. I'm not sure, but I think the casket was empty."

They got into the car, and Moose drove back up the county road to the two-lane blacktop, and then turned right. Because of the curves, the trip took almost fifteen minutes, even though it was only about five miles to the restaurant. They pulled up in front of a rustic-looking building that had a big sign over its front porch that read, "The Sagebrush Saloon."

They got out, and Noah opened the back door for Sarah. She smiled as she looked up at the sign. "An honest-to-goodness saloon?"

"Yeah, don't get excited," Moose said. "They've got a bar, and they serve drinks, but it's the food that makes this place famous and popular. You'll see."

Moose was right, as Noah concluded an hour later. The porterhouse he had eaten was probably the best he had ever tasted, and even the vegetables on the side—mashed potatoes, grilled onions, carrots and cauliflower, and corn on the cob—were incredibly good.

"Okay, we can officially add this to the list of my favorite places to eat," he said, and Sarah nodded her head vigorously in agreement.

"I told you you'd love it," Moose said. "I found it a couple months ago, and I've been here enough that most of the waitresses know me by name."

Sarah dimpled at him. "Really? And you haven't gotten a date with one of them yet? I see a couple of them that looked to me like they would strike your fancy."

Moose grinned back. "The platinum blonde," he said. "She does light my fire. I asked her out a few nights ago, and she agreed, so I'm taking her to a movie on Friday."

Sarah looked across the restaurant at the girl he was talking about, and nodded her head. The girl's hair was almost pure white, and while she was only about five-and-a-half feet tall, she was a round little dumpling. Sarah guessed that she probably tipped the scales at close to two hundred pounds, and wondered for the hundredth time what a guy as good-looking as Moose saw in a girl that big.

Not her business, though, she reminded herself. She smiled at him, and said, "Good for you. I hope it goes well."

Moose shrugged. "Well, it's like you said about us not having any real relationships," he said. "I probably wouldn't even have asked her out, but I happen to know that she's aware of what we do. Her dad works in admin, with the boss lady, and she recognized me one of the first couple times I was in here. She asked me if I was part of the 'Ed and Eddie' group in Kirtland, and when I did a double take, she grinned and told me about her dad. She said he worked in the procurement office, making sure we have all the special equipment we need. When I looked at her funny after that, she glanced around to make sure no one was looking, then made a gun of her fingers and used her thumb to show it firing. I'm pretty sure she knows what we do."

Noah looked at the girl. "And does it strike anyone else as odd that she'd be working out here, if she knows? You'd think they'd want to keep her in house. I mean, how high a security clearance do you have to have just to know about us?"

Moose looked at him, his face uncertain. "You think maybe there's something fishy about this?"

Sarah barked a laugh. "Oh my gosh," she said. "If you weren't so smitten with this girl, you'd have been asking yourself that question before now. Come on, Moose, think."

Noah took out his phone and got to his feet. "Hang on just a minute, I'm going to go outside and check this out. Just wait here for me."

He turned without another word and walked toward the door, then slipped through it and outside. He found a spot away from the building, where he was fairly sure he could be alone, then dialed Allison's number.

"It is seven thirty in the evening," he heard her say as she answered. "If no one is dying, then you'd better have a very good reason for calling me."

"It's good enough to make me risk it," Noah said. "I'm out at The Sagebrush Saloon with Moose, and it turns out there's one of the waitresses out here that he likes. Thing that bothers me is that she seems to know an awful lot about our organization, and claims that her father works for you. Before I let him get mixed up with her, I want to be sure it's neither a problem nor a trap."

Allison sighed. "Let me guess," she said, "a chunky platinum blonde?"

"Yep, that's the one. Is there anything fishy about this?"

"There's not anything fishy about it," Allison said, "but I can tell you that you just scored a brownie point for checking it out. That's Elaine Jefferson, and yes, her father works in my office. And the reason she knows so much about us is because she's actually one of our backup intelligence agents. She doesn't have the acting ability that would let her be on a permanent team, but she's as good with a computer as just about anyone we've got. She's okay. Anything else?"

"Nope. That covers it. Am I in trouble for bothering you?"

"Not this time," Allison said. "I'll never fault you for making sure your teammates stay out of trouble. On the other hand, you might want to warn him that she's got a bit of a reputation as a heartbreaker." The line went dead.

Noah went back inside and sat down again, then leaned over to speak softly. "The dragon lady says she's okay, and she's exactly what she seems to be, but she told me to warn you that you'll get your heart broken."

Moose looked across the restaurant at the girl in question, then turned to look at Noah. "Won't be the last time, and sure isn't the first." He turned to look back at her again, and Noah saw the girl toss a smile at Moose.

EIGHTEEN

THEIR BRIEFING TOOK place in Allison's meeting room. A projection screen had been pulled down at one end of the room, and a projector had descended out of the ceiling. A photograph of a tall, balding Hispanic man was being displayed.

"The man you see on the screen is Pablo Ortiz," Allison said. "Ortiz has been a major player in moving a lot of contraband into the United States for the last several years, but it wasn't until he got involved in some recent activities that the NSA decided he needed to be removed from the equation. They sent me the file, and I have to agree with them. Ortiz is involved in transporting Islamic terrorist cells and operatives across the border near Ciudad Juárez, Mexico. He uses bribery, extortion, anything at all to find ways to get these people past the border. Some of them come across the river, some are driven straight across the bridge, and some of them have actually come into the country inside tanker trucks full of milk or vegetable oil. Imagine trying to stay afloat for several hours inside a closed tanker trailer, and you'll see just how serious these people are about getting into our country."

She pressed a button on the remote in her hand, and a different image appeared. This was another man, also Hispanic, but in much better physical condition.

"This is Henrique Valdes. Henrique is probably Mexico's answer to the Terminator. As a soldier, he was one of the most formidable the Mexican army ever fielded, and upon his discharge, he went to work for their intelligence services. Unfortunately, being a good guy in Mexico doesn't pay as well as being a bad guy, so Ortiz was able to recruit him without a lot of trouble. Make no mistake, this is one of the most dangerous men you will ever encounter, anywhere. While Ortiz is the target, Henrique is going to be the biggest obstacle between you and him. You can take him out, if you get the chance, but he is not officially on the sanction."

"Is there a reason to leave Valdes alive?" Noah asked.

Allison smiled. "It's possible that there is," she said. "Henrique is actually a fairly reliable source of information for the DEA in that area. There are those who believe that he may succeed Ortiz, and could possibly become an even greater source of intelligence. If you can manage to take out Ortiz without killing Henrique, some agencies would see that as a blessing from heaven."

She pressed another button, and a picture of a tavern appeared. "This is one of the places that Ortiz is known to frequent. That's probably because it's run by his nephew, so it makes it easy for him to have some kind of control over the place. Observers have seen that Eduardo defers to his uncle on just about anything, so it's quite possible that Ortiz is holding something over his head. This tavern is in an area that is not normally frequented by Americans, so you're going to look quite out of place there. I suspect you'll find a way to use that to your advantage."

"Shouldn't be hard," Noah said. "I'm thinking a cover as a drug buyer? Make some deals while I'm there, buy up as much as I can?"

"That would definitely fit in, but be sure you read the whole file before you decide on a plan. Both of these men are very dangerous, and while Ortiz was once a major drug supplier, today his focus is on terrorism. He's been running illegal aliens into the country for years as a sideline, but now it's become more profitable than his drug businesses, because the illegals he's smuggling in now pay upwards of a hundred thousand each, to get themselves and their baggage into our country undetected."

Noah sat forward. "What about the baggage? Are we talking weapons, bombs, what?"

"We're talking whatever kind of baggage they want to bring with them," Allison replied. "On the other hand, Ortiz has been known to deal in weapons, lately. There are even rumors that he has connections for weapons with nuclear and biological potential, or at least the necessary components to produce them."

Noah whistled. "Definitely not a good guy. Are there any instructions on how you want him taken out?"

Allison shook her head. "Noah, only the team leader can decide on the mission plan. I set this organization up that way on purpose, because it's just too easy for generals to sit back in the war room and throw away their soldiers like yesterday's newspaper. We don't do that, here. Instead, you will look the entire situation over, and devise your own plan for completing the mission. I want that plan submitted to me for approval, but it's very rare that I ever disapprove one."

Moose spoke up. "You mentioned simulations," he said. "Are we going to get the chance to run through some?"

Allison pushed another button, and another tavern appeared on the screen. This one didn't look quite as rough as the other, but its dimensions were approximately the same. "We've built a mockup of that part of Ciudad Juárez, an area of about six square blocks. It will let you get a feel for where buildings are, alleys, streets, etc. That way, you can get some idea of where cover might be available, hiding places and things like that." She hit the button again, and suddenly they were looking at the interior of the tavern. "This is the interior of our mockup," she went on. "It's been constructed from detailed photographs of the inside of the original, and everything's placed accordingly. You can practice moving around in this one, and then you'll be able to move with confidence."

Noah cocked his head to one side. "If we're going to run simulations, I gather we're going to be using paintballs?" Allison smiled, and he went on. "Then, what about opposition? Do we have people playing the parts?"

"We do, yes. A fair number of our people here do just that, play the parts of the bad guys in simulation scenarios. And I should warn you, some of them are wicked with those paintball guns. Those things may break on impact, but they can still sting, trust me."

"I've run a paintball course, I know. When can we start practicing?"

"Tomorrow morning. You'll meet your referee at the Alley Town restaurant, and he'll take you out to show you this setup. He'll also supply you with your weapons and equipment, including vehicles and electronics. With the exception of the weapons, everything he'll give you will be just like what you would use out in the field, including computers, phones, all of it. Anything you ask for to use in the mission, he will give you. Those are his standing orders, and he knows it."

"And just who is this referee? Is it someone we've met already?"

Allison smiled, and Noah waited. "You met him your first day," she said. "His name is Jefferson."

She went over the mission with them several times, and finally dismissed them just before lunchtime. She had told them that they could have the rest of the day off, so they all headed out to the farm. Neil was all moved into the trailer by then, so for him, it was going home, just as it was for Noah. Sarah and Moose followed along in their own cars.

It was moving into autumn, but the weather was still decent. Noah thought it was time to fire up the grill, again—he hadn't used it since the night he and Moose had settled their differences—so he went to his refrigerator and got out a package of steaks he had planned on using that weekend. If they were to begin simulations the following day, he wasn't sure the weekend was going to be free. The steaks were thawed, so he set them to marinate while he got the grill started and warming up.

"What can I do to help?" Sarah asked, and Noah looked up at her.

"I was just going to go for steak and salad. There's a bag of salad mix ready to go in the refrigerator, if you want to just rip it open and dump it in a bowl. I got several types of salad dressing, you might get those out, too. Just set it on the table in the dining room; we'll eat inside tonight."

She gave him a bright smile, and went to get the salad ready. He had the grill ready to sear the steaks quickly, and since all of them preferred their steaks rare, it wasn't going to take them long to cook.

Neil appeared beside him, and handed him a bottle of beer. "I think you'd better enjoy this tonight," he said. "I'm not sure you want to be drinking during our simulations."

Noah thanked him, then shrugged. "From what I see so far, at least part of this mission is going to involve hanging out in a bar. If that's where I've got to meet the target, I'll have to spend some time there, let myself become a familiar face. We may get to hang out in the land of tequila for a while, and I'm gonna probably be drinking a lot while I'm there." He looked up at Neil, and winked. "Good thing I can handle my liquor, isn't it?"

Neil rolled his eyes. "Why is it that almost everything you say puts me in mind of somebody's famous last words? You know, I signed up for this because I wanted to avoid prison time. That doesn't mean I wanted to avoid it badly enough to die. Please, please don't get me killed."

"What are you worried about?" Moose asked, coming up behind them. "You get to sit back out of sight, playing games on the computer. Noah's the one who's gonna be out there taking the risks, and if he has to have a backup, that'll be on me. Even Sarah won't be in the line of fire, unless it's during a really frantic getaway."

"I don't want any of you in the line of fire," Noah said, "not if there's any way to avoid it. That includes you, Moose. I've proven to be pretty good, over the years, at taking care of myself, so hopefully you won't have to cover my back too often." He looked at the big man and smiled. "That doesn't mean I'm not glad you're available if needed, though."

Moose smiled back, then suddenly scowled. "Didn't we tell ya you don't have to fake the smiles with us?"

The smile vanished from Noah's face instantly. "Sorry, dude, it's just old habit. I've been pretending to be human so long that I can't remember to let it go."

"I think it's cute," Sarah said, returning from inside. "Let him smile if he wants to."

"And this from the girl who, just a week ago, couldn't stand the thought of being close to a man without emotions," Neil said. He eyeballed Noah and tried to look innocent. "Oh, I wonder, do you think that has anything to do with the fact that she's playing 'ride the cowboy' in your bedroom most nights lately?"

Noah turned and looked into Neil's eyes. "Neil, that was uncalled for," he said, but Sarah interrupted him.

"Oh, forget it, Noah," she said. "I sleep with you because it's fun exercise, and it's not like I have to worry about my reputation. Let the kid make his wisecracks, he's just jealous."

Neil's eyes went wide, as Noah shrugged his shoulders and turned back to the grill. "Jealous? Me? I'm not jealous," Neil said. He stood there for a moment, and then leered at Sarah. "Well, not all that jealous. As I recall, you made it clear I didn't have a shot with you back when we first met."

She nodded at him with a grin. "Yep, I did, and this is why. I like you, Neil, but you're still too immature and childish for me. Sorry."

Neil opened his mouth, but nothing came out. He tried it once more, got the same result, then turned and went back into the house.

A cell phone rang, and Noah glanced over his shoulder to see Moose answering. From the smile that lit up his face, it was easy to tell that it was a call from Elaine. It seemed their date had gone quite well, and she and Moose had become something of an item. Moose walked a short distance away to stand under a tree where he could talk privately. It didn't help a lot, because Noah and Sarah could still hear him calling Elaine his 'little love muffin.'

"Can I tell you something, and not make you mad?" Sarah asked Noah.

"Pretty sure you can, since I can't get mad. What would it be?"

"Sometimes, I wish you were more like Moose. He gets so excited whenever she calls, or whenever he's going to go see her. I wish I could make you get excited like that." She looked around at him. "Don't get the wrong idea, I'm not falling in love or anything. It'd just be nice to have somebody get excited about me."

Noah looked at her for a moment. "I get excited about you," he said. "Whenever you call and say you're coming over, I start to think about what I can do to make you enjoy yourself, while you're here. You know I get excited when you come into my bedroom—that's kind of impossible to miss. I don't have many friends, but the few guys I know here, Marco and Roger, and Charlie the bartender, I told all of them about you. I even showed them a picture of you on my phone."

Sarah looked into his eyes, and smiled softly. "But do you do that because it's what guys who have girlfriends do? Or just because you want to?"

He looked back into her eyes for a moment, with his head cocked slightly to one side. "I do it because I want to. To be honest, I haven't thought about you as my girlfriend, I just enjoy your company and I felt like bragging about the beautiful girl I'm hanging out with. That's not emotional, that's just probably ego."

Sarah's smile got a little bigger, and she leaned close and kissed him gently on the lips. "Then I really, really like your ego," she said. "Later I'll show you just how much I like your ego."

The steaks were done shortly, and Noah stacked them on a tray and carried them inside. The guys were inside waiting, and they sat down at the table and dug in.

NINETEEN

SARAH RODE IN with Noah the next morning, while Neil followed. Noah had been surprised at Neil's car when he had first seen it, because most young guys didn't go for big cars, but Neil was driving a Hummer. Noah had thought they would die off quickly, when gas prices got high enough to actually put the Hummer company out of business, but there were still an amazing number of them on the road. Neil's was fire engine red, and Noah was pretty sure it was the only red one he'd ever seen.

They parked at the restaurant, and had just gotten inside when Moose pulled in. Allison hadn't given them a specific time to be there, so they had agreed to meet early for breakfast. The hostess showed them all to a table, and a waitress arrived a moment later to start pouring coffee.

Neil slumped in his chair. "Why is it," he asked, "that people in our line of work don't get to sleep in like normal human beings?"

"Because we're not normal human beings," Moose said. "If we were, we wouldn't be in our line of work, now would we?"

Neil opened one eye and focused it on Moose's face. "You have a disgustingly valid point, and I now officially hate your guts."

"Oh, good, does that mean I can kick your ass, now?" Moose looked at Noah. "He hates me, that means I can kick his ass, right?"

Noah shook his head. "Not until after we're done with him, and that might be a while."

Neil stuck his tongue out at Moose, and Sarah suddenly burst out laughing. "Oh, my God, will you please grow up?"

Neil turned his eyes to her. "And just where exactly would be the fun in that?" He sat up again and reached for his coffee, added several packets of sugar and creamer, then stirred it up and took a sip. "I think they have the best coffee on the compound right here," he said. "Remind me to find out what brand they use."

"I already asked," Noah said, "it's called Falco, and you have to buy it a hundred cases at a time. I thought about it, but even I don't drink enough coffee to justify that. I'd still be drinking it twenty years from now, and I'm not even sure I'll be alive that long."

Sarah shrugged. "Too bad, it's really good. Maybe we should all go in together and buy a case, split it between the four of us. With that make it a better deal?"

They debated the merits of making such a large purchase, but never came to a conclusion. The waitress took their orders, and the food was back surprisingly quickly. They dug in and ate, and were just sitting there, having another cup of the wonderful coffee, when Mr. Jefferson walked in and took a chair at their table.

"Hello, Noah," he said. "It seems that all those good reports I've been getting must be true. We'll be getting you ready for your first mission, now, and I must say I'm looking forward to watching you work." He turned his eyes toward Moose, who suddenly looked like he wanted to be somewhere else. "And you would be Moose Conway, am I right? My daughter has told me a lot about you, and I want to tell you how much I appreciate the fact that she says you've been a perfect gentleman."

Moose looked confused for a split second, and then his face cleared and he smiled. "No problem, Sir," he said. "She's a wonderful girl."

Jefferson smiled back. "Yes, she is, and I'm glad you see it that way." He turned back to Noah. "So, it looks like you've already finished your breakfast?"

"Yes, Sir," Noah said. "We're ready whenever you are."

"Good, good," Jefferson said. "Let me grab a cup of coffee to go, and we can get started."

Jefferson went to the hostess station to order his coffee, while Noah and the others went to pay their tabs at the register. They all met outside a few minutes later.

"I'm in the Chrysler," Jefferson said, pointing at a new sedan. "Just follow me, and have your ID ready when we get to the checkpoint." He walked over and got into the car, while the others got into their own. A moment later, they were in a convoy following Jefferson.

The trip to the area known as Hollywood took almost half an hour, weaving through back roads and passing through several different gates. Each of them looked like it had seen better days, but when Jefferson's car approached them, they opened as if by magic. The last one, however, had a guard shack and two armed guards in what appeared to be black uniforms. Jefferson stopped, and Noah could see him showing ID to the guard.

The guard waved Jefferson through, and Noah pulled up to where he stood. He showed his own ID, while Sarah passed hers across, and the guard inspected both of them carefully, then looked closely at their faces. After a moment, he handed them back and told them to go on through, but cautioned them to stay close to Mr. Jefferson.

Neil and Moose made it through the gate a moment later, and caught up to Noah. Jefferson had pulled over and waited for them, so when he saw all of their vehicles make it through the gate, he honked his horn once and proceeded forward. Noah, Neil and Moose all fell back in behind him.

Another ten minutes brought them into what looked like a small town, but a close look at the buildings showed that most of them were simply hollow shells. There were streets laid out, but they were graveled rather than paved, and sidewalks were indicated by wooden pallets laid end to end. It was obvious that this location was used for mockups of different places around the world, and Noah was surprised to see street signs and even working stoplights.

"Somebody puts a lot of work into setting these up," he said. "I mean, it's a great idea, because it gives you a sense of your battlefield even before you get to it."

"Yeah, but from my point of view," Sarah said, "it means I'm going to be practicing my routes on gravel, but the city streets will be asphalt. That could throw me off a bit, if we have to do any precision driving."

"If that becomes necessary, I'll make sure we get a few extra days in Mexico so that you can get the feel of the streets." He looked over at her. "I have confidence in you, so have it in yourself."

Sarah grinned at him. "I haven't had any problem with self-confidence since I was a teenager," she said. "Trust me, I can handle whatever road I have to drive."

Jefferson pulled over, and Noah parked behind him. They were just in front of the mockup of the bar, and when everyone had parked, they gathered in front of the building.

"Okay, boys and girls," Jefferson said. "We're going to go inside and just get the lay of the place. There are a few people already here, including the bartender and a few of his hookers and some customers. You can interact with anyone you want to, but remember that they're all going to stay in character. Today, and today only, you can ask them point-blank questions about the character they are playing. Each of them has studied up on their character, although some of them are playing composites, because customers come and go, and so do hookers. The bartender has studied Eduardo Hernandez to the point that he can tell you almost anything about the man, and later, you'll see people playing Henrique Valdes and Pablo Ortiz in here, as well. Those two know their characters inside out."

He led them inside, and they went to a table toward the back of the room. Noah looked around, and realized that great effort had gone into making the interior look genuine. There was chipped plaster on the walls and ceiling, along with signs in Spanish all over the place, and the shelves and coolers had been stocked the way they would be in the real tavern.

A number of people were inside, and Noah heard the word *"gringo"* a couple of times. The actors were all speaking in Spanish, and seemed to be laughing at the obvious Americans. That would be in character, of course, since tourists didn't frequent Eduardo's Tavern. Just the fact that Americans had walked in would be a strong indication that they were either interested in doing some sort of business that wasn't legal, or else they were very, very stupid.

Noah had taken Spanish in high school and could speak it fluently, but it struck him that he might want to keep that fact a secret, at least for the moment. He kept his eyes moving, watching everyone, and a moment later, the bartender came toward the table.

"Señores," he said. "Oh, and forgive me, señorita, how can I help you?" The man's accent was perfect, and he appeared to be genuinely of Latino origin.

Jefferson glanced around the table. "I know it's a little early, but beers all around?" Everyone nodded, so he ordered five bottles of beer. The bartender grinned and nodded, then hurried away and returned a moment later with five very small bottles of Modelo beer.

"Do we really have to drink these?" Neil asked. "I don't think my stomach can take it, this early in the day."

Jefferson shrugged. "All we're doing is staying in character," he said. "It's doubtful that Camelot will have you actually present in the bar during the real mission, but just in case something happened and you needed to be familiar with it, we brought you along. You don't have to drink the beer, but just let it sit on the table in front of you."

"Or pass it to me," Moose said. "Sometimes, I have beer for breakfast." He tipped up his own bottle and guzzled it, then switched it for Neil's. Neil gave him a halfhearted grin and rolled his eyes.

Jefferson looked at Noah. "The whole idea here is to let you become as familiar with the most likely scenario as you can be. Ortiz is a very difficult man to get close to, and about the only time he's ever in any position that might be considered vulnerable is when he decides to go to his nephew's bar to drink and party. From what we know of him, he seems to think it's the safest place he can go, and if you study the urban layout, you'll see that the place is incredibly defensible. The back door opens onto an alley that is gated on both ends, and the door itself is made of steel, almost three-quarters of an inch thick. The only windows in the place are on the front of the building, as you can see, and the way the room is laid out, there are several tables that are completely out of any line of sight—or line of fire—from anywhere outside the building. That means that any attack on him would have to come through the front door, or crash through the big window, and Ortiz generally has enough goons and firepower with him to handle anything up to a small platoon."

Noah nodded. "And I take it the Mexican government isn't interested in taking him down?"

Jefferson grinned at him. "Are you kidding? He's in tight enough with some of the more powerful cartels that most of the government would do whatever it took to protect him. Anybody in power in Mexico is terrified of this guy, and that includes the *federales*." Jefferson took a drink out of his beer. "That's one of the things that makes him so dangerous. It's a pretty safe bet that all the fingers will be pointing our way when he gets taken down."

Noah looked around the bar once more, then back at Jefferson. "Any suggestions on how I should do it?"

"No, and no one else will give you any, either. You are Camelot, the team leader. You're the one who has to come up with a plan, and then implement it. Your mission is to eliminate Pablo Ortiz; how you do it, and what collateral damage you decide to inflict, is entirely up to you."

"So, suppose I decide to just blow up the whole bar with Ortiz in it?"

"That is entirely your call," Jefferson said. "You have literally been granted a license to kill in the performance of your duties. What that means is that you can choose any method to eliminate your target, and if there is collateral damage, then so be it."

"That was a rhetorical question," Noah said. "I'm fairly sure I can manage to kill this guy without hurting any innocent people. Now, as for Henrique Valdes, the boss lady hinted that we might be better off if I leave him alive. Apparently, he has some value to another agency, and may become more valuable once Ortiz is gone?"

"That's definitely a possibility," Jefferson said. "It's still up to you whether or not you take him out. Let me clarify one thing for you that may make the decision easier. Valdes is not a good guy. Yes, he provides us with some very valuable information from time to time, but he does so only when it benefits him or someone he wants to have in his debt. He will probably still provide us with good information, even if he replaces Ortiz, but still only when he expects to benefit from it. Now, sometimes that benefit is monetary, when we pay for his information, but sometimes it's a matter of expanding his own power base, or someone else's. Even Ortiz has benefited from information Valdes has given us, but it's a safe bet that if Ortiz knew Valdes was talking to us, Valdes would be in the foundation of a very large building."

Noah's eyebrows went up. "In the foundation?"

Jefferson nodded. "Ortiz is one of the stockholders in a large concrete company, one that's been in the news a lot over the last few years for its connections to organized crime and government corruption. The company is still going, but yes, we have a lot of information that a number of bodies have gone into the deep foundations of buildings that company has contracted for."

They spent the morning talking over different options, and Noah asked a number of questions of the bartender and some of the girls who were playing the parts of whores. They told him a lot about how the business worked, and gave him a number of names of major drug dealers and suppliers who were known to frequent the place. There were so many that it solidified Noah's plan to pose as a drug buyer in order to become a trusted customer of the place.

When it got close to lunchtime, the bartender announced that he had tacos and burritos, so they bought lunch from him and continued to discuss the many different variables. There was no way to predict, for instance, how many customers might be in the place at any particular time. It was known that Ortiz had a tendency to draw customers, common street criminals who just wanted to rub shoulders with such a powerful man. That could create a serious risk for Noah, because it could prevent his escape, or even cause him to miss his target.

Killing Ortiz with a bullet would, as Jefferson had said, point the finger back at the United States.

"Would it be better," Noah asked Jefferson, "if I can make his death look like an accident? Or natural causes?"

Jefferson seemed to think it over. "It might be, especially if you could convince people it was something natural. An accident? People like Ortiz don't have accidents, so that would look suspicious, anyway. No one would believe that he died in an auto accident, for instance, because his drivers are too well trained and his vehicles are designed to make sure he survives. Same problem with poisons: they'll turn up in toxicology, so somebody will know he was assassinated. That word gets out, and suddenly we've got an international incident, even if they can't prove we were behind it."

Shortly after lunchtime, a man walked through the front door and carefully looked at the place over. He bore such a striking resemblance to the real Henrique Valdes that Noah was certain this was the actor playing that part. The man looked carefully at the table full of *gringos*, then to the bartender, who nodded. He turned and walked back out the door, to return a moment later with six other men. One of them was obviously in charge, and Noah was sure he must be the one playing Ortiz.

Noah examined the situation from every angle he could think of, and saw almost no opportunity to eliminate Ortiz without taking out Valdes, as well. Valdes had five goons, all of them obviously armed and dangerous. If Noah could get into the right position, he could probably manage to take them all down, but then there was the danger of the bartender and other customers. People who frequented a place like this were likely to be part of the criminal element, themselves, so when one of their own was attacked, there was a good chance they would get involved in the fight. Noah would likely end up stuck right between a number of different killers, and even he wasn't optimistic enough to expect to survive.

Taking advantage of his limited ability to do so, Noah asked the men playing Valdes and Ortiz a number of questions about the way they did things. Assuming the intelligence they had studied was correct, he learned a great deal about the two men, and developed a healthy respect for the technique that was being employed, that of having actors portray the target and answer questions about themselves. He could have read all of the information he learned out of a dossier, but it would not be as alive to him as it became on hearing it out of the subject's mouth.

Noah got up and walked around the bar, looking at every aspect of it. At one point, he turned to Jefferson. "How accurate are the little details in this place?"

"We had a man in there a few days ago with a micro video camera, and he got shots of everything. He's a local, so we get updated footage every few days. As soon as we see a difference, we'll match it here, so it's pretty accurate."

Noah nodded, and continued his exploration. At two o'clock, he told Jefferson that he had his plan laid out.

Jefferson looked surprised. "Already? Most team leaders take at least two or three days, trying different scenarios out to see what is most likely to succeed. Sure you don't want to give it a little more time?"

Noah shook his head. "I don't need to. I know how I want to take Ortiz out, and it will look like nothing but natural causes. There won't be anything to suggest assassination, or any connection to an outside influence." He looked around the bar, then back at Jefferson. "This setup has been helpful, believe me. I couldn't have worked out a plan nearly as well without seeing this, but knowing that it's bound to be an almost perfect replica of the real tavern tells me I can pull this off the way I want to. All I got to do is find a way to do a little business with Mr. Ortiz, and I'm sure that won't be too difficult. I understand he used to run drugs, so I'm confident he still knows where to get them."

Jefferson stared at Noah for a moment, then looked around at his teammates. "Your team leader says he's ready to go. Any of you have any objection to that?"

Moose, Neil and Sarah all looked at each other,, and each of them shook their heads. "If the boss says we're good to go, then we're good to go," Moose said. Neil rolled his eyes, and said, "I'm still stuck on that part about how I won't actually have to be in the bar, so I'm good. I'm good."

Sarah glanced at Noah, then turned to Jefferson. "I'd like to spend a little time driving around here, get a feel for what the real city will be like. Can I do that on my own, or does the whole team have to be here?"

"Actually, you can come out here on your own. Each of your

phones has GPS, and I can send you each a special code, so that you can use it to get back out here. Your phones will also trigger the security gates, once you got those codes."

"Oh, God, you mean this outfit has its own cell phone apps?" Neil asked sarcastically. "Awesome, just awesome." He rolled his eyes, and Sarah laughed at him.

TWENTY

J ENNY, ALLISON'S SECRETARY, hung up the phone and looked over at Noah, who had been sitting there waiting for almost twenty minutes. "Mr. Wolf? Ms. Peterson will see you now. If you just go through this door…" She pointed to a door beside her desk.

Noah stood up and nodded, then walked through the door into Allison's office. She was obviously busy behind her desk, but she looked up and smiled when he came in.

"Well, you've definitely got this place in an uproar," she said. "Donald Jefferson threw an absolute fit when you said you had your plan worked out the first day. We're not used to that around here." She pointed at a chair across the desk from her, then looked deeply into his eyes. "Noah, are you really sure?"

He nodded. "Yes, I am. I'm going for a 'natural causes' death for Pablo Ortiz, one that should be accepted without a lot of questions. If I do it right, which I will, the only one who might have any suspicions will be Valdes, but I don't think he'll be complaining or raising too big a fuss. If all the Intel is right, he stands to take Ortiz's place, and if anyone thinks his predecessor was murdered so quietly, they're probably going to be looking at him."

Allison tilted her head slightly, acknowledging the logic of his thoughts. "Just so you know, I've got people running a betting pool on whether you pull this one off. We've never let an agent get out into the field as quickly as you, so it's got everyone pretty concerned. Luckily for you, it's my decision and no one else's, because I've got people who already want to see you eliminated."

Noah shrugged. "That's pretty much been the story of my life," he said. "There's always somebody who wants me gone, or out of the way, or dead. So far, I've proven to be pretty hard to kill, but I owe this last attempt directly to you. If for no other reason than that, I intend to make this mission a success."

"Well, if you do, you'll shut up a lot of your detractors, and I'll take care of the rest of them. I understand Sarah has been spending the last couple of days driving around Hollywood? How do you feel about her?" She waved a hand, dismissing her own question. "Sorry, let me rephrase that. Do you have confidence in her abilities?"

"I went out with her the day before yesterday, and rode along. That girl can definitely drive, I'll say that. On the other hand, if everything goes according to plan, she's not going to have to play Jeff Gordon. We should be able to drive out just as pretty as you please."

Allison smiled. "What about the rest of your team? Still holding it all together?"

"Yes, Ma'am," Noah said. "Neil and I are getting to be pretty close, and Moose has come a long way. I'm absolutely confident that he'll do what I need him to do, and he's even started loosening up and acting more friendly, lately. I think dating the Jefferson girl has helped a lot." He cocked his head to one side and looked at Allison. "I'm still curious about that situation," he said. "It's really hard for me to believe that so many people who know about us can live out in the world, but the secret doesn't leak."

Allison held her smile, but then she winked at him. "Noah, sometimes it pays for us to have one of our own in places like The Sagebrush. It doesn't happen often, but occasionally one of our people, especially a new recruit, tends to brag a bit. Needless to say, we discourage that, to the point that if one of our people, like

Miss Jefferson, were to overhear such bragging, that recruit might very well disappear."

"Is that what happened in this case? Did Moose go out there and run his mouth?"

"On the contrary, not a bit. Quite the opposite, in fact. Miss Jefferson was here one day when Moose had to come in, and her father told me that she asked about him that day. From what I understand, when she saw him out at the Saloon, she actually went out of the way to make sure he knew that she was aware. You'll remember, I'm sure, but I told you she was one of our computer whiz kids, so it wasn't hard for her to get into his bio. I would imagine she was delighted when she found that she is precisely the type of girl he seems to be drawn to."

"Well, good for him, then," Noah said. "I guess it just worked out."

Allison grinned. "Yes, I guess it did," she said. "Sort of like you and Sarah; that seems to be working out pretty well itself."

Noah raised his eyebrows and looked at her. "Is that a problem? If there's a rule against it, I never heard about it."

Allison sat there and looked at him for a long moment, then shook her head. "Normally, I would say it would be a bad idea for a team leader to become romantically involved with a teammate," she said, "but you are an entirely different case. I've already spoken with Sarah about it, and she seems genuinely aware that you're not likely to have any kind of feelings for her, and she insists that that's exactly what made you so attractive to her."

"That's what she told me, too."

Allison grinned. "I did caution her about one thing, that sex is actually something that we use as a tool in this business, so there may be times when you seem to be involved with other women. She assured me that her relationship with you is purely physical, and that she won't let jealousy become an issue. Noah, if it does, I want to know about it immediately. I would try removing her from your team, but if she can't be salvaged…" She let the rest of the sentence hang in the air, unsaid.

Noah nodded. "I understand," he said. "I won't let anything affect a mission, and especially not that."

She looked at him for another moment, then nodded as if dismissing the issue. "Okay, then, we need to go ahead and get this show on the road. I've already sent Jefferson to El Paso to make sure everything is ready for you when you get there. He'll provide you with your burner IDs, phones, weapons and anything else you need. We've got you booked into the Holiday Inn, each of you with your own room." She looked meaningfully at him for just a moment, and said, "For the record, we do discourage any kind of intimacy between teammates when you're out in the field. That doesn't mean we'll be watching, but it's just a guideline to prevent problems."

"Yes, Ma'am," Noah said.

Allison laughed once, then went on. "You and your team will fly out of Denver tomorrow afternoon, and meet Jefferson in El Paso tomorrow evening. He's got vehicles and everything waiting for you, so just let him know what else you need for your plans."

"Yes, Ma'am."

"Noah, this is the part where I have to say that if you or any of your team is compromised, as in captured or killed, our government will deny any knowledge of you. You don't exist, so there won't be a rescue mission. As far as Mexico would be concerned, you would probably be treated as a criminal, which could mean anything from prison time to execution, depending on what the charges are. Unfortunately, I can't even offer you the chance to back out. This is the reason we recruited you, and I'm hoping, really, really hoping, that you will turn out to be as good as I think you will."

Noah gave her his best grin. "Relax," he said. "I'll be even better than that."

She grinned back. "Good. Now, go prove that to me."

She handed him an envelope. "These are your plane tickets. Everything else you'll need, you'll get from Jefferson. Noah, I want you guys to be careful down there. This is your first mission, but that doesn't mean it's not an important one. It's got to be successful, but I want you all to come back. I have high hopes for this team."

"I appreciate that," Noah said, "and I promise you I'm going to do my best to make sure we all come back safe."

She nodded once. "Excellent," she said, and then picked up the file from her desk and began reading through it.

Noah recognized a dismissal when he saw one, so he rose from the chair and walked out of the room. Jenny looked up at him and smiled as he passed her desk again, and he returned it out of habit. When he got to the elevator, however, there was no sign of a smile on his face.

He rode the elevator down to the parking garage, and walked to his Corvette. He fired the powerful car up and backed it out of its space, then made his way out to the street and turned right. That took him out to the road that would let him head for home, and since he had nothing else to do for the day, home sounded like the place he wanted to be.

He took out his phone, and sent a message to each of his team members to meet him at his place for dinner. By the time he got to the county road, all three of them had replied that they would be there. Since it was only a little after three, he decided to fire up the grill for some barbecued chicken.

Neil was already at home, in his trailer, so he wandered over to the house when Noah got there. "Hail, Caesar," he said. "How goes it with Queen Allison?"

"Pretty good," Noah replied. "We got the final go-ahead; we fly out tomorrow afternoon. You got everything ready on your end?"

Neil broke into a big smile. "I have got things so ready that I'm making every bank in the world nervous," he said. "I've written a program that can get into every financial computer network in the world, and make fake transactions appear in any bank account I want to play around with. What that means is that Uncle Sam doesn't have to spend any money for all these drug buys you're planning to make. All you do is tell me where you want money to appear, and I'll make it appear there."

Noah's eyebrows almost met his hairline. "Are you saying you found a way to create money out of thin air?"

Neil squinted at him, and sneered. "Why would I do that? The Federal Reserve has been doing that for years; that's not new. Hell, every bank in the country, probably the world, can do that. No, I've done something even better. I can make money appear in any bank account, looking just like it came from a normal transaction, but sometime later, depending on how long I set it for, it automatically disappears. Poof! Gone like it never existed, which it didn't. Of course, the beauty of it is that you'll be long gone before anyone notices what happened."

Noah looked at him for a moment. "What happens if they spend the money before your time limit runs out and it disappears?"

Neil grinned. "Then, suddenly, a whole lot of bank examiners and federal agents from every country involved are looking for whoever owned that account, because it will be so deep in the hole that they may never figure out just how much money is really missing."

Noah nodded. "And somehow, the banks are aware of this program of yours? You said they're all scared, right?"

Neil blinked a couple of times. "Well—okay, they're not really scared, because they don't know about it, but if they did know about it, they'd be terrified. I mean, like, shaking in their boots, that kind of terrified. Holy crap, Noah, in the wrong hands, this program could destabilize the economies of some fair-sized countries!"

Noah stood there and looked at him for a moment. "Have you told our bosses about this program, yet?"

Neil blinked again. "No, not yet. Why?"

"Do me a favor," Noah said. "When you do tell them about it, don't mention that part about destabilizing economies. If the wrong people got hold of that idea, you might disappear, and I don't want to lose you."

Neil opened and closed his mouth three times, but nothing came out. He dropped into a chair close to where Noah was prepping the grill. "Have I ever mentioned that you come up with some of the most unsettling notions? Do you really think I could be in danger over that?"

"I think there are people who would decide that was a useful program, and wouldn't necessarily want its author hanging around. If you wrote the program, you could probably write one to defend against it, am I right?"

Neil nodded, but didn't say anything.

"Seriously, dude, let's just keep that part between us, okay?"

Once again, Neil only nodded.

Noah put him to work a few moments later, helping him to get the chicken cut up and marinating in a wine sauce. Noah put potatoes on to boil for potato salad after that, while Neil shucked a dozen ears of corn, coated them in butter and wrapped them in foil so they could go right onto the grill.

Sarah pulled in just a little after four, and volunteered to make coleslaw. By this time, she knew where everything was in the kitchen, so Noah simply nodded and got out of her way.

Moose showed up a half hour later, so Noah decided to move dinner up by an hour. The coleslaw and potato salad were already done, so he carried the chicken and corn out to the grill and started laying it all out, basting the meat with his own homemade barbecue sauce.

"So, I'm curious, but where on earth did you learn to cook like this?" Moose asked.

"One of the foster homes I lived in," Noah said. "The lady who ran it had a grill, and in the summertime, she liked to cook on it about once a week. I was always the one who volunteered to help, so she taught me a lot about it."

Moose nodded. "I want her name and address, so I can send her a thank you card."

"Yeah, I wish I could send her one, too. Hey, you want to get us a beer? There's a case in the fridge, and I could use one."

"I'll get them," Sarah said, and she hurried inside. Moose had started to rise, but he settled back into his chair.

"So, is this just a social dinner, or is there more to this meeting than meets the eye?" Moose asked.

"Bit of both," Noah said. "I met with Allison today, and found out we're flying out of Denver tomorrow afternoon. We'll be in El Paso tomorrow night, meeting with Mr. Jefferson."

"What did I miss?" Sarah asked as she came back and passed bottles of beer around to everyone.

"That the balloon went up," Neil said. "It seems it's time for us to stop playing games and get down to business."

Noah nodded. "I was just telling Moose. I found out today that we're flying out of Denver tomorrow afternoon, and meeting Jefferson in El Paso tomorrow night. He's supposed to have everything ready for us when we get there. I got our plane tickets. Our flight departs at twenty after four."

Noah had the grill parked close to his patio table, so that he could watch it from his chair. The four of them were sitting at the table, looking at each other. The mood was somber, and each of them was lost in their own thoughts.

"Well, we knew it was coming," Moose said. "It's just like anything else; sooner or later, you have to pay the piper."

Sarah nodded. "Yeah," she said. "Jefferson had me driving around Hollywood in a Chrysler. He said it's identical to the one I'll have down there. I can drive anything, but it's nice to be familiar with your vehicle."

"I'm taking my own computer," Neil said. "I might be able

to use a different one, but mine already knows me. That'd be like cheating on a girlfriend."

Moose laughed at him. "Neil, did you honestly just compare your computer to a girlfriend? Dude, we've really got to get you out more often. Have you ever even been laid?"

Neil rolled his eyes and sunk down into his chair. "Of course, you idiot," he said. "Didn't your mom tell you about us?"

Noah held up a hand. "Okay, that's enough. Let's try to have a good time tonight, just relax. I think if we all meet here around noon, we can be at Denver International in plenty of time to check in and go through security. That sound okay to everyone?"

"Fine by me," Moose said. "I'm probably the only one that'll have to drive over here anyway."

Sarah grinned, and kicked him under the table, and Neil just rolled his eyes again. "I don't have to drive anywhere, I just walk across the yard. On the other hand, since I have the biggest vehicle and plenty of room for all the luggage, why don't we all ride to the airport together in mine?"

Moose looked at him for a moment, then shrugged. "Why not? Maybe you'll kill us on the way; then we won't have to put up with this mission after all."

They talked about little things until the chicken was done, then Neil and Sarah brought everything else out from the house and set the table. It was a nice afternoon, and they decided to enjoy the weather. From everything they knew, it was likely to be hot in Juárez.

When dinner was over, they sat and visited for a little while, but then Moose said he wanted to go and spend some time with Elaine, and Neil decided to go to his trailer and make sure his computer and gear were properly packed. That left Noah and Sarah alone, so they cleaned everything up and loaded the dishes into the dishwasher, then sat down to watch some TV until they felt like going to bed.

TWENTY-ONE

THEIR FLIGHT WAS uneventful, and landed in El Paso at just after six. They had all been sitting together, so they all came off the plane in single file and found Jefferson waiting for them inside the terminal.

"Noah, good to see you," he said, shaking Noah's hand. "Good flight, everyone?"

They all smiled and nodded, agreeing that it was an easy flight. Jefferson led them toward baggage claim to pick up their luggage. "I brought a van with me," he said, "since I didn't know how much baggage you might have. I got vehicles for each of you back at the hotel, but I just thought the van would be easier for right now."

"No problem," Noah said.

It took them about twenty minutes to gather up all of their luggage, and Moose snagged a cart and loaded it all up. "Lead the way," he said to Jefferson, and pushed the cart as he followed along. The van was in short-term parking, and the walk took about five minutes.

Everything was loaded, and they were all inside and headed for the hotel. "I put you at the Holiday Inn, it's pretty decent. Has a nice restaurant, too. I thought you guys would like that. Pool, weight room, all the goodies."

"That'll be fine," Noah said. "I understand you've got everything else we need?"

Jefferson smiled. "It's all at the hotel. If you guys are hungry, we'll get you checked in and put your things in your rooms, then meet at the restaurant and have dinner. After that, we can go to my room and you can start looking it all over."

Noah glanced at the other three, who nodded. "Yeah, I think we're all hungry. We ate lunch early, so we could get going to the airport."

They pulled up in front of the hotel about fifteen minutes later, and were quickly checked in. Once again, Moose grabbed the luggage cart and loaded everyone's bags onto it. They were all on the third floor, and their rooms were close together, so it worked out well. Once everything was put away, they all met in the hallway and rode down the elevator together to go to the restaurant.

Dinner was pleasant, and when it was over, Jefferson pointed out that the restaurant had a very nice bar, then ordered a bottle of wine. He poured a glass for each of them, and held his own high. "To success," he said, and the others all joined in the toast.

They rode up together again, and this time, they all went to Jefferson's room. It was also on the third floor, just down the hall from theirs, a slightly bigger room. That was good, since it gave them all room to find a place to sit.

Jefferson picked up what looked like a shoebox, glanced at it, and then passed it to Noah. "Open it up," he said. "Inside, you'll find a wallet containing your ID, passport and credit cards for this mission, in the name of John Baker. Mr. Baker is from Chicago, and the wallet trash would lead you to believe that he's single and probably self-employed. He's got health insurance with Blue Cross, he's a member of two different country clubs near Chicago, and he has a couple of pictures of a teenage boy, both of which are marked as being to Uncle John from Bobby. There's also a Beretta nine millimeter automatic, but you might not want to try carrying that into Mexico. Oh, and you'll find about five thousand in cash. That's flash money, you'll need it."

Noah was busy examining the wallet, and simply nodded. Jefferson picked up another box and passed it to Sarah. "Your name is Kathy Stratton. There's a purse inside with all your ID, passports, credit cards, etc., and lots of normal purse-type stuff. Makeup, aspirins, couple different kinds of candy floating around in there, I don't know what all. However, if you take a look at this end of it, you see this ring?" He pointed at the one he meant. "If anything goes wrong, you pull that ring and a device inside the purse starts transmitting its location, as well as audio so Neil can hear what's going on. He'll have the receiver, and a way to pinpoint your location. If at all possible, we'll get you out of whatever happened."

Sarah looked at the ring, then up at Jefferson. "You won't get upset if I prefer to get myself out of jams, will you?" She swung the purse by its strap, feeling its weight. "I could beat four men to death with this thing in the time it would take to pull that ring and yell for help, and I'll be driving a car with a Hemi engine. I don't think I'm likely to need much rescuing."

Jefferson smiled and nodded. "I knew you were likely to feel that way, but our administrator being a lady who doesn't happen to possess those skills herself, she insists that we always offer a panic alarm like that to our female operatives. Besides, you might run into a situation where there's more than four men you have to beat to death. Pull that ring, and one of us will try to come and help."

Sarah gave him a sarcastic smile, and he turned to pick up another box. This one he handed to Moose. "Moose, your name is Billy Scott. ID, passport, everything, just like the others. There's a Glock forty in your box, I understand that's one of your favorite weapons. Keep it on you at all times. It's been specially treated with a film that will keep metal detectors and even gun-sniffing dogs from spotting it, at least until it's been fired the first time. If you have to carry it across the border, you should be able to do so without being caught."

Moose looked the weapon over, but didn't remove it from the holster it was in. It was a clip-on, one that he could snap onto his belt so that it would be covered by a loose shirt. He nodded, and put it back in the box.

The next box went to Neil. "Mr. Blessing," Jefferson said, "in reading your file, I learned that you were a very active participant in your high school's drama club, and have a knack for accents. Your name, as you will see you on the ID and passports and credit cards in that box, is Henri Batiste. Mr. Batiste is a French-Canadian who is now a US citizen, but has never shaken his accent."

"*Oui, oui, monsieur,*" Neil said with a grin.

"You don't have to worry about maintaining the accent around the hotel, but make sure you don't forget when you're on the phone. Speaking of which…"

Jefferson picked up another box, and opened it. Inside were four cell phones, the latest models of smartphones. He passed one to each of them, glancing at each before deciding whom to give it to. "These are your phones," he said. "You will leave your regular phones with me for now, and use these exclusively. Each of these has the numbers for the others programmed into it already, under the names they're using for the mission. You've also got numbers for me, under Jim Thorpe, and for the administrator, under the name Barbara Davis, and you'll see a lot of other numbers programmed in. If anyone gets hold of your phone and calls those numbers, we have people who will answer and act like they're old friends of yours."

The four of them took a few moments to familiarize themselves with the phones, and then Jefferson produced another box. "Noah, this is the special shopping list you gave me. I got everything you asked for, it's all there."

Noah opened the box, glanced inside and then smiled grimly.

"That's perfect," he said. "Ortiz literally won't know what hit him." He closed the box and set it aside.

There was one box left, and Jefferson picked it up gingerly. He handed it to Neil, who suddenly began to smile. "Neil, that's the special shopping list that *you* gave me, and let me tell you some of that stuff is very hard to come by. If you hadn't been able to get me part numbers, I might not have found some of it."

Noah looked at Neil, and indicated the box with a flip of his chin. "What kind of goodies you got there, Neil?"

Neil opened the box, and began rummaging through its contents. "Some absolutely amazing things," he said. He pulled out what looked like a sheet of paper covered with blue dots. "See this? Each of those dots is a microphone capable of transmitting an encrypted audio signal through a piggybacked cell tower. The cellular service won't ever know the signal is there, but it can reach my decryption equipment anywhere in the world. If anyone else were to pick up the signal, it would only sound like static." He put the sheet back in the box, then lifted a small box from inside. Opening it, he showed them all what appeared to be a wad of chewing gum, such as might be stuck under a table. "This little jewel is a well-camouflaged, high-definition video camera. Like the microphones, it can send its signal right through cellular data signals, like using Skype on your phone. It has a super adhesive on the back, so when you peel off the paper and stick it some-where, I'll get a clear color video signal for the next two weeks, unless somebody goes to scraping off the gum. You stick this up under the bar, or under a table, and I'm betting no one in that establishment will ever get around to it."

Noah nodded appreciatively. "Excellent, that's great. We'll know what's going on there, even when I'm not in the place."

"Exactamundo," Neil said. "I'm supposed to keep you sup-plied with Intel, and that's what I'm going to do. Besides, once you stick a few of these around that bar, we'll know instantly if anything starts to go wrong for you. That way, Blondie could drop off Muscles to help get you out of it."

Noah shook his head. "No, I'm going in alone," he said. "Moose will stay back with you; he's got his own wheels and ID if he has to come into town for any reason, but I don't want anyone getting a look at him if we can possibly avoid it. Same goes for you, Sarah; you'll drop me off some distance away from the bar, and I'll walk in. I don't want them getting a look at you, not at all."

"People might wonder how you get in and out of the city," Jefferson said. "What do you plan to tell them?"

"I don't," Noah said. "In a city like that, I don't think too many people advertise where they sleep, especially people who are involved in illegal activities. If anybody gets so nosy that they want to know where I go when I leave, they can follow me, but that means they're taking the risks that go along with it. I'm supposed to be a bad guy, if I have to, I'll act the part." He shrugged. "Besides, I think it would make sense for me to get a room in Juárez, let myself be seen in other places around the city. If I'm in that bar every single day, that's going to look pretty suspicious, wouldn't you think?"

Jefferson looked at him for a moment, then nodded. "Okay," he said. "There are a few hotels with some decent security, places where an apparently wealthy businessman like John Baker might stay. What about a vehicle? Or do you want Sarah to drive in each day to chauffeur you around?"

"No, of course not. I'll let her drive me in tomorrow, so that I can get a room in one of those hotels, but I'll use taxis to get around the city. Sarah, I'll let you know when I need you to come and pick me up."

Moose grunted. "I want to go on record right now that I do not like this plan. How am I supposed to cover your back, when most of the time I won't even know where you are?"

Noah shook his head. "Calm down, Moose," he said. "I've

got to play the part convincingly, and this John Baker wouldn't be trusted if he was sleeping in El Paso every night. On top of that, if I come back to this hotel each night, we run the risk of someone managing to successfully tail me. That could expose all of you and compromise the mission. I'll be needing you, don't worry; I'm quite certain there will be flaws in the plan that will require quick improvisation. That's where you guys come in. I'm not all that scared of being in Ciudad Juárez, I genuinely believe that the reason I'm not afraid to walk through the valley of the shadow of death is because I am the meanest son of a bitch in the valley."

"Well, isn't that special," Neil said. "And all this time I thought it was because you didn't know how to be afraid of anything? Isn't that what makes you so valuable to us all, the fact that you don't have emotions like fear inside you?"

"I'm with Moose and Neil on this one," Sarah said. "Look, Noah, there's no doubt you're a tough bastard, but you're not Superman. Bullets don't bounce off of you, remember? We're supposed to be your support team, but you're leaving us behind."

Jefferson grinned at Noah. "They do have a point," he said, "but of course, the final decision on the plan is always yours. If this is the way you want to play it, then so be it. To be honest, I agree with you for the most part, but if you go out there and get yourself killed on your first mission, Allison is never going to forgive any of us. She has staked an awful lot on you, so you need to do your best to make sure she collects on that investment."

Noah nodded. "Point taken, and guys, I do understand your concerns and I do appreciate them. We're still going to do it my way. And right now, what we're going to do is go get some sleep. We'll meet tomorrow morning for breakfast at seven, and then we'll start putting this plan into operation. Any questions?"

There weren't any, so they each got up and went to their own rooms, taking with them the things that Jefferson had given them, and leaving their usual phones with him. Noah got inside his room, set the boxes down on the table, and went straight to the shower. Twenty minutes later, he was in bed, and a few minutes past that, he was asleep.

He woke at five thirty, his internal alarm clock working the way it always did, and began thinking over the things he would be doing that day. He had to choose a hotel to stay in, but he didn't think that would be difficult. Jefferson would know which ones were best, and he would get his advice at breakfast. He didn't plan to take a gun with him, because it would be out of character. Smalltime drug dealers carry guns; the big ones don't, not because they're so tough, but because they're worth so much money that even their enemies are reluctant to see anything happen to them. After all, you never know when you might have something your enemy wants to buy. Things like that happened all the time.

There was a small coffee maker in the room, so he made a pot, but the stuff reminded him of what he had been given on death row. He took a single sip from the first cup, then dumped the whole pot down the toilet. Since his appetite for coffee was now whetted, however, he decided to go on down to the restaurant and get a decent cup there.

He stepped out of his room and turned to go to the elevator, but he heard his name and knew it was Sarah's voice. He stopped and turned to her, waiting so that she could catch up.

"I woke up early and couldn't get back to sleep," she said, "so I heard you moving around. When I heard your door open, I figured you might be heading down for coffee. Mind some company?"

"Not at all," Noah replied. "The rest of them ought to be coming before too long; we can either sit and drink coffee, or get an early start on breakfast. Up to you." He extended an elbow, and she smiled as she linked arms with him. They walked together to the elevator, and stepped inside when it opened.

TWENTY-TWO

THE RESTAURANT WAS just off the lobby, and was just opening. The waitress smiled at them as they came in, and hurried to set glasses of water on the table in front of them. "Hi, good to see you," she said rapidly. "My name is Tina, I'll be your server this morning, can I start you off with some coffee?"

Noah nodded, giving the girl one of his better smiles. "Yes, please, for both of us."

"Okay, I'll be right back with your coffee, and you can take a look at the menus while I'm gone." She spun and hurried behind the counter, where fresh coffee could still be heard brewing. Sarah chuckled, as the girl stood and stared at the pot as if mentally willing it to hurry.

"Well, the service is good," she said. "Hope the coffee is. I tried that stuff in the room, and it nearly killed me."

Noah nodded his head. "I made a pot of that stuff, and threw it down the toilet. It was horrible."

Tina returned a couple minutes later with their coffees, and Noah said they were waiting for friends, and would order breakfast when the others arrived. The waitress smiled and nodded, and bustled off once more.

The two of them sat and chatted for a few minutes, talking mostly about their rooms. Sarah said her bed was too soft, but other than that she thought the room was wonderful. Noah shrugged, not sure what to say about his own room other than the fact that he had slept well.

Neil was the next to arrive, which didn't surprise Noah. The boy was often up as early as he was, and had even come over and tapped on the back kitchen door a few times back at the house, joining Noah for his first cup of coffee in the mornings. As far as he was able, Noah felt that he truly liked the kid. There were things about Neil that reminded him of his pal Jerry, from his foster home days. Jerry wasn't as tall, but he was also shy and clumsy, and could be just as sarcastic.

Moose and Jefferson showed up together only a few moments later, and Noah signaled Tina when he saw them enter. The waitress hurried over, rushed off to get more coffee, then scribbled their orders down as fast as she could. "Okay, I'll get these in and we'll get them right back to you," she said, and then she was gone again.

Neil watched her go, shaking his head. Moose looked at him, then turned to look at the girl before turning back to Neil.

"Neil, you think she's cute? Want to tap that?"

Neil slowly turned his face back so that it was facing in Moose's direction, but shook his head. "No," he said. "I'm trying to figure out where on earth she could find that much energy this early in the morning. If we can follow her to its source, we might have something as valuable as gold. I mean, even meth couldn't give her that much, could it? I think she's found a whole new drug, and I want some of it." He slowly turned his face back to look at the rapidly bustling waitress.

Sarah laughed, and Moose chuckled. Noah looked at Neil, then looked at the girl. "Maybe she's just one of those people who likes early mornings," he said, and all four of the others turned to look at him. He looked from one to the other, until he had looked at all of them in turn. "What?"

"Neil was making a joke, Noah," Sarah said.

Noah nodded. "I know," he said. "I was just adding my own observation." He looked at his three teammates again. "If I hadn't been with you guys, I would've laughed along with you, but you all said I didn't have to pretend with you. I mean, if you want me to go back to it, I can."

Sarah shook her head. "No, it's fine. It was just that we forgot about that. For a second there, it seemed like you just didn't get the joke."

"I didn't, not really. I mean, I realize it was a facetious statement, about her finding a new drug, but I don't really understand exactly what makes it funny."

Moose knuckled his shoulder. "Don't sweat it, Noah," he said. "That was our bad, not yours."

Jefferson was looking at Noah. "You know, knowing about your—what condition?—knowing about it is one thing, but actually seeing it, that's something altogether different. It must've been rough, growing up like that."

Noah shrugged. "I guess it probably was, but I don't have anything to compare it to, so I can't tell you for sure. On the other hand, to me, from what I've seen of what emotions do to people, I sort of feel like the lucky one."

Neil's eyebrows went up, and he nodded sagely. "You have learned wisdom, Grasshopper," he said. "The rest of these mortals might not understand it, but I would give just about anything to be like you in that regard. I've had all the emotional pain I can take; I'd be glad to be completely unaware of what it is."

Moose looked at him. "That's why you're such a smart ass," he said. "You try to keep everyone at a distance, so no one gets close to you and can hurt your feelings. Right?"

"Why, Milton, you missed your calling, you should have been a psychiatrist," Neil said. "That's exactly what my last four shrinks all said, so you're at least as smart as them." He rolled his eyes.

"Call me Milton one more time," Moose growled, "and you won't have to worry about ever getting your feelings hurt again."

"Enough," Noah said. "Today's a big day. We get to actually go to work, finally." He turned to Jefferson. "You got a suggestion on a hotel for me over there?"

Jefferson nodded. "I did a little research on that last night, and I think the place you want to go is the Hampton Inn. They've got good security, and the taxi drivers that are allowed to pick up there aren't as likely to try to kidnap you as most of them." He blinked. "Not that I think any of them could actually manage to do it, but you might as well avoid what problems you can, right?"

"Good point," Noah said. "Okay, I'll have Sarah drive me over there in a couple of hours and drop me off. Neil, will your little transmitters work there, too?"

"Of course they will, they'll work anywhere. The way they're made, they turn on when you peel them off that paper, and then you can stick them anywhere they won't be noticed. The little micro batteries in them are good for about two, maybe two-and-a-half weeks."

Sarah started looked at him. "Two weeks? The battery in my cell phone won't even last all day, how can something that small have a battery that will last two weeks?"

Neil rolled his head onto its side and peeked at her from under his eyelids. "The battery in your cell phone doesn't cost even a tenth of what one of those little dots is worth. I guess when you're willing to spend enough money, you can get just about anything you want."

Jefferson laughed. "He's not kidding," he said. "One of those sheets, with only twenty of those dots on it, cost us almost eighteen thousand dollars. Our gadgets department didn't even know those things existed until now."

"You're welcome," Neil said with a smile. "Gratuities are accepted willingly. Especially if they're in cash."

"Okay, okay, the reason I ask is because I'd like to put a couple in the room I'm staying in, over there. Just in case somebody follows me back, or I have a reason to take someone back with me, I want to know somebody can listen in. Neil, can you show Moose how to monitor these things, so you can get some sleep now and then?"

Neil looked at Moose, then turned back to Noah. "I've got a tablet I can give him, so he can listen in. I'm not letting him touch my computer. *Nobody* touches my computer. But, yeah, that way he can sit there and listen to all the boring crap that goes on, so I don't have to. I can be doing more important things, like analyzing the intelligence that comes in."

"Okay, just make sure you guys work out a schedule so someone is always listening. You can use Sarah, too, as long as she's just sitting around here."

Tina brought out a huge tray and set it on a table beside them, then started passing their plates over. The whole process took only a couple of minutes, and she was gone again. Noah quit talking about business while they ate, but breakfast didn't take very long. Twenty minutes later, they were finished and headed back to their rooms.

Noah had told Sarah to be ready to go at nine o'clock, then went back to his room and gathered the things he'd be taking with him. He had given Jefferson his genuine ID, and now had John Baker's wallet in his pocket, as well as the passport. The other items he was taking with him went into one of his suitcases, including everything from the special shopping list. Several of those things were in bottles that looked quite medicinal, and had labels saying they had been prescribed to Mr. Baker. Other items seemed perfectly innocuous, and Noah wasn't worried about a customs inspector giving him any static about them.

And then it was time to go. Sarah tapped on his door, and stepped inside when he opened it, then flung both arms around his neck and kissed him deeply.

"You know," she said, "you could just take me with you. We can pretend we're married at the hotel."

Noah shook his head. "John Baker is a single man, remember?

Might be kind of hard to explain a wife, all of a sudden. Let's just stick to the plan, that's what I need to do."

Sarah tried to pout, but Noah simply turned away and started picking up his bags, so she sucked her lip in and glared at his back. "Fine," she said, "but if you get yourself killed, don't you come crying to me. Just remember, I tried to go with you." She waited until he had all of his things ready to go, then turned and opened the door.

He followed her down to the parking lot, and straight to the car Jefferson had provided for. It was exactly where he had told her to look for it, so it wasn't hard to find the black-and-silver Chrysler three hundred. She used the remote to open the trunk, and Noah put his luggage inside it. They got into the car, and Sarah punched up the Hampton Inn Juárez on the GPS in her phone, then began following its instructions as she drove through El Paso.

There was a line at the border, so it was almost an hour before they actually made it into Mexico. Noah was half surprised that they hadn't been stopped and searched, like several other cars he had seen. Most of those had been newer sedans, as well, and he thought for a moment that Jefferson had made a bad choice. It wasn't until they were passing those cars, and he got a look at the drivers that he understood.

Racial profiling was not only a problem in the United States, he decided, because the Mexican customs inspectors only seemed to be searching black and Hispanic drivers. He and Sarah, both being white with blonde hair, were waived on through.

They didn't talk a lot as Sarah drove, but it took her most of an hour to get to the hotel, anyway. She pulled up in front, and let Noah go inside to get his room, while she waited.

A moment later, she was wishing she had her gun. There were probably a dozen Mexican men standing not five feet away from her car, staring at her and making what she was sure were rather sexist comments in Spanish. She was starting to get a little nervous when Noah suddenly reappeared. He motioned for her to open the trunk, and she reached down to push the button, then started to get out of the car.

"Kathy, honey," Noah said with a Midwestern accent. "You don't need to get out, sweetie. Thanks for the ride, but you get on home, now. Tell your daddy I'll see him in a few days, okay?"

Sarah rolled her eyes, but smiled back at him. "Okay, Mr. Baker," she said. "You know how to reach us if you need a ride back." She started the car as he closed the trunk, and left rubber on the parking lot as she peeled out to hurry back to the Texas side of the border.

Noah, as John Baker, had taken a suite on the top floor, and two young bellhops ran to try to carry his bags for him, but he waved them away. He got into the elevator and rode it to the top floor, which was only accessible with his key card. When it opened, he turned to the right as the desk clerk had instructed him, and found his room only two doors down.

The suite was every bit as luxurious as any he had seen, and boasted not only a sitting room and bedroom, but also a huge whirlpool hot tub, as well as a jacuzzi in the bathroom. Noah shook his head, glad that he was spending Uncle Sam's money, and not any of his own.

He didn't bother to unpack, preferring to live out of his suitcases while he was there. He peeled off a couple of the sticker microphones and put one in the sitting room and one in the bedroom.

"Okay, let's test these. Neil, if you can hear me, give me a call." His cell phone rang less than thirty seconds later. "Okay, they're working alright, then?"

"I can hear you better through my monitor than I can through this phone," Neil said. "I wouldn't give you gadgets that don't work, boss. Trust me."

"I do trust you, Neil, I just don't always trust technology. You wouldn't believe the things that failed us in the field when I was in the Army."

"Oh, yes I would," Neil said. "Everything the Army got was built by the lowest bidder. The nice thing about our outfit is that they don't have a budget. When I ordered the top-of-the-line, that's what I got."

"Okay, I guess that makes sense. Good job, I'll talk you later." He hung up without another word.

He checked the time and found that it was only eleven, and decided to wait until early afternoon before going down to Eduardo's. That left about three hours to kill, and since he wasn't hungry, he decided to take a nap. He set an alarm on his phone, stripped off his shirt and shoes, stretched out on the bed, and was asleep in seconds.

The alarm went off, and he rolled up to a sitting position. He rubbed the sleep out of his eyes, stretched once, then went to the bathroom to freshen up. When he came out, he dug in his suitcase for his deodorant, used it lavishly, then slipped his shirt and shoes back on. He took three hundred dollars in cash from his stash in the suitcase, make sure he had his wallet, passport and room key, then left the room and went downstairs to find a taxi.

"*Si, Señor?*" The driver asked as he climbed into the backseat.

"I want to go to Eduardo's Tavern, do you know where that is?"

The driver looked confused. "Eduardo?"

"Eduardo's Tavern," Noah said. "49936 Avenida de la Fuentes."

The drivers face lit up with a big smile. "Ah, *si*," he said, "*Eduardo, si, Eduardo!*" The little man turned to face forward, shoved the car into gear and roared out of the parking lot onto the street.

Noah was forced to hold on to the safety handle over the door to the backseat, but he managed to smile as he did so. He knew that Mexican taxi drivers were much like those in other countries, and drove like maniacs so that they could hurry back to get another fare. That was the only way they could make a decent living, especially in areas with poor economies, such as Mexico.

Noah caught the driver's eye in the rearview mirror. "*Habla Ingles?*" he asked, and the driver's face lit up again.

"*Si, Señor,*" he said. "I speak very good En-gleesh!"

"Good, good," Noah said. "I want to stay at Eduardo's Tavern for three hours, *tres horas,* you understand?"

"*Si,* three hours, I understand!"

"Okay, you come back and get me in three hours, and I will give you one hundred American dollars. You come back for me then?" He held up a one-hundred-dollar bill and let the driver see it.

The man was nodding so vigorously that he could barely even speak, but Noah understood that he was promising to be back in three hours. He drove even faster the rest of the way, then slid to a stop right in front of Eduardo's. "Three hours! Three hours, I be back," he said, as Noah handed him a twenty-dollar bill, which was about twice the fare on the meter. The man's smile looked like it was going to split his face.

"That's right, come back in three hours," Noah said. "One hundred American dollars." He got out of the car, and wasn't surprised when it sped away as quickly as it had come. Noah turned and looked at the door to the tavern, squared his shoulders and walked inside.

TWENTY-THREE

THE MAN BEHIND the bar, Noah knew from photographs he'd been shown, was Eduardo Hernandez. The two of them stood there and looked at each other for a moment, and Noah tried to give the impression that he was nervous. He walked slowly toward the bar, carefully keeping his hands in plain sight.

Eduardo spoke, in very clear English. "Can I help you, my friend?"

Noah smiled, continuing his nervous act. "Oh, good, you speak English? Man, that's a break for me, because I don't understand a whole lot of Spanish. Listen, my name is John, John Baker, and I've been—well, somebody told me this might be a good place to come to, if I wanted to maybe buy some stuff."

Eduardo started laughing. "It's a good place to come to, if you want to buy beer or tequila, or pussy. Those we got, and lots. Whatever else you might be looking for, maybe somebody who comes in can help you, I don't know."

Noah went with him, trying to make it look as though his nervousness was fading. "Okay, okay, I gotcha," he said. "Listen, can I get a beer?"

Eduardo grunted, and pointed at a bar stool, so Noah climbed up on it and sat. A moment later, a small bottle of Budweiser was set in front of him, and Eduardo said, "Fifteen dollars."

Noah's eyes jumped up to Eduardo's, in a classic double take, but then he shrugged and pulled a twenty-dollar bill out of his pocket. He handed it over and said, "Keep the change."

Eduardo grinned, rang up the sale and pocketed his tip. He came back to where Noah was sitting, since there was only one other person in the place, an old man who had been coming around for years, and always sat on the same stool, nursing the cheapest bottle of tequila he could get.

"So what is it you are wanting to buy?" Eduardo asked.

Noah grinned, trying to look sly. "Oh, different things. Stuff I can send home, and make money on. Lots of money."

Eduardo grunted again, but his grin stayed put. "Well, I do not know for sure what you might find here, but I will tell you this. Most of my customers, they are very careful who they might talk to. If you are in a hurry, then you will probably not get to buy much here in this place. People want to get to know you before they will talk business."

Noah shrugged, still grinning. "Oh, hey, that just makes sense. I mean, I'm the same way; I won't talk serious business with somebody I don't know. I mean, you see how careful I'm being, even when I'm just talking to you, right?"

Eduardo nodded, and took a rag from underneath the bar and began wiping it down. "If you are not in a hurry, you might come here for a few days, and perhaps some will talk to you. Perhaps you will get to buy the things you're looking for." He broke into a big smile. "Perhaps you will buy so much that you will be happy, and give old Eduardo another big tip."

Noah made a silly face, one that he hoped said that further big tips might be coming up, and then sat back to nurse his beer.

Noah and Eduardo talked off and on as Noah sat on the stool. He finished his first beer, and ordered a second, throwing another twenty at the bartender and earning a big smile in return. Eduardo leaned close to him. "Do you want only American beer? I have Modelo; it is the same price, but a bigger bottle."

Noah gave him a huge smile of his own. "That would be great," he said. "I've had Modelo before, it's very good."

Eduardo grinned and slapped the bar, then went to the cooler and came back with an open bottle of Modelo. He was right; this bottle was almost twice the size of the baby Budweiser he had given Noah before. Noah held it up in salute, and took a long pull before setting it down.

"That is very good," he said. "Thank you, I really appreciate you letting me know about that." He took another pull, then stretched, leaning back on the stool, and twisting himself as if trying to pop his back. He leaned forward, then, and as he did so he pressed the bubblegum-wad spy camera up under the bar, right beside the wall where it could get a wide-angle view of everything in front of the bar.

He smiled at Eduardo. "Gotta stretch my legs," he said. "Which way is the bathroom?"

Eduardo pointed to a door in the back wall. "First door on the left," he said.

Noah went through the doorway, and found the toilet. He used it, then took the sheet of sticker microphones from his pocket and, following the instructions Neil had given him, gently stuck one onto the tip of each of his fingers, except for the thumb and index finger of each hand. He went back out into the tavern, and pressed the tip of his pinky against the outside of the door. The little microphone that had been stuck there was suddenly and permanently affixed to the door.

Noah walked around the tavern, looking at different signs on the wall, decorations that had been hung up over the years, and occasionally reached out to touch something. One sign was particularly amusing, and Noah called out to Eduardo as he stuck a microphone to it. It showed a cowboy hat sitting on top of a pair of cowboy boots, and the caption underneath read: "Portrait of a Cowboy with the Shit Kicked Out of Him."

"This is hilarious," he yelled to Eduardo, who laughed with

him. "I wish I had a copy of this to hang on my wall back home. I've got this neighbor, he's originally from Texas, and he thinks he's just the greatest thing in the world. He calls himself a cowboy, and I would love for him to see that!"

Eduardo laughed again. "That would be very funny."

Noah went back to his seat as the front door opened and three men walked in. He glanced at them, but when one of them gave him a challenging glare, he turned his attention back to his bottle.

One of the men, and Noah thought it was the one who had glared at him, rattled off something in rapid Spanish. Eduardo grinned, and replied in English. "He is just visiting," he said. "He is looking for some things to buy, to take home and sell to make money."

All three of the men suddenly turned to look at Noah, and one of them walked over to stand beside him. "I am Raul," he said. "Raul Delgado. I should tell you, we do not like new *gringos* who come to our town and think they can make us do business with them the way *they* want."

Noah turned on his stool to look Raul in the eye. "My name is John Baker," he said, "and the only reason I came here is because somebody I work for told me to. I'm not trying to make anybody do anything, that much I can promise you. I'm just here to buy some things, and arrange to get them shipped back home. That's all, I promise."

Raul put his arms over his head and stretched, leaning backward so that the loose shirt he was wearing rode up in the front. The big revolver that was shoved down the front of his jeans became visible, and Noah looked down to make it clear to Raul that he had seen it. He raised his eyes back up to Raul's own, and smiled, once more trying to appear nervous.

"Listen, Raul, I'm not trying to make anybody do anything. I'm just a buyer, and I work for other people. When they tell me go here, then that's what I do, and all I'm doing is looking for sources of the things my clients want. Now, the good part is, they give me lots and lots of money to work with. If I find what I'm looking for, and we can come to an agreement on price and make arrangements on how to get it back home, then I can make a phone call and have money sent anywhere in the world, it only takes a couple of minutes. Heck, I don't even need to know who I'm buying from, all I need to know is where to send the money, and where I get to pick up my merchandise."

Raul grinned at him, and suddenly clapped him on the shoulder. "John Baker, perhaps we can do some business. What kind of thing is if you're looking for?"

Noah tried to keep the nervousness up, as he said, "Well, you know, I'm just sort of hanging around right now to see what might be available. But if I had to say something in particular, I'd probably say I was looking for cocaine, maybe some heroin." He let his eyes flick from Raul to his two friends and back, trying to get the impression that he was afraid they might be *federales*.

Apparently, it worked, because Raul suddenly burst out laughing. "What, my friend," Raul said, "are you afraid we may be police? I can promise you this, we are the farthest thing from police." He looked at Eduardo. "Eduardo, tell him."

Eduardo grinned at Noah. "They are not police," he said. "You may be a very lucky man, because Raul is probably the best man you could meet, for what you are wanting to do. He is also probably the only one who will talk to you, because he does not fear the police, not even the American police."

Noah grinned, then, trying to give the impression that he was relaxing. He started to speak, and then suddenly looked at Raul. "Wait a minute, were you worried that I might be…"

Raul and Eduardo both began laughing. "I did not think so," Eduardo said, "because American agents have been here before. They never come in alone, so when I saw you walk in by yourself, I knew that you were here to buy drugs, but I also knew that you had not done this here before. If you had, you would have made sure that someone who was known here brought you in."

"John Baker," Raul said, "I am glad that we have met. I do not have the cocaine, but I can get you heroin. The only question is how much of it you want."

Noah sat there and looked into Raul's eyes for a moment, then smiled. "All I can get," he said, "as long as we can find a way to get it to Chicago."

Moments later, Noah was sitting at the table with Raul and his friends. The man with the glare was still unfriendly, but Raul and Pedro, the other man, were laughing and happily drinking the beer that Noah was buying for them all. Three girls came in, and Raul called out to one of them. She let out a squeal, and hurried over to sit in his lap.

Another of the girls honed in on Noah. He suddenly found her leaning over his shoulder, her hands caressing his arms as she whispered into his ear. "*Señor*, I am Felicita. You would like some company?"

Raul leaned over and whispered, "These girls are whores, of course. That means they will do anything you want, and they know how to keep their mouths shut." He chuckled as he sat back.

Noah turned and looked at the girl, and was surprised to see clear skin and bright eyes. Her hair was clean and long, and she was small, with an athletic build. He knew that most men would find her very attractive, and he had already decided that it would be in character for him to take advantage of the prostitutes that frequented the bar. He smiled at her, and pulled an empty chair close.

"Sure, sweetie," he said. "My name is John. Sit down, can I buy you a drink?"

She sat quickly, and broke into a big smile, then called out to Eduardo. A moment later, he set a glass in front of her. "Ten dollars," he said, and Noah gave him another twenty. Felicita snuggled up to him, caressing his leg under the table and making sure he knew that more than just her company was available. Noah smiled and put an arm around her, while he continued talking with Raul.

A couple of hours later, a deal had been struck that would make Raul a million dollars richer, and cause a large supply of heroin to appear at a certain loading dock in Chicago two days later. Once Noah's "client," who would be played by a borrowed DEA agent, confirmed that the product was real, Noah would tell Neil to transfer the money.

"This is good business," Raul said. "Is this all you're looking for? Are there other things that you wish to buy? Perhaps old Raul will know someone who has them." Noah grinned and started to say something, but then shook his head and took a drink from his beer bottle. Raul caught it, and smiled at him. "Come now, do not be shy, my new friend. Tell me what you wish to find, and I will see what I can do."

Noah looked up at him, and chewed on his bottom lip for a moment. Finally, he nodded. "Okay, but don't get pissed at me, okay? I've got this client, a woman, and she's wanting to buy something that's—something that's very hard to come by. Something like someone might use to make a great big bang, if you get my drift." He watched Raul's eyes closely, and caught the instant when the man realized what he was asking for.

Raul's eyebrows were high, and he searched Noah's face for any sign that it was a joke or a trick, but the tall, blonde American seemed genuinely nervous to be asking for such material.

He leaned very close to Noah and spoke softly. "I will tell you this," he said. "I do not know where to get such things. However, there is a man who might help you with what you seek, if he believes that you are true." Raul flicked his eyes toward Eduardo, the bartender. "Eduardo has an uncle, Pablo Ortiz. He comes here sometimes, just to drink and to play with the girls. He is a man who can find anything, it is said, but I would not wish him to know that I told you his name." He sat back in his chair, once again.

Noah nodded, and smiled. "Thank you," he said. "I won't say a word, but I do appreciate it."

"I hope you do not. Señor Ortiz might not approve of my giving out his name, and I could find myself in a bad position." He suddenly burst into a big smile. "But you and I, John Baker, we are now friends, and friends protect each other, *si?*"

Noah smiled just as broadly. "They do, they sure do. Don't you worry about a thing."

Raul nodded, as if coming to a conclusion. He leaned close again, and spoke in low tones. "You're still looking for more things to buy, besides what you asked about a few moments ago?"

"Yes, I still need some other things, too. Do you have…"

"I know people," Raul said. "If you wish to see Señor Ortiz, then you will be spending some time here for the next few days, for no one knows when he will come in. I will tell others that I know, people that I trust with my life, that my friend John Baker has money to spend."

"Thank you, Raul," Noah said. "Thank you, I really mean it. Like I said, I'm new at coming to places like this, so I appreciate all the help I can get."

Raul smiled and nodded, and began paying attention to the girl beside him. Noah was smart enough to recognize that he'd been dismissed for the moment, so he turned to Felicita and motioned for her to follow him to another table.

"Do you need another drink?" Noah asked her, and she nodded enthusiastically. He went to the bar and got another beer for himself, and watched as Eduardo poured a drink for the girl from a special bottle he kept under the counter.

"Twenty-five dollars," Eduardo said, and Noah gave him thirty. He picked up the glass and the bottle and returned to the girl at the table.

"I'm curious," he said. "Why is a beautiful girl like you working as a prostitute in a little dump like this?"

The girl's eyes fell to the table, and she suddenly looked as if she were about to cry. "You are disgusted by me," she said, but Noah reached out and laid his hand on top of hers.

"No, sweetie, not a bit. I'm just wondering how you ended up here, that's all. Don't worry, I like you a lot, and I'm going to be very nice to you."

With her face still pointed at the table, she picked up under her eyebrows to look at his eyes. "You like me?"

Noah smiled, and reached out to put a finger under her chin and raise her face so that he could look at it. "I do," he said. "I think you're very pretty, and you seem very sweet. You just don't seem like the kind of girl who usually ends up in a place like this."

She shrugged her shoulders, and gave him a weak smile. "My mother, she died when I was only eleven years old," she said. "I did not have a father, and no other family. I lived on the street for a while, I don't know how long, until a man named Diego found me, and he—he taught me how to make money, with the sex." She flicked her eyes toward the bar. "One day, a few months ago, Eduardo saw me, and he said I was too good to be on the streets that way, so he bought me from Diego. Now I work here, and he helps to keep me safe. He helped me get off the crack, that Diego made me use."

Noah shook his head. It wasn't hard to figure out the proper, human response to the story he had just heard. "You poor thing," he said. "But you're safe now, here with Eduardo?"

She smiled. "Yes, he keeps me safe, and he lets me keep some of the money I make. Diego, he took everything, but Eduardo is good to me. He is good to all his girls. I'm very lucky to be here." She reached out and caressed the side of Noah's face. "Can I do something for you? There is a little room, in the back, where we could go."

Noah looked at her for a moment, but kept smiling. "What

if," he began slowly, "what if I wanted you to come back to my hotel with me for the night? How much would that cost me?"

Her eyes went wide. "I would have to get permission from Eduardo," she said. "Let me go and ask him." She jumped up and hurried to the bar, and Noah could see her whispering furiously with the bartender. Eduardo looked over at him, and Noah gave him a big smile and a thumbs-up sign.

Eduardo winked at him, and smiled. A moment later, Felicita hurried back over to Noah. "He says it would be one hundred dollars, but you must bring me back tomorrow. I must be here by lunchtime, is that okay?"

Noah nodded. "That will be fine. Do I give Eduardo the hundred dollars?"

"Yes, or give it to me and I will give it to him now."

Noah pulled a hundred dollar bill out of his pocket and gave it to the girl, who hurried over to the bartender once more. When she came back, she was beaming from ear to ear. "Señor John, tonight I will show you all the things that I can do to make a man very, very happy."

Noah smiled at her. "Well, good," he said. "Go ahead and drink up, now, because I have a ride arranged and he should be here just about any minute."

TWENTY-FOUR

"HOW'S IT GOING?" There had just been a knock on Neil's door, and the skinny kid had found both Moose and Sarah waiting when he opened it. Moose was holding an extra large pizza, so Neil grinned and opened the door wide.

"Well, our illustrious leader has already bought enough heroin to kill off every addict in the greater Chicago metro area," Neil said. "The deal goes down in a couple of days, and the guy who set him up with it is working on hooking him up with other deals, too. I'd say he's got his cover working pretty solidly. Is that a supreme?"

"Supreme with extra cheese, extra sausage and extra pepperoni," Moose said. "Your little bugs are working okay, then?"

"Take a look for yourself," Neil said, pointing at a monitor on his desk. Moose and Sarah leaned close, and saw Noah sitting at a table with a pretty young girl.

"Who's the girl?" Sarah asked.

"Hooker," Neil said. "He just arranged to take her back to his hotel for the night." Neil watched Sarah out of the corner of his eye, and saw her jaw clench for just a second. "Do I detect a hint of jealousy?"

Sarah cut her eyes to him. "Maybe a little, but it's not what you think. Don't worry about it."

"I'm not worried about it. Things are about to get a little dull; he and the girl are leaving, so all we get to do is watch the Eduardo's Tavern reality show." He rolled his eyes around Moose. "Unless you want to listen to the audio from his hotel room tonight?"

Moose looked at him. "Why don't you let me take the tavern, and you can listen to the hotel room, okay?"

Neil shrugged. "Fine by me, it's going to be boring either way." He shoved a slice of pizza into his mouth and took a huge bite, then handed a large tablet computer to Moose. He tapped a few keys on his computer, then reached over and touched an icon on the tablet, and the video and audio feeds from the Tavern appeared on the tablet screen.

They watched Noah and the girl walk out the door of the Tavern, and sat there and ate as they waited for him to arrive back at his hotel room. The bartender and a couple of other men in the Tavern had a short conversation about Noah, and seemed to come to agreement that he was exactly what he claimed to be, nothing but a buyer for other people.

A sound suddenly came from the microphones in the hotel room, the sound of the door opening. The girl's voice could be heard proclaiming that the room was fantastic, and then Noah said he was glad she liked it. The next sounds they heard were not as verbal, and slowly built from an occasional moan to screams of pure delight.

All three of them were sitting there staring at the speakers, their eyes wide. After a moment, they heard:

"Señor John, you are the most amazing man."

"Felicita, you're pretty amazing yourself."

A moment later, the moaning began once more. Neil looked over at Sarah, his eyes as big as they could get.

"Is he really that good?" Neil asked, and Sarah slapped his face. She stood up and turned to walk out of the room without a word.

Moose stared after her, then turned to look at Neil, who was rubbing his cheek. "If I were you, I think I'd take that as a yes. Looks like our wheel girl has it bad for the boss man. If she can't get that under control, he'll have to get rid of her."

The action in the hotel room built up to another crescendo of happy screams, and the two men heard Noah suggest that he and the girl go down to the restaurant for dinner. Things got quiet a few minutes later, and then Moose took the tablet and its charger and went to his own room.

The next few days were more of the same. Each afternoon, Noah would head down to Eduardo's and hang out there, occasionally making a deal. Once in a while, he would call Neil to arrange for one of the phony money transfers, such as when the heroin arrived in Chicago on schedule. The undercover DEA man confirmed that he was taking delivery of some top-quality product, and less than ten minutes later, Raul Delgado was able to confirm that a million dollars plus had been deposited to his Cayman Islands account.

After that was completed, the deals came more steadily. Raul had put the word out that John Baker was a man to be trusted, a man of his word, and that word was spreading. Noah, as John, had become a fixture of the bar, and had gotten to know a lot of the regulars well.

The girl, Felicita, was constantly at his side when he was there. She had spent every night but one at the hotel with him, and the only reason she missed that one was because she was in the hospital. One of the men who had come to do business with John Baker had accidentally brought along some trouble, and a fight had broken out. Noah had been forced to hold back, and not let himself fight as well as he could, but he had joined the fray in order to stay in character. Some of these criminals now thought of him as a friend, and he had to act the part. Unfortunately, Felicita had seen another man grab Noah from behind, so she broke a beer bottle over his head.

He objected, and hit her so hard that she had remained unconscious for several hours. Noah went with her to the hospital, and sat at her side through the night. When she woke the next morning, she was amazed to find her *gringo* there beside her.

Noah had been frequenting Eduardo's for almost two weeks, waiting to see Ortiz put in an appearance. He knew that he'd been causing quite a stir in the city, because so many of the local criminal element had been showing up to meet him, to try to do business with him. At some point in the not-too-distant future, an awful lot of them were going to find themselves suddenly out of business, when all of their money disappeared. As far as Noah was concerned, Neil's little program was one of the best tools he could've imagined in the war on drugs. After all, if you hit them in their money, it hurt worse than simply taking out a few of their employees. Every drug buy he made with Neil's funny money program was likely to mean another big drug supplier closer to being out of business.

At last, his patience paid off. It was early afternoon on a Wednesday when Henrique Valdes came through the door. Henrique, he remembered from his briefing, was the chief bodyguard for Pablo Ortiz, and always came in ahead of his boss to make sure there were no police and would be no trouble. He looked around, spotted Noah, and cut his eyes to Eduardo.

"*No problemo*," Eduardo said. Henrique had heard of John Baker, of course. He looked Noah over once more, then nodded and stepped out. A moment later he was back, followed by Pablo and a couple of other men. The other girls, who had been warned off of "John" by Felicita, swarmed to the table where they always sat, and Eduardo grinned when he realized he was about to sell many more of the watered drinks.

Tequila began to flow, and the old jukebox began to play. The music was loud, and most of it was at least a decade out of date, but it was fast enough for dancing, and so it wasn't long before Pablo and the others had the girls up on their feet. If there was one thing Pablo Ortiz knew how to do, it was party, and Eduardo counted himself lucky that his *Tio Pablo* liked to drink so much. He was also glad that his uncle was always happy to patronize his establishment, and many of Pablo's business deals took place there. That meant that the bar stayed busy, and was one of the main reasons that Eduardo was able to keep so many whores working.

Felicita also liked to dance, but just as she was keeping John to herself, the other girls had Pablo and his crew. If she tried to insert herself into it now, all she would do was start trouble, so if she wanted to dance, she would have to get John up off of his barstool.

"You want to dance with me? Come on, Baby, come dance with me," she said, but Noah smiled and shook his head.

"I don't feel like dancing, not right now," he said. He nodded toward the group that was on the floor. "You can go dance with them if you want to, I wouldn't mind."

She looked over at Pablo's crew and the girls they were dancing with, but frowned. "No," she said. "I must stay with you, Señor John. Us girls, we do not, how you say, steal from each other."

Noah looked at her, then tossed his eyes over his shoulder at where Pablo and the others were dancing. "You really want to dance?"

Her eyes lit up. "*Si!* I really do," she said, and then she tugged on his arm. Noah shrugged, as if cooperating with the inevitable, and let her lead him onto the dance floor. Henrique kept an eye on him as they approached, but he didn't see any sign of danger, so he didn't go to full alert. They were all dancing, just having fun. Who cared if a *gringo* joined in?

Within minutes, they were all laughing together, and since the big joke was how poorly the *gringo* was dancing, and he was laughing right along with them, Henrique figured it was a safe bet the man didn't understand a word of Spanish. He kept an eye on Noah, just to be safe, but there was no sign at all that he presented any kind of problem to Henrique or Pablo.

Felicita and Ramona were dancing together, putting on quite a show. Pablo caught Noah's eye and winked, and the American winked back.

"You're Mr. Ortiz, right?" Noah asked, still grinning. "I hear tell you might be somebody I want to do some business with."

Pablo grinned back. "And do you have money, with which to do this business?"

"I think I've got enough. All depends on what I'm buying, right?"

Pablo shrugged and stuck out his bottom lip. "What is it you are looking to buy?" Pablo asked. "There could be many things which I might wish to sell, and many things which I may not."

Noah twirled Felicita before he answered, and let her dance away a short distance. "I'm looking for a couple of things," he said. "I need cocaine, but if you don't have the quantities I'm looking for, then I can also use heroin."

Pablo burst out laughing. "Are you serious? These are not things in which I trade," he said, "but I can help you to obtain them. However, the people I know will not be interested in selling small volumes. If you are thinking of less than seven figures, then perhaps you should go home."

Noah smiled. "I think we're on the same page," he said. "I can handle those numbers. How soon can we put something together?"

Pablo shrugged, then looked over at Eduardo. "Nephew," he called out. "Call Esteban, tell him to come down here. Tell him there is a man here who would like to do some business with him."

Eduardo nodded, and picked up the telephone, but he was kicking himself mentally. He had known all along that John was a drug buyer, and had even toyed with the idea of making an introduction to Esteban, himself. If he had done so, he might very well have received a handsome finder's fee for making the connection. Now, his uncle would get any reward, and he would be lucky to get a decent tip on the bar tab.

Still, he made the call. It was never wise to fail to do what *Tio Pablo* told you to do.

Noah and Felicita were invited to Pablo's table, and a couple of the men pulled another table up to the first so that they could all sit together. Pablo had Noah sitting to his left, and leaned over so that he could talk to him quietly.

"So, please, tell me," he said, "is it only for the drugs that you come to Juarez?"

Noah smiled down at the small girl beside him. "That was what brought me here," he said, "but it's not the only reason I stay. This little Mexican beauty might be part of that, but there are other things that I'm interested in, as well. I'm just not sure where to look for them."

Pablo's eyebrows went up a quarter inch. "And what might be these things that you are looking for? Perhaps I may know where to find them."

Noah looked into his eyes, and his smile started to fade. He forced it back into place a moment later. "I've heard stories about you," he said. "There are rumors floating around that you can get anything at all. Up until lately, I thought that meant in the way of drugs, but now…" He chewed on his bottom lip for a moment. "What would you say if someone asked you if you knew where to acquire something very special, but very, very dangerous?"

Pablo smiled, and everyone at the table, except Noah, recognized the smile as the most dangerous one he ever used. It generally meant that someone was soon to die.

"I would say that there are some questions that should be asked very softly," he said. "But, if I am asked in the right way, then it is likely that I would be able to say yes."

Noah sat there and looked at him for just a moment, never letting the smile slip for a second. "I don't know how to ask softly," he said, "so I'll just ask bluntly. I have a client who is interested in obtaining the necessary materials for making a small nuclear device. Would you be able to put me in touch with a source of such materials?"

Pablo Ortiz stared at Noah for a long moment, keeping his own smile firmly in place. At last, he licked his lips. "You ask a very dangerous question," he said. "How am I to know that you are not an American *federale*? An American agent, sent here to try to entrap me?"

Noah chuckled. "Señor Ortiz," he said, "until just a couple of weeks ago, I thought you were nothing more than a drug dealer. It was only when I spoke to Raul Delgado that I heard that you might be involved in, shall we say, more lucrative opportunities. I had asked Raul that same question, and he suggested that you might be the man to talk to. If it hadn't been for that conversation, I would have settled for some simple purchases I've made since I got here, and probably would've gone home several days ago, but I've been hoping to meet you." He leaned forward, even closer to Pablo's face, and Henrique and the others all slipped hands up under their shirts. "Tell them they can relax, Señor Ortiz. I'm all alone here, so I'm not likely to present any kind of danger. I'm sure your people are smart enough that they would've spotted anyone watching this place from outside, so unless you think I'm some sort of miracle worker, then it seems to me that it should be pretty obvious I'm exactly who I claim to be. Just a buyer, working for clients. That's me, and nothing more."

Pablo let his smile grow even wider. "It is true what you say, that we know you have no one watching you. Eduardo has been keeping his eye on you since you got here, and he has told us of the deals you've been making. If there were the slightest possibility that you were any sort of risk to me, we would not be here today." He picked up his glass and took a drink, then set it down. "I am curious about you, however. It is not often, in recent years, that an American comes to this part of our city unescorted. Do

I think that you are a miracle worker? I do not know, but this I can tell you. You're not a man who knows fear, because those who are afraid do not come here. So tell me, Señor John, why is it that you are not afraid?"

Noah chuckled again, this time a bit louder. "Oh, you misunderstand me completely," he said. "The fact is, Señor Ortiz, that I'm downright terrified. This is the first time I've ever been asked to come into this part of the world, but as I said, I have a client who is looking for the materials I mentioned. It was she who told me to come here, based on some information she had that said there was a potential source to be located in this bar. I've just been taking advantage of the situation to make some other purchases while I'm here."

Pablo sat back, and regarded Noah with suspicious eyes. "Your client for this material is a woman?" Pablo asked. "I find this to be very disturbing news, my friend. As far as I know, there is only one woman in the world who might seek such materials, and if you are working for her, then there is far more to you than I would have thought. Can you tell me your client's name?"

Noah looked down at the table, then picked up his bottle of beer and took a long drink from it. When he set it down, he looked Pablo back in the eye. "I don't know her name," he said. "I only have a contact, a man who calls himself the Dragon. He tells me what she has to say. Does that sound like the same person?"

Pablo didn't answer at first, but took another drink from his glass. "This Dragon, he is from where? Europe?"

Noah shook his head. "No, he is in Dubai."

Pablo nodded, and this time his smile was more genuine. "Then I believe we are talking about the same woman," he said. "It is very possible that I have access to what you seek, but I do not handle such things personally. In fact, the actual material is not far from your Dragon, in the same city. If we can come to an agreement on the price, delivery can be arranged in a direct manner. Would that be satisfactory?"

Noah shrugged. "I would have to check with my contact, and see what the client has to say."

Pablo nodded. "Then we'll meet again, this time tomorrow. You may tell your client that the price would be twelve million dollars. If that is satisfactory, then be sure you have the ability to transfer the funds when we meet tomorrow. If it is not, then do not return to this bar."

Noah raised his bottle, as if proposing a toast. "Tomorrow, then," he said, and then he reached into his pocket and took out several hundred-dollar bills. He gave two of them to Felicita, then rose and walked over to the bar and gave one to Eduardo. He left without saying another word, and Felicita hurried out the door behind him. A moment later, she came back alone.

Pablo called her over. "Your *gringo* no longer wishes your company?"

The girl smiled. "He told me that he will see me here tomorrow," she said, and then she looked over at Eduardo. "He also told me to ask you to have a figure in mind for which he could buy me from you. He says he wants to take me back to America, and marry me."

Eduardo's eyes became as big as the moon. "And is this what you wish? To be sold like a dog, like a pet?"

Felicita looked smug. "If he wishes to marry me, I do not care how he obtains me. Will you give him a price?"

"Of course he will," Pablo said. "If this *gringo* does return, and wishes to buy your freedom, and *if* he and I conclude our business satisfactorily, then the price will be named. Perhaps I shall even pay it myself, and give you to him as a gift."

TWENTY-FIVE

OUTSIDE THE BAR, Noah had walked calmly down the street. He stopped at the first corner, and looked around as if trying to determine which direction he needed to go, but that was just a ruse to allow him to be sure he was not being followed. Once he had sent the girl back inside, he was fairly certain that everyone there would be involved in the conversation about his plan to marry her.

He crossed the street at the intersection and made his way over to the next one. A black-and-silver Chrysler sedan pulled up in front of him, and he opened the passenger door and slipped inside.

Sarah looked over at him. "Everything okay?"

"It's all going according to plan," he said. "How is Neil?"

Instead of answering, she handed him a cell phone. "Ask him yourself," she said. "He's on speakerphone now."

Noah grinned, and held the phone up close to his face. "Neil? It's Noah, how's it going?"

"I've still got good feeds from all of the bugs you planted over the past week, including the camera bug under the bar. Your little girlfriend is causing quite a stir."

"Yeah, well, it isn't often that a little Mexican prostitute gets the chance to marry a rich American. I would imagine she's got everyone pretty curious, about now."

"I'll say," came the voice from the phone. "Ortiz just promised her that if everything goes well tomorrow, he'll see to it you get to take her home with you. She's pretty excited. He even suggested that he might buy her out from her pimp behind the bar and give her to you as a gift."

The girl behind the wheel looked over at Noah. "You're not seriously planning to marry her, are you?"

"No, I'm not," he said, "but I would like to get her out of that life. If she's a day over fifteen, I'm the king of Siam."

"Oh, wonderful, I've always wanted to work for royalty," Neil said. "Listen, your highness, the plan didn't call for you going back in and actually completing a deal like this. Or have you forgotten that?"

"Last I knew, Univac, I'm the one who makes the plan. That means I get to change it, if I feel the need, and in this case I do. You just make sure you're ready to spoof the banks once I get the transfer info. If I play this right, we not only get to take out Pablo and company, we can also lay our hands on some genuine black-market nuclear material."

"Okay, unless I misunderstood something, said material is somewhere in the Middle East. Pablo is expecting you to make the purchase, while somebody over there picks it up. Got someone in mind for that job?"

Noah grinned. "That depends," he said. "How quickly can we get Moose over there? Nobody knows who the Dragon is or what he looks like, right? I've just decided that he bears a strong resemblance to a Moose."

"I'm checking," Neil said. "Well, since Moose hasn't been compromised on this mission, it could conceivably work. I can actually get him onto a flight out of DFW in about four hours. Of course, that's going to mean getting him on a flight out of El Paso sometime in the next hour or so, which is going to require using our NetJets card. I'll have him in the air before you even get to your hotel room."

"Good job," Noah said. "As soon as he's taken possession of the material, then I'll go ahead and complete the mission on Pablo. How long will we have, once we do the money transfer?"

"Pablo's bank won't know he's been scammed for at least seventy-two hours. Depending on where the pickup is scheduled to be, Moose ought to be able to get to it anywhere in the Middle East within no more than twenty-four."

Noah nodded. "Okay, and I'm going to play a little tighter than that. Since we're talking about this much money, I think I can get away with demanding that it be inspected before we make the final transfer. If it really is somewhere in the area around Dubai, then we should be able to accomplish it within a few hours. Pablo can tell us how to reach the supplier, so once Moose has checked it with a Geiger and confirmed that it's real, I'll tell you to go ahead and make the transfer. Pablo can confirm it, and tell his people to let Moose take possession."

A new voice came through the phone. "Do I get any kind of say in this?"

Noah's face broke into a big smile. "Moose, I didn't know you were right there with Neil. Think you can handle this?"

"Can I pretend to be the Dragon? Yeah, I can pretend all day long, but that doesn't mean I get out of there alive, let alone with the product. Don't you think we need a backup plan on this?"

"Don't worry, buddy," Noah said. "As soon as we clear this line, I'm going to call Mrs. McGillicuddy. I think I can get her to put another team on you for support, since we got the chance to actually lay our hands on some of this stuff."

"Don't you just love the way he says 'our hands,' when he really means 'your hands?' Does he always act this way?"

"Neil," Noah said, "why are you asking Moose? You've known me as long as he has."

"Longer, remember, by approximately two minutes. That's a little bit like being the older twin, you know what I mean? And since you're the king of Siam, that means were a little bit like

Siamese twins. I wonder if they can ever determine which one of them is really the older one, got any ideas on that?"

"The only way to tell which one of a pair of Siamese twins is older is to see which one lives the longest. Since they're both born at the same moment, the older one is the one who dies ten minutes after his brother."

"Noah, you say the most comforting things. Okay, boss, we're on it. Talk to you later."

The phone went dead, and Noah turned to Sarah. "Everything cool on your end?"

She shrugged. "No worse than usual," she said. "When Neil saw Ortiz come in, he told me to get over here quick, so I've been cruising around, waiting for him to give me the word that you left the bar. As long as I keep the car moving, nobody bothers me too much, but when I have to stop for gas I feel like a goldfish in a shark tank. What is it with Mexican men when they see a blonde? Am I wearing a sign that says, 'Here I am, who wants a piece of ass?' Feels like it, sometimes."

"I can imagine," Noah said. "Let's run by my hotel so I can check out, then get back across the border and get some rest. Tomorrow's gonna be a busy day."

Sarah nodded, and maneuvered the car through the city until she got to the Hampton Inn. She waited in the car while Noah hurried upstairs to his room and packed quickly, remembering to remove the microphones and flush them down the toilet. He came down the elevator and checked out, then loaded his bags into the trunk of the car.

Sarah got back on the road, headed for the bridge back into the US. It took about an hour to get across, mostly because of the delay in showing ID to get back into the states. Noah used the time to put in a call to Allison.

"How's it going down there?" Allison asked.

"Pretty hairy," Noah answered. "I'm changing the game up a bit. Intel was right, I found out Ortiz definitely has a contact for nuke juice. I made a deal to make a purchase of some material, but I've got to send Moose to Dubai as fast as possible. He's going to pose as my client, who's known as the Dragon, so that he can inspect the material and take possession."

"Making an actual purchase wasn't in your mission parameters. What brought this on?"

"Spur of the moment decision. It was too easy to put the deal together, I just can't stand the thought of leaving that material out where some real terrorist can get his hands on it. I've already got Neil setting Moose up with a flight, but I'm hoping you got some assets in Dubai that can back him up."

She was silent for a moment, and he could hear computer keys clicking. "Team Aladdin is close to there, getting ready for a mission of their own in a couple of days. I can put them on him tomorrow. Noah, how confident are you that this is a real buy?"

"I'm pretty solid on it," he said. "Ortiz seemed awfully excited about the possibility of a big payday. He quoted me twelve million, which is about three million over market value. Apparently, he's in tight enough with these people that they trust him for the money, because he assures me we can take delivery as soon as I have Neil make the transfer to him."

"Okay, I'm going to back you on this. I'll be honest, I normally wouldn't allow a new asset like you to make a call like this, but we both know that I've got a lot of confidence in you. Let's just hope that computer you use for a brain is working up to its usual standards. You're putting Moose out there at some risk, but I'll grant you that the payoff sounds like it'll be worth it. I'll make sure Aladdin is briefed and ready, and I'll send Moose their contact info."

"Cool," Noah said. "As soon as I've gotten the word that he's taken possession, I'll complete my mission here."

"Good, make sure you do. Eliminating Pablo Ortiz is a top priority; he's one of the major conduits for getting ISIS cells into the US. If we can lay our hands on some real nuclear material, that'll be a bonus, but your mission takes top priority."

"Got it, Boss lady." He ended the call without another word, and grinned at Sarah. "See how easy that was?"

The blonde shook her head. "Yeah, well, you just better hope it pays off. Rumor has it that she's been known to eliminate agents who went off the reservation and did things outside of their normal mission requirements. Don't forget that if you get eliminated, there's no guarantee something nasty won't happen to us."

Noah's grin never slipped. "You worry too much," he said. "You heard the lady, she has a lot of confidence in me. Let's just get back to the hotel, so we can rest up and be ready for tomorrow."

Sarah let out a sigh, and drove on through the city. A half-hour later, they parked at the Holiday Inn and made their way to their rooms.

After freshening up, they went to the hotel restaurant for dinner together, indulging in a couple of drinks while they were there. Neil came in just as their orders arrived, and simply ordered an appetizer so that he wouldn't have to wait.

"Well, the Moose is currently winging his way toward Dallas," he said. "I had to twist some arms, but they'll make sure he gets to his gate in time to board his flight to Dubai. Queen Allison called and filled him in on who to contact when he gets there, so he's got backup." He shoved a taco into his mouth. "Now, as for your little Mexican girlfriend, I went on the assumption that you're serious about getting her out. I'll have some new ID for her before you head out tomorrow, proving that she was actually born in Odessa, Texas. I didn't bother trying to change her name, I figured that would just confuse her. Once we get her into the states, then someone from DOJ will take over and help her get established in a completely new identity. That work for you?"

Noah nodded. "Sounds good, she needs a break. Assuming she was telling me the truth, the poor kid's an orphan who got snagged off the street and turned out by her previous pimp, but Eduardo bought her a few months ago. I'm guessing she's probably been in prostitution since she was twelve or thirteen."

"That's disgusting," Sarah said. "No wonder you feel sorry for her."

"Yes, well, she's actually been one of the lucky ones," Neil added. "Girls like her who get snatched off the street in Juárez usually end up dead within a few months. The only hope they've got is to be pretty enough to get into a bar or a whorehouse, and even then they don't usually live past eighteen or so. Your girl is lucky she hasn't gotten caught up in drugs, or she'd probably be dead already."

"Her luck came in when Eduardo spotted her, and decided he wanted her in his stable. From what she told me, she had been doing meth and crack up until then, but he doesn't allow his girls to use drugs, so he got her off that shit. It's sort of ironic that her pimp may have saved her life, but at least it gives her a chance."

The three of them sat and talked for a little while, and then went back to their rooms. They each had a room of their own, but Noah wasn't terribly surprised when he heard a knock on his door a half hour later.

"Come on in," he said. "I left it unlocked for you."

The door opened, and Sarah walked in. She closed it behind her, then just stood there and looked at him for a moment. "Yeah, I know we're not supposed to do this when we're out in the field," she said, "but I just don't want to be alone. Do you mind? I mean, I know I'm not your little Mexican girlfriend, but…"

Noah was lying in his bed, reading a book. He laid it on his nightstand, then reached over and flipped the covers back on the other side of the bed. Sarah walked over to stand beside it, unfastened her jeans and slid them down her shapely legs, then pulled the shirt she was wearing over her head. She reached behind her back and unfastened her bra, let it fall to the floor, and then pushed her panties down and kicked them off. She climbed into the bed and pulled the covers up over herself as Noah reached for her, but she put a hand on his chest to stop him.

"You, um, you have been using protection with her, right?"

Noah grinned. "Every time," he said. "Condoms, plus the special cream they gave us. I'm not taking any chances, that's just not logical."

Sarah smiled and slid a little closer. "Okay, then," she said.

"So, what brought this on?" Noah asked. "You're not jealous over Felicita, are you? She's nothing but a tool I'm using."

"Yeah, I know. I'm not jealous, not really. I told you, I just didn't want to be alone. Besides, while you've been having fun with your little *señorita*, it's been a while since I've gotten laid. If you can handle an American girl, I figured it'd be nice to get back in your bed."

Noah kissed her deeply, and pulled her close. "Everything I've done with her has just been part of the act," he said. "Would it surprise you to find out that I was thinking of you the whole time?"

Sarah laughed. "Not really," she said. "Now, shut up about her and show me what you want to do with me."

They stopped talking.

TWENTY-SIX

THE MORNING SUN woke Noah as it always did, and he found himself cuddling Sarah close. He kissed her cheek until she woke, then rolled over and climbed out of bed.

"I could use some breakfast," he said. "Want some?"

Sarah nodded as she sat up on the edge of the bed and reached down for her clothes. She slipped into them, then said, "I'm gonna run back to my room and get a quick shower, meet you down in the breakfast room." She blew him a kiss and was out the door.

Noah went to the bathroom and got a quick shower of his own, then shaved before he slipped into clean clothes and left the room. He wasn't surprised, as he stepped out of the elevator, to see Sarah and Neil at a table. She pointed, and he saw that she already had a waffle and a cup of coffee waiting for him.

"So, today's the big day, right?" Neil asked. "I got a message that Moose will be landing in about two hours, and everything is in place on my end."

Noah nodded. "Yep," he said, "As soon as Moose can get to wherever he's got to go and confirm what he's looking at, I'll signal you to transfer the money. Then, once we get the word that he's taken possession, I'll take Pablo down, then grab Felicita and meet Sarah at the rendezvous point."

Neil cocked his head sideways. "Forgive me for being a party pooper, especially since I won't even be at this party, but tell me again how you plan to assassinate one of Mexico's most notorious arms dealers, right in front of several of his cronies, and then walk out unscathed with a pretty girl on your arm. Somehow, I think I missed part of the plan, here, and I'd really like to be able to believe that I'm going to see you again. Just in case you've forgotten, the blonde and I are sort of dependent on you for our continued existence and survival."

Noah smiled. "Ask me a hard one," he said. "The answer is simple. Pablo won't know he's dead yet, and since he won't know it, neither will his buddies."

Neil's eyes went wide, and he put on a sick grin. "Okay, so you're going to kill him, but he won't know it. Exactly how is it that he's not going to notice that?"

"Easy," Noah said. "Since we're going to be concluding a very lucrative business transaction today, I expect Pablo to be in a rather friendly mood. He and I will share a drink, a double shot of tequila each from Eduardo's top shelf. He's got a bottle of *Tres Cuatro Y Cinco* up there, and a tequila man like Pablo won't be able to refuse if I offer to buy it. I'll have Eduardo pour the drinks from the bottle, and I'll carry them to the table. I'll add a specially prepared swizzle stick to each glass, so by the time I get to Pablo, both of them will be laced with campsonol, a poison that acts rather slowly but can't be counteracted once it's gotten into the bloodstream. It mimics the symptoms of a heart attack, paralyzing the heart and stopping it, and it's almost impossible to detect unless you know exactly what you're looking for. Pablo is old enough, and his lifestyle is crazy enough, that no one will be surprised at a heart attack, so no one will be looking for poisons."

Neil looked at Sarah. "Excuse me, dear, but did you catch that? He did say that *both* drinks will be laced with this deadly stuff, right?"

Noah chuckled. "I did, indeed, but what I failed to mention

is that I will have a tiny amount of bentonite clay under each of my thumbnails. Bentonite has an amazing property, in that whenever it comes into contact with a liquid, it develops an electrical charge that causes it to bond with any toxins in that liquid, including campsonol. Once it has bonded, it and the toxin it bonds to will simply pass through my digestive system and be expelled the next time I take a dump. All I've got to do is allow Pablo to choose the glass he wants, then dip my thumbnail into my glass a couple of seconds before I toss it back."

Neil shook his head, and Sarah leaned her face in her hands. "Does it ever worry you, the things you know?" Neil asked. "I mean, what if you get this wrong, and use something besides bentonite?"

"That isn't likely," Noah said. "Bentonite is harmless, and actually has a number of nutrients in it. I got a snuffbox in my pocket that's full of the stuff. If I'm searched, all I got to do is take a pinch. Like I said, it's harmless, and that's how easy it is to get it under my thumbnails. Just take a pinch, and shove some up in there."

They finished breakfast, and spent the rest of the morning in Noah's room. Neil provided him with the fake ID for Felicita, which he left with Sarah. The girl wouldn't need it until it was time to cross into the United States, so he didn't want to get caught with it.

At last, it was time to put all the plans into action. Moose was in place in Dubai, and had made contact with his backup team. Everything was set. Neil would remain at the hotel, stationed at his computer and listening to everything that went on in the bar, while Sarah would keep the car as close to Noah as she could. If anything went wrong, all Noah had to do was say, "Jumping Jehoshaphat," and Neil would tell Sarah to get to the bar as quickly as possible. If that happened, it was likely that Noah would have to fight his way out, so he'd want his escape vehicle to be ready and waiting outside.

At ten minutes before two, Noah climbed out of the car in an alley, three blocks away from the bar. He walked the rest of the way, carefully making sure that he wasn't being followed. Once he was certain that he was clean of a tail, he made his way to the bar and walked through the door.

"It's good to see you again, my friend," Pablo said as Noah took a seat at the table. Felicita hurriedly took the chair at his side, and slipped a piece of paper into his hand.

Noah unfolded it, and then smiled. The price that had been named for the girl was only twenty thousand dollars, and he turned to Eduardo, smiled once more, and then nodded.

He turned back to Pablo. "I've taken the liberty of arranging another little transaction, while I'm here," he said, "and I'm sure you probably already know about it. Would it be convenient for me to simply add the additional price to the transfer I'll be making to you today?"

Pablo's smiled. "I will tell you what," he said. "If all goes well with our business, I will pay that price for you, and you may have the young lady as my gift. Is it true that you wish to marry her?"

Noah looked at Felecita, then smiled and put an arm around her protectively. "It is," he said. "Where I come from, it's not easy to obtain such a delightful little beauty with such exciting skills. I plan to take her home with me, and keep her barefoot and pregnant from now on. That's sort of a tradition, back home."

Pablo laughed out loud, throwing back his head to show how great was his delight in Noah's answer. "My friend, I think that is a tradition that we should adopt here in Mexico. But, come, let us now discuss business. You have arranged for the necessary funds?"

"I have, indeed," Noah said. "However, the Dragon is somewhat skeptical. Since you said the material is somewhere in his neighborhood, he would like to verify that it is genuine before he allows me to complete the transaction. Can you accept those terms?"

Pablo grinned. "If you had said anything else, I would

probably have had you shot. While I do not know this Dragon, I suspect that I do know his employer, and I'm quite certain that she would not authorize such a payment without being certain of what she was buying. You have contact with your man?"

Noah pulled out his phone, an Iridium satellite phone that did not bother with cell towers. "With your permission?" he asked, and Pablo nodded. Noah dialed the number, and a few seconds later he heard Moose on the other end.

"Hello?" Moose said, his accent thick.

"Mr. Dragon," Noah said, "I'm sitting here with my agent, who will tell you where to go to verify the product. I'm going to hand him the phone, now."

He passed the phone to Pablo, and the old Mexican smiled. "Señor Dragon," he said, "you are in Dubai? Is that correct?"

"I am," Moose said. "To where must I be going?"

"Not very far," Pablo said. "You are familiar with the Armani Hotel Dubai? It is on Sheikh Mohammed bin Rashid Boulevard."

"But of course," Moose said. "I am staying there myself, right now."

"Excellent, excellent," Pablo said. "The product you are seeking is in room 427. Knock on the door, and simply say that you have come about the insects. The men inside will allow you to examine the merchandise, so that you may tell my friend here that it is genuine."

"Very good," Moose said. "Of course, you know that it is quite early, here. Will they be expecting my visit?"

"Yes, Señor Dragon. I made sure they understood that someone would probably want to inspect it at this time."

"Very good. Will you stay on the line with me? The room you speak of is only a few doors down."

Pablo nodded into the phone. "Of course, I would be delighted."

They heard the sounds of doors opening and closing, and then Moose's footsteps as he walked down the hall. There were other footsteps around him, and Noah knew that he would have a couple of men with him. If he had been alone, it might have raised suspicions. There came the sound of a knock, and then Moose could be heard saying, "I have come about the insects."

A door opened, and several voices could be heard speaking at once. A moment later, things got quiet and they heard Moose say, "Give me just one moment." There was a rustling sound, and then a sound like static from an old radio.

"The product is genuine," Moose said. "I will wait here while you conclude your business."

Pablo smiled and handed the phone back to Noah. "Señor Dragon would like to confirm to you that the product is indeed what you seek."

Noah smiled, took the phone and said, "Mr. Dragon?"

"My client will be very pleased with this product. Please conclude the transaction so that I may take possession immediately."

"Yes, sir, I sure will, and I'll call you back as soon as it's done." Noah ended the call and smiled at Pablo. "Looks like we've got us a deal," he said. "Have you got transfer instructions for me?"

Pablo reached into a pocket and withdrew a sheet of paper, which he unfolded and laid in front of Noah on the table. There was a string of numbers on it, and Noah recognized them as SWIFT codes and foreign bank account information. He dialed another number, and when Neil answered in a very practiced French accent, he said, "Henri? This is John. We're ready to make the transfer I discussed with you last night. Use this information." He read off the codes and numbers from the paper in front of him, and Neil read them back to confirm them. A moment later, Noah looked at Pablo and smiled. "Check your bank," he said.

Pablo looked at Henrique, who was punching buttons on a smart phone. A moment later, he passed the phone to Pablo, who broke into a huge smile.

"Well, my friend," Pablo said, "it appears that our transaction has been quite successful." He looked at Felicita, and flicked his eyes to Noah. "This girl is now yours, as my gift. I hope she comes to realize just how fortunate she is."

"Oh, *Señor*, I do know," she said. She looked at Noah, her eyes filled with love and leaking tears. "Señor John, I will make you the most happy of men."

Noah leaned over and kissed her, then looked up at Pablo with a smile. "Well, this has been a good day all around," he said. "Will you allow me to buy us a celebratory drink? I've noticed a bottle of *Tres Cuatro Y Cinco* up high over the bar. I'd be happy to purchase it for you, if you'll share a drink with me from it."

Pablo laughed. "How could I refuse? Eduardo, fetch it down."

Noah laughed as well, then got up and went to the bar. "Eduardo," he said, "two double shots!"

Eduardo climbed up onto a stool and got the bottle, then poured the drinks. Noah reached for the cup full of swizzle sticks that was sitting on the bar, and snagged the two gold ones he had slipped into it the day before. No one in this bar used swizzle sticks, so he had been fairly sure they would be safe there. He dropped one into each glass, and carried them back to the table. He extended his right hand toward Pablo, but wasn't surprised when Pablo reached for the glass in his left.

They each swirled the amber liquid once with the swizzle stick, then took them out and laid them on the table. They clinked their glasses together, and together they tossed them back. No one noticed that Noah dipped his thumb into his glass while he was stirring it.

He sat there with Pablo for another thirty minutes, and then looked at Felicita. "Are you ready, sweetheart? We've got a lot of paperwork to get done, so I can take you back home with me. We might as well get started today." He turned to Pablo. "Excuse me, *Señor*, I should ask your permission to leave."

Pablo looked over at Henrique, who was once again punching buttons on the smart phone. When Henrique smiled and showed Pablo that his bank account still showed the presence of the money, Pablo smiled at Noah.

"Señor John," he said, "may you and your lovely young lady find great happiness, just as you have given it to me this day. *Vaya con Dios, Señor.*"

Noah rose from the table, holding the girl's hand as he did so. A moment later, after she had grabbed a small bag from behind the bar, they were out the door and walking swiftly toward the corner. Alerted by Neil that the deal was done and Noah was out and on the street, Sarah pulled up in front of them as they arrived, and he hurried the girl into the backseat of the car, then slid in beside her.

"Felicita, meet Sarah," he said. "Sarah, Felicita. You got that little present for her?"

Without a word, Sarah picked up the Texas driver's license that had Felicita's name and picture on it and passed it back to him. He showed it to the girl, and she looked confused.

"Señor John? What is this?"

"This, Felicita, is your ticket to a new life. We're going to take you into the states, and if anyone asks you, you were born in Odessa, Texas, exactly nineteen years ago today. I'm your boyfriend, and I brought you to Ciudad Juárez for your birthday. Do you understand?"

She looked at the driver's license, and then up at his face. "And then you will marry me?"

Noah smiled. "You bet, baby, just as soon as we get settled in back home."

He glanced up, then, and Sarah's eyes caught his in the rearview mirror. She said nothing, but the look she gave him called him a heartless bastard.

It took them an hour to make it across the bridge, but then they were in Texas, and Felicita began to cry. Noah held her, letting her weep on his shoulder as Sarah drove directly to the Western District of Texas office of the Department of Justice. She had called ahead as they came off the bridge, and a pair of agents were standing in the parking lot when they pulled in.

Noah looked at the frightened Mexican girl. "Felicita," he said, "there is something you need to understand. I am not the man you think I am."

She looked up at him, confused. "You are not Señor John?"

He shook his head. "No, I'm afraid not. My real name doesn't matter, but it isn't John. And, Felicita, I'm afraid that I'm not going to be able to marry you, after all."

Felicita began to cry again. "But, but you said—please, please do not send me back there, I cannot go back there…"

"Shh, calm down, you're not going back. Listen to me, Felicita, I am a special agent of the United States, and I was sent there to do a job. It's done now, but I liked you, so I wanted to get you out of that life. Now, these people," and he indicated the man and woman who were standing outside the car, watching them, "they're going to take you and help you start a whole new life. If you want to go to school, they'll help you do that, or if you just want to go and get a job, they'll help you with that, too. But I can't stay with you, and I won't be able to see you again."

He opened the door and pulled her out of the car, then introduced her to the agents who were waiting for her. The woman took Felicita and put an arm around her, then walked her into the building, even as the girl kept looking over her shoulder at Noah. The man stood beside Noah until they were out of earshot, then grinned at him.

"So, I understand she was a big help to you on whatever your mission was?"

Noah nodded. "Yep," he said. "She provided exactly the diversions I needed, just when I needed them, and she didn't even know what she was doing. You guys make sure she stays safe, okay? I'd hate to think I brought her out of one bad life into another one." He rolled his eyes to the agent's face. "I might have to come back and find out what happened."

He turned and got into the front passenger seat beside Sarah, then pointed straight ahead. She put the car in gear and drove out of the parking lot, leaving Felicita behind.

"You know you broke her heart, right?" Sarah asked as she drove.

Noah shrugged. "Yeah, well, I figured it was better it be broken by a false promise than by a drug, a knife or a bullet. One of those would've gotten her, sooner or later."

Sarah looked at him, and the expression he saw from the corner of his eye might have been a sneer, or could have been a grin. "And you claim you don't ever feel anything."

Noah leaned his head back against the headrest and closed his eyes. "You don't have to feel something emotionally to know the difference between right and wrong, Sarah. Just because I don't have a conscience doesn't mean I don't know what compassion is."

The blonde girl shook her head. "Yeah, okay, whatever."

TWENTY-SEVEN

THE BIG HUMMER pulled into the farmhouse driveway at just before noon the next day, and all four of them followed Noah into his house.

"Oh, I think the drive here was longer than the flight," Sarah said. "At least this big monstrosity of yours is comfortable."

Neil grinned at her. "Monstrosity? That gives me an idea. I've been trying to come up with a name for it. I'll call it Hummer-stein."

"That's cute," the girl replied. "I'm just glad we're out of it."

"Me, too," Moose said. "No offense, Neil, but your driving scares me to death." Moose had met them at the Denver airport that morning. His flight from Dubai had arrived only a half hour before their flight from El Paso.

"Hey, it scares me to death, too," Neil said. "Why do you think I insist on driving the biggest thing on the road?"

"Okay," Noah said, "anybody who wants a fast lunch is looking at microwavable burritos or peanut butter and jelly. Who wants what?"

"PB&J," Sarah called out, and the other two guys echoed her. Noah got out a loaf of bread and began smearing peanut butter and jelly onto different slices, and then slamming them together. He put two sandwiches onto each of four paper plates, and carried them to the table. Sarah got up from where she'd been sitting and got bottles of root beer out of the refrigerator for everyone.

"It's good to be home," Sarah said, and then she looked at Noah. "Well, I'm not home yet, I just meant it's good to be back here."

Noah shrugged. "You stay here enough," he said. "You can move in if you want to."

She looked at him for a moment, then smiled. "Let me think about it, okay?"

"Okay. You all remember we got debriefing in the morning, right? Nine AM at the admin building."

Everyone agreed that they knew, and it wasn't long after they finished their sandwiches that they all decided it was time to truly go home. Neil started up the Hummer to drive the three hundred yards to his trailer, while Moose and Sarah got into their own cars and headed back to their own apartments. Noah watched them drive away, then went back inside and cleaned up after lunch. When he was finished, he went to the library, selected a book and sat down in one of the big, overstuffed chairs to read for a while.

Jefferson had met with them the night before, after Noah and Sarah had dropped Felicita off at the DOJ and made it back to the Holiday Inn. He collected all their fake IDs and phones, gave them back their own, and gathered up the weapons and other equipment. While they would be flying back, Jefferson would have to drive in his big van. It had special government plates that prohibited it from being stopped or searched, which was how the organization could move equipment around the country so easily.

"Good work on nabbing the nuclear material," he said to Noah. "How did the rest of the mission go?"

"It went slambang," Neil said. "Pablo Ortiz collapsed five minutes ago in the bar, and Valdes is administering CPR. Eduardo the bartender called an ambulance, but God knows how long it will take one to get there. From the way everyone is panicking, I'd say they already know he's gone."

Jefferson nodded. "Excellent. Is anyone making any comments about Mr. Baker? Is there any suspicion?"

Neil shook his head in the negative. "None that I can see," he said. "Eduardo called someone, a woman, and he's been telling her that Uncle Pablo dropped dead, just like everyone had been warning him he was going to one of these days. It actually sounds like everyone is happy about it."

"I got the impression that maybe old Uncle Pablo was the money behind the bar, and probably took a lot of money out of it," Noah said. "If I'm right, then maybe Eduardo gets to keep the place all to himself now."

"Valdes is probably happy, too," Jefferson said. "He's probably going to step right into Pablo's shoes."

Noah nodded. "Yeah, about that," he said. "He's got Pablo's bank account info, so if he takes over, all that money becomes his, right? What happens when it all disappears in a few days? If we're planning on keeping him as an asset, we need to be thinking about that."

Jefferson grinned. "Other people are way ahead of you," he said. "Allison talked to somebody at the NSA, and they decided to make the payment for the nuclear material a real one. That way, the actual suppliers get paid, and Valdes doesn't come out looking like a bad guy. Well, no worse a bad guy than usual, anyway. NSA gets to keep him as an intelligence asset, and the sudden disappearance of millions of dollars doesn't make people start wondering what really happened to Pablo Ortiz."

"Okay, good. So what's next?"

"I got you all on a flight back to Denver in the morning," Jefferson said. "You should be back home around noon, and you can rest up tomorrow, but you go for debriefing at nine the next day. The conference room at Allison's office. Which reminds me, Noah, she wants you to call her. Now."

Noah raised his eyebrows, and took out his phone and called his boss. She answered on the first ring.

"Put me on speakerphone," she said, and Noah did so.

"Okay, everyone can hear you," he said.

"Team Camelot, I just want to tell you—well, those of you who are there—that your first mission has been an unequaled success. We've never had a first mission go so well, let alone produce so many side benefits."

"Side benefits?" Noah asked.

"Yes," she said. "I just got word from another agency that Raul Delgado was found dead this morning. It appears that someone he owed money to was quite upset that the money wasn't available. Delgado was one of the major distributors of methamphetamines coming across the border into the USA. Excellent work, Camelot. I'm looking forward to debriefing you when you get back." The line went dead.

They went to their rooms after that, to get packed and ready to leave in the morning. All of them were tired, as much from the stress of the last two weeks as from anything else. They went down to dinner a little later, and when they came back up, Sarah walked into Noah's room with him.

"Would you mind if we didn't have sex tonight?" Sarah asked him. "I'd really just like to cuddle with you, if that's okay?"

He turned down the covers and slipped out of his jeans and shirt, but left his underwear on as he got into bed. A moment later, she shed everything but her panties, and slid into bed beside him. Noah turned on his side and wrapped her in his arms, and just held her until she drifted off to sleep.

Once he heard her breathing slow, he allowed himself to go to sleep, as well. They awakened the next morning, shoved down a quick breakfast, and then climbed into Jefferson's van for the ride to the airport.

Noah came back to the present. He had been sitting in his library for a few hours, reading *Swiss Family Robinson* with part of his mind, while he was going over the mission with another part. He wasn't concerned about the debriefing, but wanted to be sure he had the mission firmly fixed in his memory before he got there.

As the sun was going down, he decided to go and grab a shower, so he walked into his room and stripped. In the bathroom, he turned on the shower so that it was hot and filling the room with steam, then stepped into it a moment later.

The tap on the glass of the shower door came as a slight surprise, and he pushed it open, ready for violence if it came his way, but it was only Sarah. "The door was unlocked, I hope you don't mind."

She was standing there naked, and he swung the door wider so that she could step inside with him, then pulled her close and kissed her under the spray. They washed each other, and when they were done, Sarah took Noah by the hand and led him to bed. She pushed him back onto the bed, then climbed into it beside him, pulling herself up onto him.

The sun woke them as it came through his bedroom window, and Noah was surprised that he had slept so late. He chalked it up to being comfortable and secure, and decided he must have needed the extra rest. They got up and went to the kitchen and made coffee, but then they both said they were too tired to bother fixing breakfast. They went back to the bedroom and got dressed, then got into Sarah's car and drove to Kirtland. A couple of fast food breakfast sandwiches hit the spot, and by the time they were done it was time for the debriefing.

They parked in the underground garage, and rode the elevator up to Allison's floor. Jenny the secretary smiled as they came in, and told them that they were being awaited in the conference room. They went down the short hallway and entered the room, where Allison was waiting.

Neil was already there, and they sat down at the table across from him. Moose showed up only a minute later, and took the seat next to Neil.

"This is going to be one of the most informal debriefings I've ever done," Allison said. "More than anything else, I just want to tell you again what a fantastic job you guys have done. You have lived up to my expectations, and even exceeded them. I've been hearing from every department head today, and they're all saying the same thing."

Noah raised his eyebrows. "Which is?"

Allison grinned. "That I'm a freaking genius for recruiting you, and then giving you three of our best for your support team. You guys have done more than just carry out your mission, you've also made the world a safer place for all of us, and in several different ways." She looked at Neil. "That little program of yours is pretty exciting," she said. "I've already had other agencies asking if I know anything about all of these drug dealers who are suddenly complaining that their money is vanishing. I'm telling them I don't know anything, and I want to keep it that way. This is a tool that could be extremely dangerous in the wrong hands, and while I may be an egotistical bitch, I personally believe that the wrong hands would be any hands other than mine. We're just going to keep that our secret, okay?"

Neil smiled from ear to ear. "Yes, Ma'am," he said. "I'm actually very glad to hear you say that."

Allison turned to Moose. "Moose, I want to give you a special pat on the back. You went halfway around the world into a completely unknown situation, impersonated an international arms dealer, secured and delivered a fissionable quantity of nuclear material, all without batting an eye, when you were ordered to do so by your team leader. As I recall, just a few weeks ago, you pretty much hated his guts, didn't you?"

Moose shrugged. "I guess it's hard to stay mad at a guy who can kick your ass. Besides, I completely understood where he was coming from. We had the chance to get that stuff off the market, we couldn't pass that up."

Allison looked at him for another second, then turned to Sarah. "Sarah, I was particularly proud of you on this mission."

Sarah's eyes went wide. "Me? Why me?"

Allison grinned. "Because you handled it, my dear. And if you think about it, you'll know exactly what I'm talking about."

Sarah turned pink, but grinned.

"Noah," Allison said. "You surpassed every expectation I had. That logical brain of yours caused you to see and take advantage of opportunities that the rest of us overlooked. Because of that, the DEA has managed to take almost twenty million dollars worth of drugs off the street in the last two weeks, and we've managed to secure nuclear material that could have been used to make more than one small nuclear device. On top of that, we now know who that supplier is, a known antiquities dealer from Egypt. Moose actually carried the material out of that hotel, because it was packed inside an ancient leaden urn."

Noah nodded. "It's like I told you, Ma'am, I'm just here to do a job. We all are."

Allison looked at them all for a few moments, and then smiled once more. "That's very good," she said. "That's very good, indeed, because I'm already working on your next mission, and it's one that all of us believe only Team Camelot can pull off. Unfortunately, you're not going to get a lot of time to train."

Noah looked at the other three, who all looked to him, then turned back to Allison. "Can you tell us anything about it?"

She looked at them for a moment longer, then nodded. "The president of an African country is being pressured to form an alliance with Russia and Syria. That's an alliance the United States does not want to see happen, but we've just learned that the man's daughter is being threatened by some outside force. If he does not agree to the alliance when the summit meeting on it is held in three weeks, our intelligence indicates that she will be murdered. In a moment of weakness, he confessed this situation to one of our diplomats over there, and when it was sent back to the State Department, our president got hold of it. He called me and asked me to step outside our normal operations, and send a team in to find out just what kind of threat it is, and eliminate it." She paused for just a moment, looking at each of them in turn. "The problem is that you'll be going in with less than optimum intelligence. At this point, we don't even know for sure where the girl is, so this is as much an investigative mission as anything else."

"I'm just curious, but wouldn't this be something more suited to an outfit like the CIA?" Noah asked.

Allison gave him what he interpreted as a sad smile. "Normally, it would be," she said. "Unfortunately, in this case, we cannot risk whoever is behind this pressure finding out that we even know about it. That means we can't use any asset from an agency that our enemies know anything about, and so far, the only one they don't know about is us." She got to her feet, and stood there looking at them. "I'm afraid that this is going to be your next mission. Your briefing, such as it is, will take place the day after tomorrow."

GET A FEW FREE BEST-SELLERS, AND EXCLUSIVE NOAH WOLF CONTENT

Building a relationship with my readers is the very best thing about writing. I occasionally send newsletters with details on new releases, special offers and other bits of news relating to the John Milton series.

And if you sign up to the mailing list I'll send you all this free stuff:

A copy of the prequel to the Noah Wolf thrillers, The Way of the Wolf. Learn and walk through Noah's horrific childhood, shady upbringing, and what exactly happened to mold him into the cold blooded killer he is today.

A copy of the opening novel in my bestselling Sam Prichard series, The Grave Man. If you liked Noah Wolf, then you'll love Sam!

Just for fun, I'll also throw in the *second* novel in the Sam Prichard series as well, Death Sung Softly. That's a quarter of series absolutely yours and ready to read for free.

Finally, you'll be eligible to enter exclusive giveaways I have for only my readers. The odds of winning are great since only subscribers on my mailing list are eligible to enter. Prizes include Kindles, Amazon gift-cards, Bestselling paperback and ebooks, and much more!

You can get the three novels, eligibility to the giveaways, and exclusive Noah Wolf content, for free, by signing up at

www.davidarcherbooks.com/vip